P9-DNC-224

ONCE MORE

UNTO THE

BREACH

ONCE MORE UNTO THE BREACH

Meghan Holloway

The following is a work of fiction. Names, characters, places, events and incidents are either the product of the author's imagination or used in an entirely fictitious manner. Any resemblance to actual persons, living or dead, is entirely coincidental.

Copyright © 2019 by A. Meghan Holloway
Cover and jacket design by Mimi Bark

ISBN 978-1-947993-60-0
eISBN: 978-1-947993-75-4
Library of Congress Control Number: 2019938202

First trade paperback edition May 2019 by Polis Books, LLC
221 River St., 9th Fl., #9070
Hoboken, NJ 07030
www.PolisBooks.com

POLIS BOOKS

To Michael,
For planting the seed, joining me on this coddiwomple,
and encouraging me every step of the way

To E.A.D.,
For telling me stories

To L.O.C.,
A man I've only known through stories

To Aidan and in memory of JJ,
My own beloved Ottos

To the men and women of the Greatest Generation,
For living lives of honor, sacrifice,
and commitment

And to my grandmother,
Who was so proud that I am an author and so excited about this story,
but who never had the chance to read it herself

6 April 1940

Dear Nhad,
I arrived in Paris today. There is a disquiet and edge here.
It is as if the city is holding its breath. Waiting.
-Owain

i

Once more unto the breach, dear friends, once more;
Or close the wall up with our English dead.
In peace there's nothing so becomes a man
As modest stillness and humility;
But when the blast of war blows in our ears,
Then imitate the action of the tiger...
Henry V, Act 3, Scene 1, 1-6

27 August 1944

I hated Paris as much as I did any city, with its buildings like encaging bars and the congestion of people making it feel as if the air were rationed. And never more so did I hate the city than when it was filled with gutted shops, sandbag barricades, and coils of barbed wire.

The sun had not yet risen above the chimneys when I reached Rue de Vaugirard.

Be wary near Palais du Luxembourg, the old man had warned, *and the Panthéon. The fighting, it is heavy there with la Résistance.*

I shook off the fog of memories and swept my gaze from the streets to the rooftops as I skirted the palace. The streets were eerily quiet, and I knew the expansive gardens, though I could see little of them, were empty of the Luftwaffe. I followed the curve of the grounds, gaze continually moving.

The heightened vigilance threatened to drag me back decades, and it was a relief when a shrill whistle split the air. An unseen enemy was always the more dangerous.

I looked ahead just as the sun gleamed over the bell-like curve of a grand stone structure at the end of a wide, straight street. Then I turned to face the men separating themselves from the cover of foliage and shadowed alleys.

"*Hé! Qui es-tu?*"

"*Où vas-tu?*"

The men approached aggressively, two of the seven with the straps of their rifles banded across their chests, one with a thick, gnarled staff propped on his shoulder. They had a bone to scratch, and I had crossed their territory at the wrong moment. As was often my lot, I stood head and shoulders above them, and the sidelong glances and fanning out around me hinted at their unease.

Their faces were drawn tight with weariness, hunger, and suspicion. Such was the face of resistance.

"Eh?" The one who had spoken first did so again, thrusting his chin at me. "*Qui es-tu?*"

They were all bristled and lean, younger than they looked, I wagered, but whittled and hardened from four years of fighting. They murmured amongst one another, and I caught the words *carlingue* and *allemande*.

"I do not speak French," I said, widening my stance and shifting my weight onto the balls of my feet. I kept my arms loose at my side, hands open. "*Je ne parle pas français.*" The phrase came to me suddenly, and I remembered with startling clarity the boy who had taught me the words almost thirty years ago. He had been even younger than I, and he had been laughing over my stilted pronunciation when a German bullet punched through his helmet and skull. "I do not understand."

"You are American?" The one who spoke was the shortest of the seven, and though his stature hinted at youth, his eyes were like river stones.

"No." I shifted to keep them all in my line of sight as the one with the staff began to edge around me. "I am Welsh."

10

"Welsh." The first one who had spoken was obviously their leader, and he conferred with the others now in a sharp burst of words. When he turned back to me, his face was twisted in a sneer. *"Tu es anglais."*

Anglais. English. "No." My voice matched his for hardness. "I am not English. I am Welsh."

He spit on the ground. *"L'anglais* are cowards." He finished with a torrent of words in his own language.

I did not need to understand French to understand the tone, and I braced myself. I was expecting the staff and heard the whisper of air as it rushed toward my head.

I had spent my life with a shepherd's staff in my hand. It was a tool I knew well—well enough to also know how to use it as a weapon. I caught it before the blow could land, and with a swift twist and jerk, I yanked it from the man's grasp. He was off balance, so it was a simple enough thing to sweep his feet from under him.

I flipped the staff in my hands and thrust the thicker end into the gut of the man rushing me. He went down wheezing, and I caught the next in that sensitive region between the throat and the shoulder. He cried out, and I knew his right arm had gone excruciatingly numb.

Then the butt of a rifle caught me in the temple.

I staggered and went down on a knee. As I struggled to get my feet back under me, a boot caught me in the jaw, and the world wavered.

I knew as soon as I opened the door to his bedroom.

The bed was neatly made, the quilt Aelwyd had sewn before he was born smoothed across the narrow stretch. When I looked in the bureau, I found it empty. His coat and boots were gone from the hook and shelf by the door.

I strode across the yard, cupped my hands around my mouth, and shouted his name into the hills. Only the echo responded.

The road squelched underfoot as I walked to its summit south of the house. From the crest of the hill, I could see the track as it twisted through the valley. The hills were brown in the grip of winter, the sky

11

the color of a cold sea. The lane was a seam that followed the curve of the land as it undulated in swells and peaks like an endless wave. The grazing sheep were skirted with mud and smelled of the moorland.

It was empty for as far as I could see, and I staggered as the full realization struck me like a blow.

He was gone.

A kick in the ribs jerked me back to awareness as the four uninjured men dragged me into the closest alley. Another kick caught me low in the back, and I groaned. The alley spun around me, but I managed to catch the next boot aimed at my face, yanking the man off his feet.

"*Arrêtez! Arrêtez!*"

The new voice did not penetrate the blows until a gunshot rang through the alley and a shard of brick glanced across my cheek.

I gathered an elbow under me as the men ducked and moved away. A woman stood at the mouth of the alley. The pistol in her hand was aimed above the men's heads, but now she leveled it at the man closest to her. "*Arrêtez. Ou le prochain sera dans votre tête.*"

An argument broke out, and the angry voices made my head pound as if it were on a blacksmith's anvil. My stomach rolled as I forced myself up onto my knees, and I half-crawled, half-shuffled to lean against the stone wall. I propped my elbows on my bent knees and cupped my head in my hands.

I did not realize consciousness had started to fade until a gentle touch on my shoulder startled me. "Sir?" The woman. Her voice was soft and accented, but the lilt was not French. "Are you well?"

I lifted my head quickly and glanced behind her, only realizing I had caught her elbow and dragged her to my other side when she let out a startled yelp. The alley was empty.

"They've gone. It's safe now."

My sight wavered as I turned toward her. Even with my vision blurred, I noticed her eyes. They were the color of the sky in Wales before a storm, so dark and turbulent they were more gray than blue.

They studied me intently.

She leaned in close, cool hands cupping my face, brow furrowed as she peered into my own eyes. "You need medical attention, and we can't stay here. Others will have heard the shot, and it's best not to be caught in a crowd these days. Can you stand?"

American. Her voice was low and smooth, but forthright and no-nonsense. She had to be American.

"Aye, I can stand." She straightened and held her hand out to me. It was covered in blood, as was her arm above her elbow, staining the edge of her dress's sleeve. "You are bleeding."

Her eyes flickered. "It's yours."

I looked at my hand to find it stained red. My face felt wet, and when I touched my right temple, I winced and felt a rivulet stream down my cheek.

"Don't. You'll only make it worse."

I staggered to my feet and leaned against the wall as the ground tilted beneath me. Before I could protest, the woman wedged herself against my side and draped my arm over her shoulders. "Quickly now. Lean on me."

The top of her honey-colored head reached my breast-pocket, but her grip was strong. "More will come?"

"It's possible, but not likely. You landed some blows yourself, it seemed." She tilted her head back to look at me and smiled, and it was as if I were home watching the sun break through the dense morning mist that blanketed the hills.

"The pistol…" It was nowhere in sight.

"Let me handle the pistol. You focus on walking. Is there somewhere I can take you?"

I stumbled to a halt, almost pulling her off balance in my haste, and fumbled for my pocket, only relaxing when my fingers traced the crinkled edges of the letter. My head pounded in rhythm with my heart. The woman peered up at me, curiosity blatant in her face.

"I have to reach *27 Rue Tournefort*."

13

"Tournefort…I know it. But it is at least a kilometer away, and you need your head tended to."

"I must—"

"You can barely stand on your own. I have a friend who lives nearby. She's a nurse." I resisted when she tried to guide me forward. "Please. I'm in the Ambulance Field Service. I know a concussion when I see it. If you come with me now, I will take you to Rue Tournefort myself once Dionne checks your head."

My stomach felt as if it were attempting to crawl up my throat, so I acquiesced. "Thank you, miss."

"Charlie will do."

"Charlie?"

She did not answer immediately, instead peering out the mouth of the alley. "This way."

"My rucksack." It lay in the street, and I swayed where I stood as she fetched it and slung it over her shoulders before returning to my side.

She led me down the long, straight street. The sun now gilded the dome of the stone structure ahead and pierced my eyes. I blinked in relief, eyes watering, when, after a block, she turned north onto a narrow side street. "Charlotte Dubois, but everyone calls me Charlie."

I had known a lad in school named Charlie. He had looked like the south end of a north-bound wild boar and had the personality to match. He had been *dim gwerth rhech dafad.* "Charlotte. Rhys Gravenor."

"You are Welsh. They said you were English."

"I told them otherwise."

"Shame they didn't believe you." She turned into an alcove. "Just here." She produced a key from the pocket of her dress and fit it into the lock. The door opened with a metal groan into a carpeted foyer with a winding staircase wrapped around a lift. My apprehension must have been apparent, for Charlotte glanced at the glass and wood box. "It hasn't worked in years. Careful going now. Dionne's flat is at the

14

top."

The steep, circular climb was dizzying, and by the time we reached the sixth level, I was weaving on my feet.

"Steady, steady," she murmured, leading me to the last door at the end of the hall. She knocked, and moments later, a dark-haired woman opened the door.

"Retour si tôt? Ou—" The woman broke off as she caught sight of me and then launched into a hushed, rapid exchange with Charlotte in French. I fought to keep from leaning too heavily against the slight woman at my side. The Frenchwoman stepped back and opened the door wider. "Take him by the window, where the light is best."

The flat was small with a sparse, threadbare look, though the place was clean and welcoming. The ceiling was steeply slanted, and as we moved to the window, I had to stoop lest my head brush the ceiling.

I sat down heavily in the chair the Frenchwoman dragged over, too disoriented to be concerned about dwarfing the delicate frame. I winced, and the woman's shrewd gaze did not miss the movement.

"Charlie, bring some water and cloth. And my medical pouch, *oui?*" She turned back to me as Charlotte disappeared behind the only door aside from the entry in the flat. The kitchen was in a corner of the room and a curtain was hung over a threshold, behind which I guessed was the bedroom. "Lean forward, *s'il vous plaît.* You were hit in the back?"

I did as instructed and propped my elbows on my knees. She untucked my shirt from my trousers and pushed it up under my arms. "Kicked. In the right kidney."

She clucked her tongue. *"Oui, le rein.* A bruise is developing." He fingers were warm as she palpated the area, and even though her touch was light, I grimaced. "You will be sore, and there may be some blood."

I nodded and straightened, rolling my shirt back down my torso as Charlotte re-entered the room.

The Frenchwoman moved around to face me. "Your jaw is swelling and bruised as well. Your teeth, they are loose? Broken?"

15

I ran my tongue over the back of my teeth. "No."

"*Bien*. Charlie, you will clean his head while I will make a poultice for his face and back." She disappeared behind the curtain and reappeared moments later with a number of green leaves in hand.

"Comfrey?"

Charlotte placed the basin of water in my lap, a medical pouch on the floor beside my feet, and dragged the one other chair from its place before a tiny table to sit in front of me. "Dionne always says that it is best for healing wounds, as long as the skin is not broken." She dipped a cloth into the water and carefully wiped the blood from my face and neck.

"My mother says so as well."

I studied her. Her skin was pale with the faintest dusting of freckles across her cheeks. Her eyes were mesmerizing. In the shadowed alley, they had appeared so dark as to be gray. Here, with the morning light glancing over her forehead and nose, they appeared as pale a blue as the sky in winter. Her brow furrowed, and as she leaned closer, dampening the cloth in the water again and dabbing around the gash at my temple, I could smell the crisp aroma of peppermint.

"You are American."

Her gaze flicked to mine and then back to her work. She smiled and again her face was transformed, as if lit by the sun from within. "I am indeed."

She leaned back and studied my face and then bent to retrieve the medic pouch. Dionne spoke again in French, and Charlotte used a pair of crooked bandage scissors to trim a square of gauze before passing the rest to the other woman. She plucked an iodine swab from a box of tinctures, snapped the tip, and shook the contents to the end of the cotton. She applied the iodine, placed the square of gauze over the gash, and ripped a piece of adhesive plaster to secure it with the edge of her teeth with quick precision born of much practice. She smoothed the adhesive into place and peered into my eyes once more. "How is your vision?"

"Blurred at times."

"Dizziness? Drowsiness?"

I started to nod and thought better of it. "Aye."

She retrieved the basin of water, now pink with the stain of blood, and disappeared into the wash room. Dionne approached with two compresses, the comfrey poultice layered between pieces of gauze.

"Hold this." Dionne placed one compress on the swelling of my jaw "Now lean forward." She rolled my shirt up again and placed the second on the bruising over my kidney and secured it in place with the adhesive plaster.

The clean, fresh aroma of the comfrey filled my head.

"What is this now?"

My mother straightened from arranging a compress of comfrey over a swelling knot on Owain's forehead. She wiped her hands on her apron.

"Billy Hughes was being a diawl to the new boy at school."

"Language, Owain," my mother said.

"You know it is true, Mamgu."

My mother met my gaze, and the look on her face said that even though she reprimanded him, she agreed with him.

I hid a smile. "And?"

"And I stopped him."

I glanced at his knuckles. They were smooth and unscathed. I rubbed the back of my neck as I pulled out a chair at the table and sat next to him. "You let him hit you again."

He hung his head. "I did not let him."

"But you did not hit him back."

"No." His voice was small.

I sighed and leaned forward to prop my elbows on my knees. "Machgen i."

"I am bigger than all of the other children, Nhad. I must have a care."

"I know you do. But putting Billy in his proper place when he

17

deserves it would not be amiss."

"I do not want to hurt anyone."

I ruffled his hair and tilted his head back so I could peer into his face. At sixteen, he seemed both ancient and painfully young. "You've a gentle heart, you do, and I am proud of you for being so kind." He smiled up at me. "But I do not like to see you hurt."

"All's well, Nhad. I am not hurt, just a little bloody."

"Rest is the best treatment for a concussion." Charlotte's voice startled me back to awareness.

I rubbed my brow and squeezed the bridge of my nose. "I cannot afford to delay."

"Rue Tournefort will still be there tomorrow."

I met her gaze. "I have waited nearly five years."

We strode quickly, keeping to side streets. "The fighting was intense near the Panthéon just the other day," Charlotte said, voice low. "We must be cautious."

"You do not need to come."

She was silent as we navigated an alley littered with rubble. When she paused to scan the adjacent street, she said, "You don't speak French. You may have need of me."

I caught her elbow. She had cleaned my blood from her arm, but the light blue fabric of her dress still carried a stain of rust on the edge of the sleeve. I noted absently that my fingers met where they were wrapped around her elbow. "Thank you."

She dipped her head to the right. "This way." I relinquished my grip on her arm and followed her through the late afternoon streets. I had allowed the two women to convince me to rest for several hours while the poultices did their work and the ringing in my head settled to a dull throb.

She stopped and pointed to a sign over our heads on the stone exterior of a building. White letters on a blue background proclaimed RUE TOURNEFORT.

We arrived at the end of the street, but it took us only minutes to traverse the two blocks to reach the door labeled *27*. I knocked heavily on the door, not bothering to curb the rising urgency, and Charlotte touched my arm.

"I need to know what to say if someone answers. Why are we here?"

"I am looking for someone." I swallowed. "A young man. My son."

She stared at me in ringing silence as the echo of my knock and words faded. We both startled when the door creaked open. An old woman peered through the gap.

"*Bonjour, madame.*" Charlotte spoke with her for several moments. The woman's gaze darted to the street behind us when Charlotte mentioned Owain's name, and she avoided looking at me as she shook her head.

"*Non, non, je suis désolée.*" She moved to close the door, but I wedged my hand against it.

"Rhys," Charlotte said quietly.

"Please." I ducked my head to catch the old woman's gaze. "Please. He is my son." Keeping one hand on the door to prevent her from closing it on us, I withdrew the letter from my pocket with the other. "He was here, two years ago. He sent me this letter. Tell her, Charlotte. Tell her I am trying to find my son."

Charlotte translated quickly, and the old woman finally looked up at me directly. She glanced into the street once more and then opened the door further to usher us within. When we were seated around her table, the old woman began to speak to Charlotte, but her gaze stayed focused on me.

"Her grandson knew your son," Charlotte said. "They met working at the local café and became friends. They had similar opinions on the war."

You bloody will fight, or you are no son of mine! I will not call a coward my own. The memory of my shouted words reverberated in

19

my mind, and the pounding in my temples started anew. I rubbed my forehead.

"Rhys?"

"Go on."

Charlotte hesitated and then continued. "He moved in to help her after her grandson was killed in the bombings. She says he was like a son to her."

Owain had always cared most for the things broken and hurting. My throat ached. "Ask her to continue, please."

"She says he met a woman here, a young Frenchwoman named Sévèrin. He would not tell her because he wanted to keep her safe, but she thinks the woman was Jewish. And she believes your son became involved with the Resistance."

"Where is he now? Does she know?"

The old woman spoke again, and Charlotte's voice sharpened as she conversed with her.

"What did she say?"

Charlotte sat back in her chair, and her gaze was hesitant as it met mine. "She says she has not seen your son since Vel' d'Hiv."

"Vel' d'Hiv?"

"*Rafle du Vèlodrome d'Hiver*," the old woman whispered, reaching across the table to grasp my hand with her gnarled one.

"Tell me, Charlotte."

"Vel' d'Hiv was when the gendarmes conducted a mass raid and arrest of the Jews here in Paris. She has not seen your son since July of '42."

"What are you thinking?"

I rubbed the back of my neck. I had been as a blind man upon leaving the old woman's home, and Charlotte had tucked her hand into the crook of my elbow and led me back to Dionne's flat. "Owain is not Jewish. That roundup should not have touched him."

"Perhaps it did not. Maybe the timing is mere coincidence.

20

When did he send you the letter?"

I withdrew it from my pocket and offered it to her.

She handled the creased, stained paper with care, turning the envelope over in her hands. "This has traveled some distance."

I had studied each stamp. They were from multiple locations at different dates. There was one from here in Paris, one from Lisbon, two from Africa, one from Bermuda, another from Manhattan, and one from Sutton Coldfield.

"Well, I'll be." She tucked a loose lock of hair behind her ear. "In September of '41, mail became restricted. The first stamp is from November of '42. I am stunned it made it to you."

Two years too late. I shook off the thought.

"Do you need a light for that?"

I glanced down and found I was rolling the cigarette I carried back and forth between my fingers. "No, thank you." I tucked it into my pocket. "The man she mentioned after telling us of Owain's disappearance. Where did she say we could find him?"

She handed me the envelope without questioning its contents. "Alfonse. She said that your son mentioned *l'épicerie* with a red awning on Rue Pavée multiple times."

"Is it near?"

"It is in Le Marais, on the right bank, but only a couple of kilometers away."

"Le Marais? What does that mean?"

Charlotte placed a bowl of the stew Dionne had prepared while we were out on the table before me. The nurse had left soon after we returned to fill her overnight round at the hospital. Charlotte sat across from me at the tiny table. My knees bumped hers, but she waved away my apology. "Le Marais is the name of the district. It…it is the Jewish Quarter."

I sat back in my chair. "Then this Alfonse may know if Owain's disappearance is linked to the roundup."

"If he is still there." Charlotte's voice was quiet, and she blew on a spoonful of stew before eating.

I had no appetite, but I forced myself to eat. The stew reminded me of my mother's *cawl*, though without the lamb. Even so, the fare was far heartier than any I had eaten of late. I was not certain if the gnawing in my gut was from the head injury, hunger, or disappointment. "I will try to find him tonight, then."

"Wait until morning." She cut me off before I could argue. "It is dangerous to ask these questions. Even now. That is why she denied knowing your son. She was afraid we might be with the *carlingue*. Fears like that do not abate after a few parades and speeches. People are even more leery to open their doors at night to a stranger. We will have better luck if we wait until morning."

"We?"

She kept her gaze on her bowl, eating with the careful pacing of one long-familiar with rations. "You do not know the city or the language. I am offering you my assistance."

A fervent edge clipped the smooth cadence of her voice, and I searched her downturned features. Her face was expressionless, save for the pleating between her brows that gave away her tension. Unease crept into my mind, but she was right. A guide through Paris would benefit me.

"Very well, then." I was careful not to let hesitation tinge my voice. "I accept your offer."

The street below the apartment was quiet, but even with the hush I could not sleep.

I swallowed a groan as I stood. My head and jaw throbbed. My lower back ached and pinched, but the bed Charlotte had offered me was more comfortable than the cot in the old man's wood shop, though it, too, was built for a person shorter than I. I had refused the bed at first, but Charlotte had insisted, saying she had spent many a night on Dionne's settee and it was better suited to her size than mine.

Grimacing as I stretched, I crossed to the window. I let out an unsteady breath and patted my trouser pocket for the cigarette. I tucked it, unlit, into the corner of my mouth, the taste of the paper and tobacco a familiar comfort. I had promised myself after the Somme I would never set foot in France again.

My rucksack leaned against the wall, and my shirt was hung from a peg over a dress. The dress was green and soft, a fine contrast to the thicker, coarser fabric of the shirt the old man's granddaughter had given me. Charlotte had cleaned the blood from it after dinner.

I retrieved the letter from the pocket and leaned against the window ledge. The fifth arrondissement's buildings were clustered together like my Balwens jostling in the pen waiting to be sheared. The moonlight that did circumvent the rooftops was faint but enough to read by.

I did not need to read the contents. I knew them by memory. I tucked the letter back in my pocket and stared out into the night, watching the sky gradually lighten over the shadows of the idle chimneys.

And then a jolt of memory had me padding to the doorway of the bedroom and pushing the curtain aside to peer into the apartment. Though she had reminded me of her Colt M1911, Charlotte slept with abandonment, sprawled on her stomach with a thin arm and sock-clad foot dangling over the edge of the settee. Her movements in sleep had her dress rucked up to the back of her knees and pulled taut across the curve of one hip; the fall of her hair had parted to expose the angle of her jaw and the fragile-looking skin of her nape.

I shook out the threadbare quilt that covered the bed. The August day's warmth lingered even in the dark hours, but Charlotte murmured as I moved across the flat and covered her, shifting and drawing the quilt up to her chin.

She made a picture of vulnerability, but I could still remember that ferocity she had shown in the alley and, later, the straightforward manner that was so American.

And she had known my son's name before I said it.

23

Meghan Holloway

4 June 1940

Dear Nhad,
Paris has been flooded with refugees from Dunkirk.
Yesterday, bombs fell on the city.
It was as if hell were raining from the sky.
-Owain

ii

The shop with the red awning on Rue Pavée took little time to find, but the windows were boarded up—a crude Star of David was painted in garish yellow over the door—and no one answered my knock.

"What should we do?" Charlotte startled when I leaned my weight against the door, pressing against the joint where the bolts entered the frame, and popped the door open. Her eyebrows winged over her forehead before she glanced around, but the few people on the street kept their gazes averted from us.

I forestalled her when she started to precede me through the entry. "We do not know what may greet us." She moved aside to allow me to pass, and I entered the shop.

The place smelled stale, as if it had been boarded up for some time. But there was no stench of rotted and spoilt food. There were few staples left on the shelves, and no produce in the bins. The shop was clean, if dusty, and the glass from the broken windows had been swept into a pile against the wall.

"Someone has been here since the place was boarded up." Charlotte's voice was hushed, and I nodded. She snuffed out the meager light by closing the door behind us, and we both stood still to allow our eyes to adjust to the dark.

I checked the back storeroom, and it, too, was deserted.

"Rhys." Charlotte's urgent whisper drew me back into the shop, and she pointed toward the ceiling.

I looked up, ears pricked, and after a moment, I heard it: the quiet creak of a footstep. I glanced around the front room but saw no doors other than the one through which we had entered. I retreated into the storeroom, Charlotte close on my heels, and hidden in the shadows of the back corner of the room was a narrow door.

Standing off to the side, I turned the handle. The door opened soundlessly, and after a moment, I glanced around the corner. The narrow staircase leading to an upper floor was empty, but it was dimly lit by a window from the flat above. I could not see into the flat and could only see the edge of the window and the adjacent rooftops. There was no sound of movement.

"Wait here," I whispered to Charlotte, and carefully edged up the stairs, keeping an eye on the doorway above me.

The flat was empty save for a rumpled cot in the corner. There was another door leading off of the flat, and I watched it for several breaths. No shadows flickered in the doorway, but still I waited, and in the silence, I thought I could hear the low sound of harsh breathing.

The young man who suddenly erupted through the doorway appeared more startled by my presence in the flat than I was by his, and a tremor shook his hand as he lifted the gun and took aim at my head.

"*Haut les mains!*" I stood silently watching him, and he crossed the distance between us in hurried strides. "*Haut les mains!*"

He had never fought a man in close quarters. I could see it in the darting of his eyes and how he had positioned himself too close to me when I had the clear advantage of height on him. He was young, no older than fifteen or sixteen, and frightened. He jabbed the gun at me and repeated the phrase.

"He wants you to put your hands up."

Charlotte's voice startled him, and the gun started to swing away from my head and toward her. I stepped into him, grasping the boy's wrist, shoving upward so the gun was pointed toward the ceiling and then twisting his arm against the natural bend of the joints. He cried out and lost his grip on the weapon, and it clattered to the floor.

I released him and kicked the gun toward Charlotte. She stood at the entry of the flat, her own pistol leveled at the boy. "I thought you were staying downstairs."

Her gaze did not leave the young man. "I prefer to not be left behind." Her voice was calm and even, her hand perfectly still on the gun. It was a ready stance, one born of long practice, and I wondered again why she had offered me her help.

"You cannot barge in here!" the boy said in heavily accented English. "You have no right to do so!"

"I am looking for someone, and it is imperative I speak with a man named Alfonse. I was told I would find him here."

"Why should I tell you anything, you—"

"*C'est assez, Pierre.*" The new voice spoke from the shadowed doorway, and Charlotte's gun swung toward the man who came forward. He held his hands up in a placating gesture. "I am unarmed."

"As you can see, I am not," she said, voice and hands unwavering.

He dipped his head toward her and then turned to me. "I am Alfonse, the man you seek." He studied me, gaze shrewd. "Come. I know why you are here, and it is best we sit and talk. You do not need your weapon here, *mademoiselle.*"

I nodded when Charlotte glanced at me, and the reluctance was clear in the pinch of her brow as she lowered the pistol. We followed Alfonse through the doorway in which he appeared into a bare kitchen. He opened a door across the room to reveal an empty pantry and stepped within.

"Rhys," Charlotte said, voice low, "I do not think—"

Her warning cut off abruptly as Alfonse slid aside the back panel of the pantry to reveal an adjacent, hidden room.

"Such subterfuge and caution have become necessary, I am afraid." Alfonse stepped back and gestured for us to precede him.

I ducked through the pantry and into the hidden room. It was a long, wide room with numerous cots set up along one wall and at the far end of the room under a dust-shuttered window was a table and chairs.

Against the wall opposite the cots, shrouded paintings, sculptures, and trunks were carefully stacked.

Charlotte passed me and approached a painting, lifting aside the shroud to peer at the contents of the frame.

I did not recognize the art, but I heard her indrawn breath. "What is this place?"

Alfonse and the boy followed us into the room, the latter sulking to the corner to slouch onto a cot. Alfonse closed the panel behind him. "It is a sanctuary of sorts, if you will. And a storehouse. Come, please, be seated." He led the way to the table and chairs, studying me as we sat across from one another. "The resemblance is uncanny."

"Then you do know Owain."

"Know him, yes. We have a connection now, you and I."

"How so?"

"Owain is my…How do you say it in English? My nephew through marriage?"

I sat back in my chair, and Charlotte glanced at me, reluctantly letting the shroud fall back into place and taking the seat at my side.

"My niece, Sévèrin, is your son's wife." He smiled at me.

I rubbed my forehead and pinched the bridge of my nose. My jaw was stiff and ached when I spoke, and my head throbbed, making my stomach swim sickeningly in my midsection. "Then he is alive?"

Alfonse glanced back and forth between Charlotte and me. "There are no guarantees, but he was alive when I saw him months ago. When word of Normandy came, they left in haste. You were told differently?"

Charlotte spoke for me when I remained silent. "We were told he disappeared after Vel' d'Hiv."

"*Oui*, it was necessary. Owain cut all ties afterward with those he had known before who were…not involved in his work. It became too dangerous after Vel' d'Hiv."

"My son is not Jewish."

30

"No, he is not. But what he is doing goes against the edicts of this Nazi France." His lips curled over the words.

I glanced at the trunks and art against the wall. "I must find him."

Alfonse followed my gaze. "As you can imagine, what Owain is doing is dangerous. It is something he is willing to die for and he would not want you to endanger him—or yourself—by seeking him."

"You must know something of what took place between Owain and me."

Alfonse hesitated, but the boy spoke from the corner. "Owain would not want you here. He told my father of you, of how you cast him out. I listened."

"Pierre!" the older man hissed.

I met the boy's defiant stare. "I do not need to be reminded of an exchange I had with my son by a young whelp who knows nothing of my family." My voice was even, and he flushed and looked away.

"Please, forgive my son. He is a boy and is therefore ignorant in many ways."

"If you know what happened between us, then you must know how imperative it is I find him. As a father, you understand this."

Alfonse rubbed his mustache and looked to his son. "*Oui*. Yes, I understand this. But I can only tell you what I know. He would never tell me more than the first rendezvous. He said it is better if no one knows the entire route in case of capture." He gazed at the wall lined with trunks and art, but I did not think he saw them. "His cargo…it is precious. Do you know Forêt de Fontainebleau?"

"I do," Charlotte said.

"There is a small town in the south of the forest, Larchant. To the east of the town lie marshes. There is a ruin of a church at the edge of the marshes…"

"Look there." Charlotte pointed up the river. "That is one of my favorite sites in the city."

The spire of the cathedral was black against the overcast sky, and

31

the bell towers stood behind the spire like solemn sentries. I leaned against the stone rail of the bridge beside her.

"I used to draw this eastern view of Notre Dame often. I love the flying buttresses. Did you know they prevent the walls from falling outward? Something so beautiful, and with such an essential purpose."

Owain had wanted to be an artist as a boy. Paper and pencil had always been tucked into his pocket, and he had set more than one quilt alight drawing in bed after he was supposed to be asleep. I wondered if that was part of what drew him to Paris.

She tucked a loosened lock of hair behind her ear. "I own my ambulance, and I have access to the hospital's petrol reserves."

I rubbed the back of my neck, the unease that had been lurking since last night blooming into suspicion. We had not even known one another for a day. And yet she made this offer and knew my son's name. I hid my suspicion under the guise of curiosity. "Why are you in Paris?"

"I came to study at the Sorbonne in '36." She pointed north. "Dionne's place is near the university, and I lived with her for a time. She and I are cousins. I was finishing my studies when we heard word that Poland was invaded." She shrugged. "May came swiftly, and then when the bombs fell in June...I suppose I hoped the Parisians would take up arms..." What appeared to be disappointment tightened her face for an instant before she shook herself. She was, after all, American. Aside from we Celts, I had never met a people more ready to fight for their homes. "Well, so it was. I wanted to do something, and the American Hospital needed people for the Ambulance Field Service."

"That was brave of you."

She made a noncommittal sound and was silent for several moments, gaze on the cathedral. "Do you know what my work with the hospital has largely amounted to?" She did not wait for my response. "Not a hill of beans. For four years, I have helped tend the hogs since the garages at the hospital were converted to sties. I've planted so many vegetable gardens I have lost count." She held her hands out before her, studying them with an absent look on her face. Her hands were small and fine-boned, and callouses marred her palms. They looked grossly out of place on such elegant hands that appeared better suited for white lace gloves, playing the piano, and holding a teacup. She looked up at me and that direct gaze was gray once more.

"Do you play the piano?"

My question startled her, but then she gave me that dawn-like smile. "I do indeed." Her slow drawl thickened. "I can play the piano, draw, paint, sew, and dance. My mother insisted on those. But my father also insisted on making certain I could shoot, drive, and take an engine apart and put it back together again. I could be of use to you."

Her smile and sweet voice assuaged the gathering suspicion. That was what would make her dangerous, I realized. I did not know what motivated her, and her very presence imbued trust. Accepting her help would be foolhardy. But it would also speed my journey. "What the boy said was true. I did cast out my son. I told him I did not want to lay eyes on him again until he grew up and took on his responsibilities like the man I had raised him to be."

Charlotte straightened from where she leaned against the bridge. "But you're searching for him now, are you not?"

———————

"Here we are."

I watched from the doorway of Charlotte's room at the American Hospital as she ducked out from beneath her narrow bed, a hunk of metal and wires in her hand. My means of transportation was a cantankerous pony and a wagon I had been repairing for thirty years, but I could guess. "You disable your ambulance?"

"Of course. It's habit now." She stood and glanced around the featureless room. Aside from the bed, only a bureau and a sink graced the small space.

My own rucksack was on my back, and I held the satchel she had packed with a heavy coat, boots, her two dresses—one green, the other a darker shade of blue than the one she wore—and a pair of socks that appeared to have been darned more times than my own. She had rolled her undergarments into the green dress with neither modesty nor fanfare. Her practical nature was appealing, but as I followed her gaze around the room, I imagined this tiny, bereft lodging was a far cry from the life she had known in America. Her smile, though, was wistful when she turned to me.

"I doubt I will return, and I must admit, I will miss this little room." She took a deep breath. "Well then." With the rise and fall of her chest, I noted that though her form was slight, she was shapely. Her figure reminded me of the fiddle I had left by the hearth at home. The children always begged for a song in the evenings. "Shall we be off, then?"

"Aye."

I followed her back through the hospital's bustling halls, gathering four more satchels of provisions from the store room, and then she led me out to a long row of ambulances. They all looked identical, but she approached one confidently and patted its side as if it were a beloved steed instead of a piece of machinery.

"Most call their girls Katy, but that is not terribly original."

"Is it not?" Katy sounded original enough to me.

"This is an Austin K2/Y. Hence, Katy."

"And you call yours?"

"The more dignified Kathryn. She takes a little patience and understanding, but she has never let me down." She lifted the side panel of the hood and leaned within, reinstalling the part she had removed to disable the ambulance.

"I see. I have such a beast. Her name is Braith. She's black and white, and she prefers my mother's flowers to hay and cannot resist mud puddles."

She chuckled. "Is Braith a Welsh name?"

"Aye."

"What does it mean?"

"Black and white."

This time, her head tilted back, and her laughter was a full peal, unrestrained and delighted. She closed the hood and brushed her hair back from her forehead, leaving a streak of grime across her pale skin. "Of course. You are funny as all get out, Rhys Gravenor."

I had never thought so, but I could not resist returning her smile.

She rounded the boxy vehicle, unlocked the padlock, and threw the bolts before pushing the double doors wide and folding out the rear steps. The back of the ambulance was cavernous with two stretcher platforms on either side spanning the length of the interior. The upper stretchers were at the lowest position, hovering over the bottom platform, but I could see cranks at the ends to set them into their higher position.

It was stifling within, and though the interior was scrubbed clean, there was a faint metallic odor.

"Incoming!"

A whine sounded overhead in unison with the warning, and I threw myself over the boy. The percussion of the exploding shell reverberated through me and stole my hearing for long moments. Dirt rained over me and where it hit my skin, it stung as if shards of glass were scraping across the exposed flesh.

Someone shoved past me, pausing to reach down and yank the gas mask from the belt of the injured man I had thrown myself over.

"Halt!" My voice sounded muffled to my ears.

Arthur grabbed my arm when I would have gone after the other man. "He's already dead, Rhys."

The boy had begged me not to leave him only moments ago. I hung my head. Dirt littered his sightless eyes, and I moved to brush it away and close his lid but stopped. My hands were covered in his blood.

"Rhys?" Charlotte's soft query startled me back to awareness, and I fought the urge to flinch when she touched my arm. "Are you well? You looked as if you were somewhere else."

Back in the foxholes, but only in my mind. "Merely distracted for a moment."

Her gaze searched my face before she climbed the rear steps into the back of the ambulance. She slid a section of paneling aside over both stretcher bearers. "Once we are underway, the air will circulate." She pointed to the two vents overhead. "The fans help as well. The smell is always worse in the summer."

I handed her the supplies we had gathered—how little we had been able to collect made me appreciate how self-sustaining my farm was—and as she stowed the satchels and bedrolls, I wondered if she were incredibly perceptive or if I were so transparent.

"I keep the P.O.W. racks filled, but we may need more petrol."

"P.O.W. racks?"

She took my proffered hand as she descended the steps, and after she folded them back into place, I swung the doors to. "Petrol, oil, and water." She pointed to the padlocked shelf of canisters behind each rear wheel. "Wait here for me, and I will retrieve the petrol orders."

The canvas doors of the cab were rolled up and tacked to the frames. There was only one seat, the driver's, and a spare tire was stowed behind the seat. A door led into the rear of the ambulance, and a crowbar, hatchet, and helmet hung on pegs beside the door. A metal box with a cushion on it served as an extra seat.

I climbed within and settled onto the box. There was enough room to stretch my legs in front of me, and I leaned my head back against the rear wall of the cab.

Married. I allowed myself to digest the news. My son had a wife, a woman he loved and to whom he had pledged himself. I rubbed my thumb against the bare base of my third left finger and suddenly wished for the binding of the simple gold band I had not worn in years. It was not practical to wear it while working, and I could not have borne its loss. It sat on my bureau at home next to my photograph of Aelwyd.

"We will marry one day," I told her when we were six. I had

always been thankful she had found that plan agreeable.

I heard Charlotte's approach a moment before she climbed up into the seat behind the wheel. She held up a piece of paper triumphantly. "An order. If the creek don't rise, we should have plenty of petrol to make it to Larchant and further if need be."

The engine stirred to life, and I fought the urge to grip the edge of the door as we began to move. It was not my first time in a vehicle, but I still found the sensation unsettling and slightly sickening.

She glanced at me. "I studied art and literature at the Sorbonne." Her hands were confident on the wheel and gear shaft, shifting skillfully and seamlessly. "I spent almost every day in the Louvre before the war. Even when there were still only rumors, they began to move pieces out of the city. By the time the Nazis arrived, the Louvre was practically empty." She stopped the ambulance and engaged the brake. "It will be less conspicuous if you wait within while I fill the petrol orders."

I nodded, mind racing. Charlotte hopped out of the cab and disappeared from sight. I heard a smattering of French and then the vehicle jostled as the back was opened.

When Charlotte climbed back into the cab, I said, "You recognized the painting in the attic on Rue Pavée."

I sat slightly behind her, so she turned in the seat to face me. "The Jews have—*had*—some of the most priceless collections in Paris. Perhaps in all of Europe, even. But when they were labeled as stateless, they lost property rights. Everything they had previously owned was considered ownerless. There were massive raids." She tapping her fingers against the wheel. "I did recognize the painting in the secret room. And that connection makes me wonder if your son has been smuggling Jewish art collections before the Nazis can confiscate them."

I could easily imagine Owain becoming involved in such an operation, but Charlotte's conclusion was swift and neat. One most likely born of prior knowledge. And I had no way of knowing if her guidance would lead me toward my son or further away. "Were you involved in that effort?"

She glanced at me sharply. She did an admirable job of clearing any expression from her face, but her brows were expressive. In the short time I had spent in her company, I could already discern a pattern. The knit in her brow smoothed after a moment, and her gaze remained on mine. "Yes. I did not just spend time at the Louvre. I worked there."

She said no more, and I sensed no deception in her voice or eyes. But when I asked, "Did you know my son?" her gaze slid away from mine.

The ambulance's engine rumbled to life, and she disengaged the brake. "No, I didn't."

I did not know why she lied, I only knew that she did.

26 June 1940

Dear Nhad,
A swastika flag hangs at the Arc de Triomphe,
and people have fled the city by any means
available—automobile, cart, and foot.
The streets seem deserted. I listened to Pétain on the radio
order an end to the fighting.
And then a week later, I caught a glimpse of Hitler in Montmartre.
-Owain

iii

Henri

"I will not ask again, *monsieur*." I rolled the sleeves down my forearms and rebuttoned the cuffs. "Who was the man here earlier, and what did he want?"

I had always found fear a far more useful tool than pain. Wariness was evident in the old Jew's eyes. He met my gaze evenly, though, and said nothing.

His son, however, had not shut his mouth throughout the entire interrogation, screaming and threatening. "My father will tell you nothing, you traitor. *Enculé*."

I sighed. Children had always tested my patience. Even my own two had known better than to interrupt me or meet my gaze when I spoke to them. I drew my pistol and fired a bullet into his head.

The father screamed, spittle flying, his face turning red as he strained at his bonds toward the slumped form of the boy. He hung his head, his sobs harsh and broken, and when he looked up at me, the hatred was evident in his dark eyes. I noted it absently. Perhaps once, years ago, I would have relished it. But hate, I had come to realize, like war, was simply a fact of existence.

"You will get nothing from me now," he whispered, voice hoarse.

"Then you are of no use to me." My next bullet pierced his forehead, and I paused a moment to admire how precise the shot was between his eyes.

It was like a painting, I thought, taking in the scene before me. I

41

was dissatisfied with the composition, though, and holstered my pistol to rearrange the scene. I tipped the son's chair over onto its side, and then pushed the father's chair back so that the beam of light coming through the window brought the hole in his head into stark relief.

I stepped back and tilted my head. The chiaroscuro of the attic, the deep shade of blood pooling around the boy's head, and the sorrow stamped permanently on the man's face were beautiful. My fingers itched for a brush. One day, if I made it home from this wretched place, I would paint this while sitting in my vineyard with my dog at my feet.

Sorrow pierced me when I remembered. Gerhardt would not be there to curl at my feet before the fire every night once I returned home. The man who had shown up at my flat a month ago had tossed my beloved schnauzer's collar on the table before me. It was matted with blood. Next, he slid a small cigar box toward me, and dread twisted my stomach even before I lifted the lid and found the horror within. That delicate shell of ear was so familiar to me. Had it really been six years since I held Mila in my arms, soaking in my wife's softness, whispering my love for her in this very ear that now sat gorily before me?

"I thought you would appreciate the artistry. Didn't your Van Gogh cut off his ear?"

Rage swept through me so swiftly and violently I almost lunged across the table and ripped his throat out.

"That is one ear," he said. "There are many more pieces of her we can remove and send to you if you do not return what you have taken. You have six weeks."

I had two weeks left before their deadline, and I had found everything but the Friedrich collection. Desperation ate at me. Gerhardt's collar and the small cigar box weighed heavily in my pockets and felt as if they burned through fabric and flesh straight to the marrow of me.

I did not bother cleaning up after my work. I searched through the frames and trunks but found nothing worth saving. I studied the scene once more to commit it to memory and then left, blending in with the passersby on the street with ease even as I studied each face I passed. The man I had seen on the street earlier had features so similar to the man I sought that I knew if I could find him, he would lead me to Owain.

Meghan Holloway

28 September 1940

Dear Nhad,
Most have returned to the city from the countryside.
Rations and curfews have been put in place.
German propaganda is all I see and hear.
The French are frustrated but silent.
-Owain

iv

There was one checkpoint as we left the sprawl of Paris and headed south. It was manned by a trio of young American soldiers, their faces drawn from war but still holding the earnestness of boyhood. All three of their faces lit when they saw Charlotte.

I was not the only one affected by her smile, I noted, as she laughed and beamed and complimented them while they looked over our identification cards.

When they allowed us through and we drove on, she turned the smile toward me, though this time it held a rueful edge. "I find it helps to smile when I ask for something."

I chuckled and felt a stir of pity for her parents.

"And it costs me nothing to smile and charm, especially when our boys seem to need it so."

"Women represent home," I said without thinking. "Home and softness. Warmth. Something to which we can return."

She glanced at me as she shifted gears. "You fought in the Great War?"

"Aye. At the Somme." I had been in other skirmishes and battles, but the Somme was the one that still found me in sleep most often. I forced my thoughts from the mire, lice, and blood.

"I'm sorry." Her voice was soft. "My grandfather fought in the War between the States."

"Your civil war?"

"Yes. He would never speak of that time."

"Sometimes the past is better left where it is and not brought home."

Charlotte was not one to mince air, and silence descended between us, comfortable and light. To avoid watching her, I studied the passing landscape. As long as I did not look down at the ground rushing past, my stomach stayed where it was.

The city gave way to outlying villages which eventually flattened into a plain of what once was likely farmland but was now churned into mud that had been sun-dried into a wasteland. The road was rutted, and dust billowed under the agitation of the tires. The ambulance swayed with the same lulling motion of my wagon at home. I smiled to myself, even as I felt the weeks of exhaustion settle about my shoulders like a cloak.

I fingered the swelling of my jaw as I yawned. The motion caused the joint to crack.

"You should rest. You are likely worn slap out."

My head was starting to droop, but it jerked up at Charlotte's words.

"I know you did not sleep last night. I woke when you covered me and saw you at the window."

I rubbed the back of my neck. "Sleep does not come easy to me."

Sitting at an angle behind her, I could not see her smile, but I caught the movement of the curve of her cheek as she did so. "Your accent is getting thicker."

"I am not the one with an accent."

She laughed and shook her head. "Sleep. It is open road for some kilometers before we reach the forest."

"If there is anything amiss…"

"I will wake you. Rest. There is nothing that needs done."

I closed my eyes and drifted. I slept as I usually did: only a few steps from wakefulness where dreams come with ease and the guise of reality.

I dreamt of home.

A section of the fence in the north pasture was beginning

to crumble. The spring was a wet one, and multiple stones had been knocked awry by sliding mud.

The boys had helped me clean away the rubble and remove the loose rocks. Davey and Neville, too small to help Stephen and Peter haul the stones we had collected, were mixing the mortar while I removed the loose masonry.

The wind was brisk and still held the chill of winter as it swept over the hills. It whistled in my ears, so I didn't hear her calling at first.

Neville tugged at my shirtsleeve.

"What is it, cariad bach?"

He did not answer, of course. The tow-headed lad had not spoken since he had arrived with the other ten children four years ago. He tugged at my sleeve again, and this time I turned and followed the direction of his pointed finger.

My mother was laboring up the hill, the hem of her skirt caked in mud.

Straightening from my crouch, I placed a restraining hand on each boy's shoulder as they started to race toward her. The frantic way Mam waved and shouted my name had unease settling in my gut. "Wait here."

I strode toward her, catching her arm as she slipped on the wet turf.

"Rhys," she gasped, and clung to my arm.

Concerned, I set her back from me. Her face was pale, her eyes red-rimmed. "What is it? News about one of the children's parents?"

She shook her head and wordlessly handed me the paper she clutched.

It was a letter, stained, an edge torn. The ink that scrawled my name and the location of the farm was faded, but I recognized whose hand had penned it. My own fingers were unsteady as I unfolded the paper.

But as I tried to read the letter, it caught flame, singeing my hands before it turned to ash. And as the ash fell through my grasping fingers,

49

it turned to blood.

I lurched into wakefulness, fumbling for my breast pocket, only relaxing when I felt the crumple of paper. The letter remained where it had been since I received it, worn but whole and unscorched. It was a dream I had been having for months now. I withdrew the cigarette from my pocket and tucked it into the corner of my mouth.

The sun was in its waning descent toward the horizon. The ground was still flat but trees now hemmed the track of road on either side.

"I don't mind if you smoke," Charlotte said.

"I do not smoke." I tucked the cigarette back in my pocket and leaned forward, bracing my elbows on my knees, in time to catch the quirk of her brow. "Did I sleep long?"

"Only perhaps an hour. I was about to wake you. We should stop before the sun sets. Traveling at night is risking being shot."

"The Germans are known to be in these woods?"

"The Resistance. They tend to strike before they ask questions."

I touched the bandage on my forehead. "Aye. Is there water nearby?"

"The Seine is over yonder to the east."

"Let's make camp close by."

She took the next turnout leading toward the river, and we wound our way deeper into the forest. Boulders hunched like silent sentries as we drew closer to the water. We edged around a grouping of boulders taller than the ambulance, and then the track suddenly exited the trees and widened into a clearing on the water's edge. Charlotte started to drive into the clearing, but I stayed her hand on the gearshift.

"No, that is too exposed. Pull back around the boulders. We will set up camp there."

She reversed the big vehicle as if it were a small Jeep, backing between the boulders and copse with no hesitation.

"When did you learn to drive?"

She set the brake, and the engine rumbled into stillness. The forest was quiet with only the conversation of the birds and the sigh of the water to fill it. Some of the tension that had tightened my chest in the last weeks loosened, and I took a deep breath.

"My grandfather had a tobacco plantation. My father has it now. But my grandfather let me start driving his Fordson when I was eight." She chuckled. "My mother and grandmother were madder than wet hens when they found out."

We exited the cab, and she followed me through the trees to the water's edge. I motioned for Charlotte to wait in the trees as I stepped into the open. The birds continued their whistling and warbling, and all was still.

The river was wide and moved with a slow, lazy current. I could see the bed for only a couple meters before the water deepened. On either shore, all I could see were trees.

When I turned back to Charlotte, she had her gun in hand and she scanned the riverbank as well.

"All seems well," I said.

The water was blissfully cool, and I drank deeply before splashing my face and letting the water run in rivulets under my collar. Charlotte sighed, and when I turned to her, the gun was no longer in sight and her hair was wet.

"Do you think it's safe to swim?" Her eyelashes were damp and spiked together, and a bead of water trailed down her cheek.

"Let's search the area first, and then we can take turns in the water."

We walked a kilometer perimeter around the site but found no signs of encampments, Resistance or German. I shortened my stride, conscious of the woman at my side, and she kept pace with me without complaint.

Charlotte retrieved our rucksacks from the ambulance, and then we took turns in the water. She handed me her Colt, and I sat on a boulder with my back to the water. I forbore not to focus on the whisper of cloth as she disrobed behind me and then splashed into the water. She gasped.

"Cold?"

"Freezing! But pure bliss."

I retrieved fresh clothes from my rucksack and cautiously removed the bandage from my right temple. The gash felt raw and tender under my palpations, but no fresh blood stained my fingers when I drew my hand away. "You've not been in the River Tywi."

"Is that in Wales?"

"Aye. Its source is in the Cambrian Mountains. It flows through my valley and is cold enough to steal your breath and shrivel your—" I stopped, recalling to whom I was speaking. "It is bitterly cold, it is."

She laughed, the sound dancing with the sweet song of the water. "Where I'm from, the heat and humidity make it feel as if you are wrapped in wet cotton in the summertime. The bayou was in our backyard, but you'd better have a care trying to swim there or you would be a gator's supper."

Her rucksack slouched at my feet. "A gator?"

"It is a creature like something out of a nightmare. Huge and prehistoric with a bite fierce enough to take down a horse."

I could not fathom such a creature. "And you swam with such a beast?" I leaned over on the pretense of untying my boots and slipped my hands into her rucksack.

"Not on even the hottest days! We would crawl under the fence and swim in the neighbor's cow pond."

I leafed through the folds of her clothes with care, cautious not to disturb the meticulous way she had packed the satchel. "You have siblings?"

"A younger sister. It's her cow pond now. She married the neighbor's son." I heard more splashing and then a sigh. "I imagine I'm an aunt by now, but with the mail restrictions I do not know."

I knew of mail restrictions. "When all of this is over, will you return home?" I did not know what I expected to find tucked away and hidden in her rucksack, but all I encountered was the few items I had

52

seen her pack.

There was silence for so long I thought she may not have heard me. When she spoke, she was close behind me, her voice muffled as she dressed. "I suppose so."

I quelled the urge to startle and jerk my hands from the rucksack. The movement would give me away. I stayed bent over my knees, withdrew my hands and made certain her satchel appeared undisturbed, before I quickly untied my laces.

"I have not thought about it, to tell you the truth," she continued. "The war seems to have lasted so long I grew used to not thinking about anything but one day at a time. Do you think it is over?"

I straightened and set my boots aside. "The war? I think with the foothold the Americans have in Europe now it will only be a matter of time before the Germans are pushed back."

"You'll return to Wales after you find your son?"

She touched my shoulder, and I stood to allow her the use of the boulder. I left her pistol on the rock and stacked my clean clothes on the grass. Her hair was darker wet and slick against her head and neck. Unpinned, it draped about her shoulders. Her eyes appeared larger and a dark blue with her hair smoothed away from her face. She wore her green dress now, the light blue a wet bundle in her arms, and the color suited her.

"You may borrow my soap, if you like. You will not come out smelling of flowers."

I chuckled and accepted the cake from her, waiting until she was seated and turned away before stripping down and plunging into the river. The water was cold and refreshing, and the brisk temperature soothed the ache in my head, jaw, and back. I bathed first, then gave my trousers and shirt a scrub before swimming into deeper water.

"Will you?" Charlotte called, reminding me of her question. She drew a comb through her hair, and I turned away from the temptation to admire the curve of her waist and the intimate movement of the wooden teeth through her hair.

"Aye. 'Tis home." There had been a time when I was a lad when I had wanted to leave, had disdained the toil of my father and grandfather and his father before. But hunched in a trench, I had promised myself that if I made it home, I would never leave. The farm had, at first, become a beacon, and once I returned, it became my lifeblood. I was tethered to that stretch of soil. Pluck a thread of my valley, and I felt the reverberation to my core. I did not care for how stretched those threads felt with such distance between home and where I now stood.

"Rhys."

The alertness in Charlotte's voice had me swimming back to shore in powerful strokes that propelled me through the water. When I reached the shallows, she was standing facing the woods, though she did not have her gun in hand.

"I'm here," I said, voice low, only pausing long enough to yank on my clean trousers.

"Slowly. I do not want to frighten him."

I approached her cautiously, glancing down at her when I reached her side.

She tipped her chin. "Just there."

I followed her direction and saw a dark shadow just within the line of trees. I relaxed and whistled softly. "Here now, *bach*. Here."

The dog edged out of the woods, eyeing us warily. He was tall and leanly built, his black curls dense and littered with twigs. He cautiously wagged his cropped tail.

I knelt, talking softly to him, only realizing I spoke in Welsh when Charlotte whispered, "What are you saying to him?"

"I told him he is a handsome lad and he is safe here. We mean him no harm."

As we spoke, he wandered closer, and when I slowly stretched out a hand, it was the deciding factor for the beast. He crossed the last distance between us at a run. He pressed his angular head into my hand and then pushed past my arm and buried his head against my bare chest.

"The poor lamb." Charlotte dropped to her knees and ran a gentle hand down his back. "Bless his heart. He has half the forest in his coat. Where did he come from, I wonder? I think he is a poodle under all of these leaves and twigs.'

"Aye." I felt his withers, along his back and loins, and inspected his paws. "No injuries. He appears in good health, though perhaps a bit hungry and in need of some care." I cupped his muzzle and lifted his head from my chest to inspect his teeth. He stood passively, showing no hint of aggression or unease. His teeth were in good condition, and I put him at about five or six years of age. His eyes were limpid brown, and he met my gaze with the age-old wisdom and patience canine's possess. I rubbed his ears, and he closed his eyes and leaned into my hand. "Well then, if you can start a fire, I will catch the three of us supper."

Charlotte and the dog both beamed. I stood and retrieved my clean shirt, shrugging my arms into the sleeves and buttoning it before tucking the tails into my trousers. Charlotte collected her wet dress from where it was draped over the rock and my wet garments stretched over the grass and patted her hip as she moved into the trees. "Come, pup. We will have to think of a name for you."

The dog glanced back and forth between us. His tail thumped in the dirt, and he whined. "Go on with you now," I said. "I do not blame you for your choice."

He loped after Charlotte.

A fired burned in the middle of a cleared circle of ground behind the ambulance when I returned to our camp with five carp. Our wet clothes were draped from the side mirrors of the vehicle, and woman and dog sat beside the fire. She used the comb she had drawn through her own hair to work out the mats and debris in the poodle's coat. He lay peaceably on his side, his back leg sticking straight up in the air. She hummed as she went about her task, and I was caught by the picture the pair made.

As I banked the fire and gutted and cleaned the fish, I caught the tune of her humming and smiled. "Puccini?"

She glanced at me, and with her hair soft about her face I could not miss what a fine sight she was, all wispy hair, dark eyes, and sun-like smile. I could not trust her, but I could not resist admiring her. "You know your opera." The dog placed his paw on her thigh, coaxing her back to the task. Already he looked less like an abandoned wild creature and more like a pampered pet with his coat free of the worst snarls.

"My father bought my mother a gramophone one year for *Nadolig*. For Christmas. She loves opera, though I cannot say I care for all of it. Sounds like the wailing of a *cyhyraeth*."

"A *cyhyraeth*?" She stumbled over the pronunciation.

"A spirit who moans and shrieks when it is a person's turn for death."

"Like a banshee?"

"Aye. The Irish have their banshees. We Welsh have our *cyhyraeth*. They make a noise as disagreeable as opera." Her head tilted back as she laughed, exposing the pale, delicate line of her throat. Simply to watch her laugh again, I said, "In the summer, when we left the windows open at night, my mam's gramophone gave the closest neighbors a terrible fright."

My efforts were rewarded, and the dog sighed at the delay and rose to pad over and investigate the fish. I rubbed his ears. "You will have your share, *bach*."

Charlotte wiped her eyes. "Wagner is one of my favorite composers when it comes to the *cyhyraeth* wails." Her pronunciation was smoother this time. "But his work does not sound soothing when hummed. And I endeavor to not fault him for being German."

It was my turn to laugh.

————

Night closed about us swiftly in the shelter of the trees. Charlotte changed the bandaging over the gash at my temple, and then while I buried the fire and cast the fishbones aside, she climbed into the rear of the ambulance and laid out our bedrolls on the stretcher bearers.

"What do you think of Algernon?"

The dog and I looked at one another, and I grimaced. I was certain if the poodle could have managed such an expression, he would have as well. "Algernon is not a name fit for a man, let alone an innocent beast."

"You've said no to all the others as well."

"You are not calling the poor animal Archibald, Beauregard, or Cedric."

"Digby? Eugene?" I knew she was having one on me when she said, "Fauntleroy?" There was a moment of silence and then a snicker from within.

"This is what I attempted to impart upon my son," I said to the dog, who watched me with seeming avid interest if his tilted head and pricked ears were any indication. "Women are fair creatures. Lovely and strong. But passing strange as well, and it is best not to forget the latter."

Charlotte leaned out of the back of the ambulance, her smile wide and full of cheek. "That is sound advice. But I will have you know women prefer the term *mysterious*."

Mysterious. Secretive. I did not know why she kept her knowledge of my son from me. "I will keep that in mind."

We stared at one another for the span of several heartbeats, and in the fire-light I thought I saw her face flush.

"Well." Her tone held a practical crispness I appreciated. "The bedrolls are laid out."

"Get settled. The dog and I will walk round the perimeter once more before we turn in."

"Don't startle me upon returning, please."

I had no desire to have a personal encounter with her Colt. "I will whistle when we approach." I demonstrated, and the dog's ears went up.

The moon was waxing gibbous, but little of its light reached through the barrier of the limbs overhead. The forest was alive in the dark, and the sounds of the night creatures, the scents of the earth and water and woodsy air were comforts. I walked more surely and more at ease, even in the dark, than I had since crossing the Channel.

The dog paused and whined low in his throat.

"What is it now, *bach*?"

A finger of moonlight snuck past the boughs and gleamed in his eyes as he looked up at me. I put a hand on his head and felt a quiver run through his body. I expected him to take off into the night, but he continued with me, a black shadow on silent paws, as I circled back to camp.

A pinpoint of light drew us through the dark like a beacon, and as we approached, I realized Charlotte had lit a lantern. I whistled, and when we reached the ambulance, the dog leapt into the rear. Charlotte was already abed, and I thought she was asleep until she started laughing as the dog climbed onto the stretcher bearer with her and prodded her with his nose.

She propped herself up on an elbow. "Humphrey, there is not enough room for the both of us! What do you think of that name? Or perhaps Lawrence?"

He gave no indication of approval for her name recommendations but proved her wrong by tucking himself into a ball in the bend of her knees. He curled up with a heavy sigh and rested his head on her hip. She stroked his long, narrow muzzle. "Do you think we should look for his owner? Perhaps he is lost."

"Poodles are smart dogs, they are. If there were a home to return to, he would already be there."

"My father had a coon hound. He loved that dog, though she did not care much for anyone but him. I have never had a dog of my own. You?"

"Aye. I have two at home who help me with the sheep. Bess and Bracken. Bess was expecting her first litter of pups when I left. We have always had a menagerie. Owain was forever bringing home animals."

I closed one of the ambulance doors and climbed within, leaving the other ajar to hear anything that might approach. I removed my boots and stretched out on the bedroll Charlotte had prepared for me.

She settled onto her side, hands folded beneath her cheek. "Is Owain your only child?"

I reached out and snuffed the lantern. An acrid waft of smoke curled over my head and escaped through the vent like a ghostly kestrel fleeing into the night. I lay on my back and tucked my arm under my head. "No." The word left me with an almost soundless breath, lost to the night like the waft of smoke. I cleared my throat. "No. There were two others. Twins. I lost the pair and my wife at their birthing."

"I'm sorry. I should not have asked."

"You could not have known. It was many years ago, but I still visit their grave often." Especially within the last few years. "I had the babes buried with Aelwyd. She would have wanted it that way. The priest was none too happy, but…Well, I made him see reason." And had spent several nights in the local gaol after having done so. I flexed my left hand with remembered soreness.

She was quiet for so long I thought she had fallen asleep. Her voice was a mere whisper when she spoke. "We will find Owain."

"Aye, we will." I would not consider any other possibility. And I would discern why she sought him along the way.

———

I woke, as was my habit, before first light. Charlotte slept on, but the dog followed me outside and lay on the shore watching as I caught fish that were slow moving in the dark, cool water.

On our stroll back to camp, the dog halted, tail and ears alert. I glanced around but heard and saw nothing that hinted at danger or another presence. The dog looked up at me, though, and then bolted deeper into the woods, lost from sight quickly in the morning shadows. I whistled and waited for his return, but it did not come.

The fish were cooking over hot coals when Charlotte emerged from the ambulance. The amber light of the new sun glinted on her head and gilded her hair. She lifted a hand in greeting and moved into the woods toward the water. When she returned, the hair about her face was damp and her eyes were clearer.

She sat beside me on a fallen log and leaned toward the fire to smell the fish. Her stomach rumbled. "Where is Galahad?"

I smiled at her choice of names. "Not Lancelot?"

She grimaced. "I never cared for Lancelot. And I always thought Guinevere had cotton for brains."

I chuckled and then broke the news to her gently. "He took off into the woods this morning." Her face fell. "I am certain he will return for breakfast. He ate two fish last night."

But the dog did not return, not even when Charlotte ventured into the brush calling for him. Disappointment was evident in the set of her shoulders as she folded the bedrolls while I doused the embers of the fire.

"We should set off, then, I suppose," she said after checking the petrol tanks and oil.

Before I could suggest one last trek through the woods to find the dog, the distant sound of barking reached our ears.

"That's him! Here, boy! Here!"

He did not respond to her calls for the barking continued but drew no closer.

"Come," I said. "We will find him. But have a care. We do not know what he has found."

Charlotte followed me into the woods, and we both called for the dog, adjusting our course to the direction of his barks. We followed the sound downriver and deeper into the forest. The trees grew less dense, and the boulders dominated the landscape.

"There!" Charlotte pointed ahead and raced forward.

The dog's barking ceased when he saw us, and his tail began to wag. He stood under the edge of an overhang of rock.

"There you are, you silly beast." He leapt up and placed his paws around her waist like a child embracing his mother. "I thought

60

for certain—" Her words cut off, and she stiffened.

"Charlotte?"

She did not respond or turn at my query, just stared into the shadows of the overhang. I lengthened my stride to reach her, stopping abruptly when I caught sight of what held her transfixed.

A soldier lay in the belly of the cave-like rocky protrusion. He was gravely wounded if the amount of dried and caked blood on his clothing and the gray pallor of his face was any indication.

His uniform was German. And the pistol he held in a trembling hand was pointed at Charlotte.

Meghan Holloway

19 October 1940

Dear Nhad,
The OJ published two new "laws" yesterday.
"On the status of the Jews" is the phrasing they used.
I am uneasy. This denaturalizing of a people can only mean ill.
-Owain

V

I stepped in front of her and held up my hands when the gun jerked. My shirt tightened across my shoulders as Charlotte gripped the back.

"I have my gun," she whispered.

I did not take my eyes from the soldier. He met my gaze for several taut moments, and Charlotte's fingers tightened in my shirt. His face was heavily lined with pain, and his eyes were wide and darting. I recognized the wildness in his eyes as fear, and his breath came shallowly and quickly. I could see the struggle it took for him to hold the pistol. "No. Leave it."

The gun dropped to the ground, the arm too weak to hold it up any longer.

"Otto," he whispered. "*Kommen Sie.*"

The dog trotted obediently to his side. The man's eyes closed. He was not a young man. He was closer to my age, perhaps older, and wore the uniform of an officer. A tear leaked from the corner of his eye as he hugged the poodle to him.

"*Bitte.*" He looked up at me, and I could see he fought to keep a tremor from his voice. He nudged the dog toward me. "*Nimm ihn. Bitte.*"

"What is he saying?" Charlotte asked.

"He knows he is dying." How long he had been here and how he had survived even hours after the wound, I did not know. "I think he wants us to take the dog."

"*Bitte,*" he said again. The poodle whined and licked the man's forehead. "*Er heißt Otto.*"

"Take him, Charlotte. His name is Otto."

She released the back of my shirt. "Here, Otto. Here, boy."

The dog whimpered and glanced between us uncertainly.

I nodded at the man. "We will take him. He will be safe."

He may not have understood my words, but he understood the tone for his eyes closed again. "*Danke. Vielen Dank.*"

I knelt beside him. The odor emanating from his wound was unmistakable. I had met death enough to recognize its cloying perfume. A bullet had exited his body with grueling, widespread damage in the center of his abdomen. With careful hands, I rolled him to his side. The bullet had entered at the small of his back. A spine shot.

I eased him down and rubbed the back of my neck before turning to look at Charlotte. She knelt beside Otto, an arm around his neck. "Take this." I picked the Luger up from where it had dropped into the dirt and handed it to her.

"What are you doing?"

I caught the man's arm and lifted him to a seated position. "I apologize. This will hurt." I hefted him up and over my back, taking care to balance his upper legs on my shoulder rather than his gory abdomen. I paused to balance myself with the weight and then rose to my feet. I jostled him as little as possible, but still he groaned.

"Rhys?"

I answered her honestly. "I do not know."

———

The wooden planks rumbled under the tires, and the bridge creaked ominously, listing to the side when we reached its center.

Charlotte did not flinch or hesitate but kept driving at a slow, steady pace. When we jounced onto the sandy road on the opposite bank, though, she took a deep breath and rolled her shoulders.

"Well done."

She darted a small smile in my direction as she shifted gears. She had been silent for hours. The road had narrowed as we drove south, and the trees crept closer about the track. The way was rougher, wilder, and she had been tense the entire time, constantly searching the terrain. Her hand on the gearshift was white knuckled.

We both scanned the road before us. We had ventured west of the river, but streams still traced their way out from the Seine. The sound of the one we had just crossed faded as the ambulance rumbled down the road. It was midday, but the canopy of trees cast deep shadows.

"There," we said at the same time when we caught sight of the turn-off.

Charlotte braked and downshifted. Alfonse had said it was a lane, but it was no more than a path, and branches slapped the hood and scraped along the sides as we turned onto it. The way was rutted and uneven, and the ambulance bounced and rocked through the overgrowth.

There was a groan from the back and a hoarse mumble in delirious German. From the corner of my eye, I saw Charlotte's fingers tighten on the steering wheel and gearshift, and she maneuvered carefully over a rough spot in the path. Even so, I had to brace a hand over my head to keep from hitting the roof.

"I still do not like this."

"I know."

"If the Resistance finds him with us…"

I pointed. "Just ahead."

It was just as Alfonse had described. The church in the meadow was half in ruins, the ancient stone brought down by time rather than the fighting. The forest was working to reclaim the ruins and would soon threaten to overtake the section left standing as well.

Charlotte brought the vehicle to a halt still within the shelter of the trees and killed the engine. "If the Resistance finds him with us, they won't only kill him. They will shoot us as well. They will not ask questions."

I cracked the door into the back of the ambulance. We had raised the stretcher bearer and placed the wounded officer on the lower stretcher. Otto lay across his legs, and he thumped his tail when he saw me. I closed the door and turned to Charlotte. "Do you want to wait here?"

In reply, she slipped out of the cab. I followed suit and rounded the hood to pause beside her. Before I could check the action, I cupped my hand around the back of her neck. She glanced up at me, but her face was in shadows and I could not see the color of her eyes. She held her Colt at her side.

"We will not let them find us."

I felt her hesitate, and then her hand came up and she squeezed my wrist. Her skin was cool against mine. She stepped away and moved within the shadows along the perimeter of the meadow. I watched her for a moment before circling the opposite direction and focusing on the church.

There was no movement, no sounds from within the ruins. Charlotte met me at the far side of the meadow.

"It looks deserted. Perhaps Alfonse was wrong," she whispered.

I put a hand on the butt of the Luger. I had taken the German's holster from his hip and buckled it about my own. "Stay here and keep watch. I want to take a look inside."

I picked my way across the crumbled, briar-filled courtyard, avoiding being in direct line of sight from the yawning entry. I reached the wall and pressed my back to the warm stones. Slipping the Luger from the holster, I crept along the side of the building. I paused when I reached a section of the wall that had weakened and caved outward. With one last glance around, I climbed over the rubble and ducked within.

Nothing stirred. The bell tower had collapsed into the nave, and the result was as if a shell had exploded. The damage to the interior was extensive. The choir and the apse still stood, though the stained glass was long since gone from the windows. Moss made the stone slick underfoot, and vines draped the walls like finely woven tapestries.

It was cool and shadowed, and only one pew remained intact.

The others were rotted or splintered. On the remaining pew, though, was a stack of neatly folded blankets, and on the overturned altar was a lantern.

The apse was laden with hulking shadows, squared edges sharp under the canvas drapery protecting what lay beneath. I holstered the Luger and approached the curved recess, my footfall muffled by the carpet of moss. I grasped the edge of the canvas and pulled. The heavy protective fabric unfurled like a wave, eddies of dust drifting upwards to catch in the sunlight like a spray of sea foam. I stepped back, coughing into my elbow, and took in the storehouse that had been unveiled.

Dozens of crates were stacked shoulder to shoulder in the space. The sizes were varying—some taller than me, others no larger than a child's height. All were tightly slatted and nailed shut. I could find no identifying markings on the crates, but I could hazard a guess at their contents.

I retreated from the chapel. "Bring the crowbar from the ambulance."

"What did you find?"

"Bring it and see."

I watched Charlotte's face carefully as she took in the crates, noting the excitement that lit her eyes and the satisfied curve of her lips. I took the crowbar from her and slipped the edge into the seam of the crate, leaning down on the tool to pry the nails loose.

As soon as the top was ajar, Charlotte lifted it and carefully eased aside the fabric wrapped around the contents. Her breath caught as she unveiled the sculpture within the crate.

I set the crowbar aside and knelt beside her. "Is it from the Louvre?" I could not see much detail about the piece looking at it from such an angle. It was bronze, the figure of a man clasping a woman to him with his face tucked into the curve of her neck.

"No." Charlotte's voice was but a whisper. A sheen of moisture glinted in her eyes. "This is a Camille Claudel. She died in an asylum last year. I tried to send her a letter a few years ago, but her brother wrote back to me instead." She caressed the heads bent together with a gentle finger. "I thought she had destroyed all of her work." She took as much care with wrapping the sculpture back in its protective layers as one would with swaddling an infant. When she sat back on her heels, I replaced the top of the crate. She reached for the crowbar. "I want to check the others."

"Help me bring the German in. Then I'll open the other crates."

She straightened and turned to eye the blankets and lantern. "At nightfall, we can light the lantern."

We carried the German into the church on a stretcher with Otto trotting ahead of us.

"Is he a war dog, then?" Charlotte's voice was strained as we climbed over the rubble, but her grip never faltered.

The poodle navigated the rubble with agile ease and darted into the ruins of the nave.

"Aye, I wager so."

We laid the German in the corner of the choir. His eyes were open but glazed, and he struggled to focus on Charlotte. "Analise." He sighed and closed his eyes but continued to speak to the woman he thought was present until his voice faded along with his consciousness.

"I do not understand why you are trying to save him."

I followed her back to the ambulance and gathered our satchels and bed rolls while she disabled the vehicle. "I am not saving him."

"But you—"

"He is beyond saving. The man is dying. It is only a matter of time. I do not know how he has lasted this long."

Her brow was knit as she turned to me, and her voice was heated. "He is the *enemy*."

"Aye. But I could not leave him to that fate, Charlotte. Deserved or not, I could not leave him to such a grueling end, alone with animals picking at his flesh before he is fully gone."

She sighed and rubbed her forehead, looking away.

"I know you are angry, and I—"

70

"I'm not angry," she said. "I am frightened. Here, I will take the bedrolls."

I relinquished them and remained rooted to the spot where I stood, watching as she crossed the sun-dappled meadow, light and shadow playing over her, and then disappeared into the church.

While Charlotte went through the crates in the apse, I set snares in the woods and caught two rabbits and a quail. I dressed the game and cooked them over a fire in the twilight. As Charlotte and I ate—each of use sharing our portions with Otto, who took the food delicately from our fingers but ate enthusiastically—the German awakened.

I tucked two blankets under his head and shoulders to prop him up.

"*Danke, danke. Ich heiße Wilhelm.*" He jerked a thumb toward his chest. "Wilhelm."

"Wilhelm?"

"*Ja.*"

"Rhys."

Charlotte touched my shoulder, and when I looked up at her, she handed me one of the canteens. "He may be thirsty." She nodded to the man and smiled, though it was strained at the edges. "Charlie." She glanced at me, and her smile became easier and brighter. "Or Charlotte."

The man drank messily, water spilling down his chin, and we both ignored the liquid pooling in the gore of his abdomen.

"Night is falling," Charlotte whispered, looking up at the empty arch of windows. The sun was taking her last breaths, bleeding into the sky the deep red and purple of her last light of day before the cool balm of moonlight soothed the wound of her passing. "This must have been a lovely church once."

"Aye. We best light the lantern."

I covered Wilhelm with a blanket, ensuring all traces of his uniform were hidden from sight. I met his gaze and held a finger to my mouth. He nodded in understanding.

Charlotte and I secured the lids on the crates. Twenty-six sculptures were secreted away in the midst of the ruins. If Charlotte sought a specific piece, she did not find it here. Though she recognized some of the works, sharing the history of the ones she knew with me, she did not linger over them and did nothing more than study them.

I knew more than curiosity drove her to check the contents of each crate. And I knew she searched for something, because her brow was pleated with disappointment as we drew the canvas back into place to shroud the hidden art and retreated from the apse.

The night had deepened to pitch before I heard movement from outside the church. Charlotte and Otto sat in the floor beside me. She was working her comb through his coat, but the dog sat up now. He did not growl, but he stared into the darkness toward the fallen bell tower, alert and watchful. I touched Charlotte's shoulder. "Someone comes," I said, voice low.

She tensed and moved the skirt of her dress aside to show me that her gun rested on the stones beside her. I fought a smile.

A man stepped from the shadows and stood at the edge of the dim pool of light emitted from the lantern. He appeared ancient, stooped and gnarled with age, his face weathered by time and long years spent working in the sun. He carried a staff and leaned heavily on it, but when he spoke, his voice was strong.

"*Demain, dès l'aube, à l'heure où blanchit la campagne, je partirai.*"

Charlotte's brow wrinkled.

"What did he say?"

"He makes no sense. He is quoting poetry: 'Tomorrow, at dawn, in the hour when the countryside becomes white, I will leave.'"

I stood. "Sir, I—"

He squinted and moved further into the light. "Owain?"

"His father." I looked to Charlotte.

"*Son père.*" She brushed off her dress as she gained her feet and translated and then listened to the old man's response. "He says

72

the resemblance is startling and that you should have a care. It could be dangerous to be mistaken for your son."

I gestured to the pew I had vacated. "Please."

The man moved at a shuffle, his staff ringing against the stone. He sat, passing a hand over Otto's head before resting both over the gnarled end of the cane. He thrust his chin at where Wilhelm lay and spoke.

Charlotte hesitated, glancing at the German before responding. They exchanged words for a moment before she turned to me. "His name is Benoit, and he owns the land this church is on."

"How does he know my son?"

While they spoke, I glanced at Wilhelm. His eyes were closed. I did not know if he truly slept or merely feigned it. Otto padded across the room and lay by his side with his chin on the German's shoulder.

"He says it was Owain who approached him several years ago about using the church. It is a safe haven, a resting point. He said that the site has been part of your son's network since '42. He said the Germans have never suspected and have never come to question him." I could see the effort it took her to not look to the pallet in the corner.

His network. "Ask him why it would be dangerous to be mistaken for Owain and where I can find him."

Charlotte relayed my question. "When he was last here, Owain told him it would be his last transport, that the Americans were coming and it would be different once the Germans were driven out. He says he last saw your son in June and expected to see him on his return, but he should have been here weeks ago. He never returned. He is afraid of what may have happened to him."

"Returned from where? Does Benoit know where Owain goes from here?"

When Charlotte asked the man, he met my gaze. "Vichy."

———

Benoit returned in the morning with food, petrol, and a rifle. He handed me the latter. It was a Lebel Model 1886, an 8mm bolt action rifle I recognized from the Great War.

When he spoke, his voice was somber. Charlotte translated. "He wants you to have the rifle. He lost all three sons in the last war and a grandson in this one. He said from what he knows of Owain, he is a brave man, and he knows you must be a good man to come so far to find your son. He says he would be proud for you to carry his rifle."

The words struck me. "I am honored."

He and Charlotte conversed further. "He says to find the librarian at the missionary house in Vichy, that she will be able to aid us."

A groan came from the corner and the three of us glanced toward the pallet. Wilhelm's head tossed restlessly, but thankfully he uttered no other sound. Charlotte looked at me from the corner of her eye but responded calmly to Benoit's query.

He bade us farewell and clasped my hand tightly in a gnarled, work-roughened grip. When he was gone, Charlotte turned to me. "He wanted to know if our friend was injured. I said merely ill."

"We need to get rid of the uniform."

The trousers would be covered and would not garner notice, but the coat was undeniably German. I undid the top four buttons. He wore a plain shirt underneath. The bottom half of his coat had shredded with the exit of the bullet.

Charlotte knelt at his head and lifted his upper body onto her lap to ease the garment from his shoulders. I used a knife and carefully cut away the cloth from where it had crusted and dried into his wound. I did not want to tear it free and renew the bleeding.

Wilhelm moaned as we worked to the remove the identifiable outer layer of his uniform, and Otto whined where he lay across his master's legs.

"All is well, *bach*," I said. I sliced up the sleeves and worked the coat from under him.

Wilhelm's eyes opened, but I did not think he saw us. He looked up at Charlotte and smiled. "Analise, *liebchen, engelchen*." He continued to murmur to his absent love.

Though she held herself stiffly, when a tear escaped from his eye and slid down his temple, Charlotte wiped it away. Her hand trembled and then settled against the side of his face. "Shh," she whispered. "Shh." He stilled and quieted immediately, and she looked up at me, eyes dark and lost. "We should burn the coat."

I buried it instead in the rubble of the shattered nave. Wilhelm rested more easily and made no sound when we carried him to the ambulance and loaded him on the stretcher bearer.

I started to stow the French rifle with our supplies, but instead I rounded the ambulance and placed it between the back of the driver's seat and the spare tire. Largely hidden from sight but within my reach. While Charlotte replaced the part she had removed from the engine, I filled the tanks with petrol and then retrieved the map. Charlotte joined me at the back of the ambulance as I spread it across the floor.

She traced a finger across the country. "The demarcation line was here. We will come upon it along the river here going into Moulins, but I do not know what to expect now. I have not ventured that far south since before the war."

"We may come upon Allied forces as well. And the Germans will be retreating even still."

We both looked at Wilhelm's prone figure. "As long as he is with us," Charlotte said, "I think it is best to avoid villages. He is slipping further into delirium, and as soon as someone hears him speaking German…"

"If it happens, we will say we found him and are transporting him to authorities."

"People will question why we did not simply kill him outright."

"Let them. He is already a dead man."

She nodded and leaned back over the map. "I think we can make it here by the day's end. To the east of Bourges on the Loire." Otto hopped out of the back of the ambulance as Charlotte climbed up and latched the left door and then closed the right. He followed her around the vehicle.

I folded the map and tucked it back into the satchel, stowing the rear steps before circling to the cab. Otto sat between us, and when I rubbed his ears, he looked up at me with his tongue lolling and mouth open as if smiling.

Within an hour, we left the forest behind. The land stretched south in a flat, featureless expanse with only the occasional village and oasis of trees for relief.

My jaw was not as stiff today, but the bright sun overhead produced a pulse that beat in my temples. As the sun approached its zenith, I realized the haze in the sky to the west was not simply an illusion in the rising temperatures of midday. It was dust.

I leaned over and retrieved the rifle from where I had stowed it.

Charlotte glanced at me, brow knitting when she saw the Lebel across my knees. "What is it?"

"Look to the west."

Her hands tightened on the wheel. "That's not a storm blowin' up. Something approaches."

"Something large."

She downshifted, and the vehicle began to slow. "Should I—"

"Keep going. We—" My ears pricked to a growing hum, and I scanned the sky. "Get off the road. Now." I opened the door into the back of the ambulance, pushed Otto within, and closed it behind him.

"Hold on."

I gripped the doorframe as Charlotte shifted gears and spun the wheel. We lurched off the road and into the adjacent field, bouncing violently over the rutted land. We raced toward a copse of trees in the middle of the field.

The hum grew to a thunder, and then four fighter-bombers pierced the dusty haze and roared toward us.

12 November 1940

Dear Nhad,
There were thousands of students in the processions yesterday
along the Champs-Élysées. The Germans were brutal in their response.
But the French have found their voices.
-Owain

vi

We skidded into the shelter of trees, snapping saplings under the carriage, just as the fighters screamed past overhead. We bounced to a jarring halt, and Otto howled in the back of the ambulance.

I leapt out.

"Rhys!"

"Stay down!" I shouted as I ran to the edge of the trees. I shaded my eyes and looked to the sky. Relief almost made me stagger. "Back out of the trees! It's the Americans. They will not fire when they see the cross."

The planes were looping to circle back over us. The ambulance's engine whirred.

"Quickly, Charlotte!"

"We're stuck! Something is caught underneath!"

"*Coc oen.*" I sprinted back to the ambulance, tossing Charlotte the rifle as I ran past. I shoved my shoulder against the hot metal of the front grill, ignoring the burn, and gripped the tow bar, pushing with all of my might. "Hit the accelerator!" I shouted above the growing thunder of the approaching fighters.

There was a groan of metal, and then with an ominous crack the ambulance leapt backward so quickly I fell to my knees. "Go, go, go!"

She sped in reverse out of the shelter of the trees and into the open daylight just as the fighters buzzed our position. All four pulled up sharply, climbing and looping away from us.

I got to my feet, heart thrumming, and hurried to the driver's side of the ambulance. Otto was barking wildly in the back.

"You are hurt."

Charlotte blinked at me, eyes wide. "What?"

I reached up and wiped the blood from her check. A narrow cut followed the line of her cheekbone, a layer of skin scraped off. "You have a scram here."

She started at the sight of her blood on my fingers and pressed the back of her hand to the wound. "A tree branch must have caught me." She leaned back and cracked the door. "Hush your mouth, Otto. Settle now." She climbed down from the seat and staggered when her feet hit the ground. I caught her elbow and held on until she was steady. "I think we broke a spring."

"Can it be fixed?"

"Yes, but—" Charlotte's eyes widened, and she stared behind me.

I turned to find tanks, Jeeps, and scores of men marching toward us. The ground rumbled beneath our feet and the din of an approaching army grew.

Charlotte gripped my arm. "Wilhelm…"

"We could turn him over to them, but there is no need. He is a wounded soldier who is almost dead."

She searched my face and then nodded.

A Dodge command car broke from the mass and veered toward us. Two flags flew on either side of the hood. Both were red and white. One had three stars; the other was emblazoned with the number *3* on it. A tall man stood in the car, and the sun gleamed off of his polished helmet. As the Dodge drew even with us, his high cavalry boots hit the ground before the vehicle had even come to a complete stop. He strode toward us in ground-eating strides with the slightly splayed stance of a man who had spent much of his time on horseback. He wore a revolver on each hip, and both were ivory-gripped. A bull terrier leapt out of the Dodge and trotted close at his heels. I swallowed a chuckle when I saw the G.I. dog tags around the canine's neck.

I thought the decades old habit had been forgotten, but as he approached, I snapped a sharp salute.

80

"What's happened here?" His *here* sounded more like *heah*.

"We did not realize you were American, General, sir."

"Those Thunderbolts and Mustangs are a damn fearful sight. Is the ambulance wrecked?"

"No, sir," Charlotte said. "But I think a spring is broken."

He focused shrewd eyes on her. "You the one driving this thing?"

She straightened her shoulders. "I am, sir."

His face seemed etched in a perpetual scowl, and the lines on his forehead and around his eyes were deep. But at her affirmation, a surprisingly boyish smile split his face. "I'll be damned. We have so many god-awful drivers it's a relief to come across a good one. Damn fine evasive measures, miss. If you were a man, I would be proud to have you in the Third."

I hid a smile as Charlotte's cheeks flushed. "Thank you, sir."

"You carrying wounded in the back?"

"One," I said carefully. "Gravely wounded."

"Is there anything a field surgeon can do for him?"

"No, sir. A spine and gut shot. It is only a matter of time."

"Fucking shame. I'd like a word with him."

I saw Charlotte stiffen from the corner of my eye. "He is in and out of delirium, sir."

"I'll be brief."

I nodded at Charlotte, and after a moment's hesitation, she unlatched the rear door. He did not bother with the fold-out steps as he climbed in. Otto lay across Wilhelm's legs, but he sat up when the door opened.

"Handsome boy you have here." The general rested his hand on the dog's head for a moment and then leaned over the unconscious German. He placed a hand on Wilhelm's shoulder and removed his helmet, holding it over his heart. "You've done well, son. Rest easy now." He repositioned his helmet, smiled at Otto, and then climbed down from the ambulance. "That's a fine German pistol you're

81

wearing."

Inwardly, I cursed my carelessness, but I kept my voice even. "I took it off a German soldier."

"Well done, man!" He clapped me on the back hard enough to stagger a smaller man. "Those Kraut sonsabitches will soon have neither their guns nor their lives when the Third is finished with them. Carry on." He strode back to his command car. "Willie, come along." The bull terrier looked up from sniffing around one of the ambulance's tire and raced after his master.

Charlotte leaned into me. "Was that…?"

"Aye."

We watched as he shouted for a group of men to join him beside his car. They hurried over and listened attentively, glancing over their shoulders at us almost as one. Then he climbed into the Dodge, the dog bounding in after him, and roared off.

The group of soldiers approached us, and the one in the lead spoke. "The Old Man said we're to help you get the ambulance back in working order."

"We'd be much obliged," Charlotte said, her accent thickening winsomely.

"Private, help move their wounded," the one in the lead instructed.

A short, stocky boy stepped forward and climbed into the back of the ambulance to take the head of the stretcher. I took the other end, and we carried Wilhelm into the shelter of the trees. He groaned as we placed his stretcher on the ground but made no other sound. Otto took his place lying at his master's side.

Charlotte was sliding out from under the ambulance when I returned, and I noted all six men hurried forward to help her to her feet.

"It's the rear right spring," she said. "It is cracked in two."

"Can you fix it?" I asked.

"No, I can only replace it. Which I could do if I had the part."

"We can get it for you, ma'am."

"Thank you…"

"Corporal Orin, ma'am."

"Thank you, Corporal Orin. You can get me a rear spring? They're longer than a front spring."

"Yes, ma'am, Private Edwards here is the best mechanic we have," the corporal said, gesturing to the boy who'd helped me with the stretcher. "He can fix it for you himself."

"That won't be necessary." She smiled at the private, and his ears turned red. "But some assistance would be greatly appreciated."

As the private hurried away to find the part, the corporal asked, "What may we do to help, miss?"

"Just Charlie will do, please. We'll need to chock all the wheels save the rear right one and jack up the axle till that wheel is just clear of the ground."

"Currer, Ellis, you two find some rocks we can stack to take the weight of the frame once we have the jack in place."

"I will get my toolkit."

———

The Army's eastward forge streamed around the ambulance while repairs were being made as if men and tanks were a ceaseless current and we were a rock on the riverbed around which the water diverged. Once the spring was replaced, we thanked the soldiers who had helped us and continued south, soon breaking free of the flow of troops. I watched in the side mirror as the ribbon of raised dust grew closer and closer to the horizon.

Wilhelm had regained consciousness as he was loaded back into the ambulance, but he had wisely kept silent.

The rest of the afternoon passed without event, and the shadow we cast upon the road lengthened. Twilight crept over us in the wake of the sun like a cool, dark cat pacing after a golden bird upon the windowsill.

"It's a risk, but the moon has been bright enough to drive by,"

83

Charlotte said. "Shall we continue?"

I agreed, and we drove into the night. The moon was a bright pearl clasped at the hollow of the night's deep blue throat. The open plain across which we drove was bathed in the soft light and the road stretched before us like a pale stream.

"Tell me a story."

I glanced at Charlotte. The moon seemed to caress her face and her hands at the wheel. "I have no talent for tales."

"Tell me about your home, then."

"Ah." I closed my eyes and took a deep breath, imagining my lung were filled with the earthy aroma of soil, wet sheep, and rain-drenched heather. "I almost lost Owain once before, when he was just a small lad of six..."

My mother met me at the door as soon as I crossed the threshold. "Are they not with you? Your father and Owain?"

"No." I had begun to unwind my scarf and coax my fingers from my mitts, but I halted. "They have not returned home? They should have been back hours ago."

She twisted her apron in her hands. "I know. I walked the lower pastures calling for them. Should I fetch the neighbors to help us search?"

"Not yet. Let me get a torch, and I will search. You stay here, put a kettle on. It is bitter out."

I set back out into the waning light of the gloaming. The wind was biting, and it carried my voice away as I called for them. I searched our northern fields to no avail, climbed the last stone fence that marked the edge of the Gravenor land, and set off into the hills. The dark and the cold deepened, and it was full night by the time I reached the stone fence denoting the Driscoll's land.

The moon was cloaked in dark clouds that refused to relinquish her light onto the hills. I flicked on the torch and panned the beam across the field. The gleam of curious gazes of sheep caught in the light, but there was no sign of my father or son.

Thunder rolled over the hills, and the sky to the west flickered ominously. "Ffaddyr! Owain! If you can hear me, machgen i, answer me!"

All was quiet for several long moments, and then I heard the faint sound of barking. My knees threatened to buckle, and I braced a hand on the stones to steady myself.

"Rhiannon! Here, fy merch!"

The barking came again, closer this time, and from the north. I lengthened my stride and continued to call for the collie until her lean body separated from the shadows and raced into my light. I knelt as she came to me and ran my hands over her. She was uninjured, and as soon as I said, "Where are they, Rhi?" she raced back into the night along the fence line.

I followed her some distance before my light caught on two figures. My father was slumped against the stone fence with his staff across his knees as if he had merely leaned there to rest and had fallen asleep. Perhaps he had. My father and Owain frequently reminded me of a pair of cats, always finding a pool of sunlight in which to bask and slumber.

But it was not sleep that claimed my father. I knew even before I reached him. I staggered and bent double, bracing my hands on my knees as a sob threatened to resonate through my chest like thunder did over us in that moment. The small figure at his side stirred, visibly shaking, prodding me from the welling grief.

"Owain." My throat was tight.

"I cannot get Tadcu to wake, Dadi."

I knelt beside them and caught his small body close. He clung to me, and I stripped off my coat and wrapped it around him. "Are you hurt?" I shone my light at his tear-streaked face.

He shook his head. "We were trying to find the lost ewe, and Tadcu said he needed to rest. I fell asleep when we sat down, Dadi, I did not mean to. And when I woke up, I could not get Tadcu to wake." His voice trembled.

85

"Hush now. Do not fret. I will take care of Tadcu. Did you not know the way home?"

He wiped his nose on the sleeve of my coat. *"I did, but I didn't want the pwca to get Tadcu. Billy Hughes told me they roam the hills. He said they change shape and come upon you when you are not watching for them and steal you away forever."*

Rhiannon nudged my side, and I rubbed her ears while I fought the urge to tell Owain that Billy Hughes might as well have stones between his ears. *"All is well now. I need you to be a strong lad and follow me home. I will carry Tadcu, and I need you to stay close to me. Carry the light, and hold on to Rhi. Mamgu is waiting for us."*

He looked up at me as I stood. *"Is Tadcu going to wake up?"*

I rested my hand on his head and had to clear my throat before I spoke. *"No, machgen i, he is not."*

I carried my father down the hills to home, his weight heavy in my arms. My mother met us in the yard and swept Owain into her arms before hurrying ahead of me to open the door. She wept as I placed my father in his bed. I took Owain from her, and as we left the room, she was crawling into bed, drawing a quilt over my father's prone form.

I had Owain drink a cup of tea as I bathed him in the washtub. He was quiet, his head hanging as if it were too heavy for his fragile neck to hold the weight. He felt so slight in my arms as I wrapped him in a blanket and sat in front of the stoked fire with him in my lap. Rhiannon took up her place at my feet.

"You did a very brave thing today, Owain." He burrowed closer to me, tucking his head under my chin. *"But I would have lost you had I not been able to find you tonight, and that is something I could not bear. I was very frightened."*

He was quiet for several long minutes, but his fingers plucking at my shirt assured me he had not fallen asleep. *"I was not frightened, Dadi. I knew you would find me."*

"I am sorry about your father," Charlotte whispered in the

ensuing silence.

"Do not be. He died exactly how he would have wanted, had he had any say in the matter."

———

We were both quiet as the kilometers passed by under the ambulance's wheels. We reached the outskirts of La Charité-sur-Loire some time later and parked in the deep shadows cast by the ramparts at the far edge of the village.

An owl called hauntingly into the night and remained unanswered as I sat at the back of the ambulance and watched Charlotte and Otto roam along the ancient wall. Woman and dog were merely shadow against shadow, but the murmur of Charlotte's low voice reached my ears and I smiled to hear her conversing with the canine at her side.

"I thank you for looking after Otto."

I froze at the heavily-accented but clear English words spoken behind me, my hand going to the pistol holstered at my hip. Wilhelm sighed and rolled his head toward me as I stood and climbed into the back of the ambulance.

"He has been my closest friend, like a child, for many years now, and I did not want him to stay with me as I died in the woods," he whispered. I shut the door behind me. He must have sensed my mind racing over everything said within his earshot. "I mean you no harm."

"You have been able to understand us this entire time."

"I am an officer and an educated man. I speak many languages."

"Why tell me now?"

"Because I do not wish to die in silence." We both glanced toward the closed door at Otto's playful bark and Charlotte's laughter nearby. "Do not tell the woman. It would only cause her more suspicion."

I nodded. "Do you have family, anyone I should try to send word to?"

His smile was bittersweet, and the low lantern light deepened the lines in his face. "Only the dog you have agreed to care for."

"He will not be abandoned," I promised.

"I know." He shifted, features pinching in pain, and I adjusted the blankets over him when a shiver coursed through his frame. "Thank you. For everything. Your son should be proud to call you father."

Before I could respond, Charlotte opened the door and glanced between the two of us. "Is everything well?"

"Aye. He was restless and fading into delirium again. I did not want the sound to carry. We do not know who may be listening."

Otto leapt into the ambulance ahead of her and settled with a sigh across Wilhelm's legs. She closed the ambulance doors behind her as she climbed in and opened the vents before kneeling and drawing out a satchel from beneath the stretcher bearer. She fished within and extended a handful of leather to me.

"German or not, it is safer if you keep the pistol hidden. You can wear this under your shirt."

I unbuckled the hip holster and set it aside before turning my back to her as I unbuttoned my shirt. I shrugged it off my shoulders to allow it to hang around my hips, caught by the shirt tails tucked into my trousers. I wore an undershirt and slipped the shoulder holster on over it. I felt a touch at my back and the fit of the holster changed as Charlotte adjusted the straps.

"Your draw will be slowed tremendously, but it is a risk we will have to take. It is less risky than the wrong person seeing you with a pistol."

The fit was comfortable, and the Luger fit snuggly within the pocket. I shrugged out of the holster and placed it beside my bedroll before buttoning my shirt. When I turned back to Charlotte, her cheeks were pink but she did not avert her eyes.

"Is this how you carry the Colt?" The curiosity had plagued me since Paris.

"A thigh holster and a false pocket," she said, smile full of cheek. "I had no desire to part with my Colt and equally no desire to be executed. Carrying it hidden was my solution."

She was a remarkable woman, even with her secrets, and when she allowed me to lift her onto the raised stretcher bearer over Wilhelm, her hands lingered on my shoulders while mine lingered at her waist. I forced myself to withdraw and extinguished the dim light of the lantern before settling onto the bearer on the opposite side of the ambulance.

Silence descended around us with the darkness, and I heard a rustle as Charlotte shifted on the top stretcher. My senses felt pricked toward her, and I could tell when the exhaustion of the day caught up with her. Her breathing became deep and even. I focused on that easy rhythm and allowed it to lull me into slumber.

25 December 1940

Dear Nhad,
Nadolig Llawen. I miss you and Mamgu, Bess and Bracken.
I miss home. But I cannot return. Not yet.
I find I have a need within me to prove
I am not the coward you think me.
-Owain

vii

We followed the Loire south, against its northward flow, until we reached the point where the river joined its left tributary. The Loire flowed from the east, and once we found a place to cross the eastward branch, we followed the southern tributary, the Allier.

It led us through Moulins and through smaller villages that were silent and still. We drove around unmanned checkpoints. The tree growth grew denser, and the brown river narrowed and widened as it undulated through the countryside. Along several stretches, sandy shoals served as small islands in the center of the river or as peninsular shores where the water was low. The river carved a serpentine path through alluvial forest and then gradually widened and straightened as we entered the outskirts of Vichy.

We arrived at midday and parked in an alley at the edge of town.

"We may need to leave in haste," I reminded Charlotte when she moved to disable the vehicle.

Her indecision was clear on her face. "But better to need to spend a few moments at this than risk coming back to find the ambulance has been stolen..."

I had to concede her point, and while she disabled the vehicle, I slipped into the back of the ambulance. Otto's cropped tail thumped in greeting, and I rested a hand on his head as I handed Wilhelm the rifle. His look was questioning, and I kept my voice low.

"We have hidden the ambulance out of the way, but I do not know who may happen upon this alley."

He nodded and spoke to the dog in brisk German. Otto's

demeanor changed in an instant at the command, and he went from loving pet to trained war dog in a shift of muscle.

I exited the ambulance by the rear doors and closed them behind me. Charlotte rounded the vehicle. "Do you know where the library is?"

She shook her head. "No, but I imagine near the town centre. We will head there and ask if need be. Keep your eyes open. The Milice here have a more brutal reputation than the Gestapo."

We moved cautiously through neighborhoods in the grip of unease. Suspicion, shame, and jubilation were stamped on each face we saw in varying degrees.

An old woman watched us from a doorway and called sharply to three young boys playing with a hoop and stick in the street. They froze, the hoop clattering to the ground, as they watched us approach until the woman called again, and they raced past her skirts into the precarious safety of home. She followed them and secured the door after her.

The wooden hoop lay like the sun-bleached carcass of childhood innocence in the street where it had fallen. As we passed, I picked it up and leaned it against the closed threshold through which they had retreated.

"Rhys, that woman." Charlotte caught hold of my arm and clung, her unease evident in the taut grip of her fingers. "Why is her head shaved?"

I followed her gaze and saw the woman on the opposite side of the street walking with her arms folded across her chest and her shoulders hunched as if braced for a blow. She walked swiftly with her gaze down.

"Stay close to me," I said, voice low.

Charlotte nodded and did not relinquish her hold on my arm as we navigated the streets. "Do you think she was a Jewish sympathizer? Is that why her head is shaved?"

"Perhaps, but I do not know."

A stooped, gnarled man swept his doorstep with painstaking care ahead of us, and when we reached him, Charlotte paused. *"Pardon, monsieur, savez-vous où est la bibliothèque missionnaire?"*

When he cocked his head toward her voice but peered past her shoulder, I realized his eyes were sightless. They conversed for several moments. When he finished telling her how to find the library, she thanked him and turned to me. "He said the missionary house is on Rue Mounin, near the thermal baths. The library must be part of the house." She smiled. "He said that he has heard that the building is large and white and has the name *Bethanie* on it, but that has never aided him."

I chuckled. "I suppose it would not."

We found the missionary house easily with the old blind man's directions, and a woman greeted us as soon as we entered the arched doorway. After Charlotte conversed with her in hushed tones, she led us through the building to the library. The place was still with the hallowed quiet generally reserved for a church. The smell of old paper permeated the room, and light streamed through the high arched windows. We wandered further within, and Charlotte finally released her hold on my arm. The shelves were set up like a set of ribs down the long, narrow room.

The woman who escorted us called out. When there was no response, she spoke to Charlotte in hushed tones and withdrew from the room.

"She invited us to wait here while she finds the librarian." Charlotte wandered down the long spine of the room, glancing down the rows of shelves.

I followed and slipped between the shelves to study the collection. I could not read any of the titles on the heavy leather tomes save for one on a shelf above my head. The leather was worn along the edges of the cracked spine. The gilded script read *La Bible.*

It was large and weighty, and when I pulled it from the shelf, I realized the pages bulged around a thin panel of wood tucked within. I cradled the spine in my hand and opened the book with care.

The fine pages wafted aside to reveal a painting hidden in the center of the book. It was a portrait, done in dark, muted colors.

I kept my voice low when I called Charlotte's name, and after a moment, she slipped around the shelves and joined me. I held the bible out to her wordlessly.

Her brow wrinkled as she approached, and then her eyes widened as she took in what I held. Her indrawn breath was audible.

"Rhys." Her voice was a breath of sound, and awe laced her tone. "I think…I think this is a Rembrandt."

"The Dutch painter?"

Her fingers hovered over the painting without touching it. "Painter, printmaker, draughtsman. The man epitomized the word master in the arts." She eyed the laden shelves around us. "What else is hidden here?"

"*Bonjour?*" a soft, feminine voice called from out of sight.

Charlotte started, and I carefully closed the bible around the painting and slipped it back onto the high shelf.

Charlotte exited the row ahead of me as the speaker stepped around the shelves at the far end of the room and came toward us. She was young and plainly dressed, but her face was lovely and accented by the dark scarf wrapped decoratively around her head. "*Puis-je vous aider?*"

Charlotte answered her. "*Demain, dès l'aube, à l'heure où blanchit la campagne, je partirai.*"

The woman flinched as if Charlotte had struck her and then her eyes went wide when she focused on me. Her throat worked visibly before she spoke again. "*Vois-tu, je sais que tu m'attends. J'irai par la forêt, j'irai par la montagne. Je ne puis demeurer loin de toi plus longtemps.*" Her voice trembled.

When Charlotte relaxed, I knew her response was what Benoit told Charlotte to look for. She started to speak again, but the woman held up her hand, indicating silence. She glanced over her shoulder at the empty doorway.

"You cannot be here," the woman whispered in heavily accented English.

"I am—"

"I know whom you are. You cannot be here. They are watching."

"Who is watching?" Charlotte darted a glance at me.

The woman shook her head, wringing her hands.

"You recognized me," I said.

"Owain favors you strongly. He is not here, if you seek him."

"When did you see him last?"

She shrugged and paced past us to straighten a shelf of books. "It was last month that I saw him. We do not see him regularly, and we do not always know when he will come and need shelter."

"We?" Charlotte asked.

A knock sounded on the door and it cracked open immediately to reveal a middle-aged man dressed in the vestments of priesthood. "Nanette?" As he spoke, Charlotte glanced back and forth between the two of them. The young woman swallowed, throat working, and her voice was hoarse when she responded to the priest.

He came further into the room at her words. "You are Owain's father?"

"I am. I am searching for him. If you have any word, any knowledge of his whereabouts, it would aid me."

"He and Séverin were here possibly five weeks ago, it was. We—"

The young woman yelped as Charlotte reached up suddenly and yanked the scarf from her head. Her hair, like the woman's on the street, was closely and roughly shorn. The woman's eyes closed, and she fell to her knees before the priest.

His face paled, and his hand trembled as he reached out as if to touch her head, but only allowed his fingers to ghost over her shorn hair. "Oh, Nanette. What have you done?"

"My god," Charlotte said. "You are not a Jewish sympathizer.

97

You're a Nazi sympathizer."

The woman looked up at the priest, and a lone tear rolled down her cheek. A torrent of French fell from her lips, but I interrupted her. "Did you betray my son?"

She flinched, and she turned to me but did not lift her gaze to meet mine. "I had to."

Charlotte drew her gun and pointed the pistol at the woman's head. She bowed her head, shoulders slumped. The priest knelt beside her, shielding her, and before I could put the question to her, he asked, "Why?" in a voice that cracked.

Words poured from her in a sodden torrent, and I watched the priest's face crumble at her explanation. He swallowed audibly, and this time he allowed his hand to rest on her head. "You foolish, foolish child."

"Where would Owain have gone from here? Look at me," I said, voice hard when she began to cry, waiting until her damp gaze met mine before continuing. "You know the next stop in his network?"

The priest answered for her. "There are caves along the Rhône in a village called La Balme-les-Grottes."

I turned and walked away, striding through the building and out into the afternoon sunlight. I bent double, bracing my hands on my knees as I struggled to draw air into my lungs. I flinched at the soft touch on my back, and as I straightened, Charlotte's hand fell away.

"Why did she betray Owain?"

Charlotte sighed. "They threatened the priest and the library, telling her they would drag the man and the entire collection into the streets and set both alight."

There was no comfort in knowing she had exchanged my son's life for another's. "If what she says is true, we need to leave. I cannot afford to delay. Not now that…" My voice caught.

"I know." She tucked her hand into the crook of my elbow. "Free French or Milice, I do not care to be waylaid by either. They do not ask questions. They interrogate."

Her footsteps were hurried as we moved along the narrow streets, but I covered her tense fingers with mine and slowed the pace. "We will only draw attention if we race."

She nodded, gaze straight ahead, spine rigid. We picked the streets we traversed at random, pausing only long enough to ensure we were not turning into an alley that ended at a stone wall. I made certain that at every turn, I darted a glance over my shoulder.

"How quickly can you get the ambulance running?"

"It will take me a moment to replace the distributor cap."

"Then we need to split up to allow you that time."

"We are being followed." Her steps faltered, but she did not look back.

"Aye. Only one man, though he is the only one I have seen. That does not mean there are not others."

"The Free French will think we are German contacts of hers. The Milice will think we are part of your son's network."

"And we cannot afford either assumption."

"Can you find your way back to the ambulance?"

I looked to the sky. The rooftops were not nearly so high and dense as in Paris, and the sun's westward list was clearly visible. "I can find it. Quickly now, when we take this next corner, you take the cross street and get back to the ambulance. I will follow shortly." We made the turn and picked up our pace. The next street leading north was narrow, but it crossed through to the street running parallel to the one we were on. I glanced back. The man who had been following us since we left the missionary house had not yet turned the corner. "Go!"

She bolted from my side, racing up the side street. I strode on, only looking back once I was well away from the street Charlotte had taken. The man still followed, glancing down the side streets as he passed. He made no effort to conceal himself from my view but followed me doggedly as I wound my way through the city, pressing ever north.

The city center fell behind me, and I was soon in the outskirts of Vichy, drawing closer to where Charlotte had hidden the ambulance. I turned a corner and then quickly ducked into an adjacent alley, pressing back against the rough stone. I unbuttoned my shirt partway for easier access to the Luger I carried in the concealed holster. It felt heavy at my side.

When the man passed by the mouth of the alley, I moved. I was a head taller than he, and catching him around the neck, using his own forward momentum to swing him around and slam him into the stone wall was a simple matter. He staggered but shoved off the wall and sent an elbow flying back at me. He was used to fighting shorter men, for his elbow would have connected with my shoulder had the blow landed. I stepped out of his range but pressed my own advantage of longer arms by reaching out and clapping both palms over his ears with a force like a double blow of hammers against an anvil.

He went down like a sack of stones, cradling his head, and I gave him several moments for the ringing in his ears to cease. "Who are you, and what do you want?" I kicked his leg. "Why are you following me?"

He merely smiled up at me before his gaze darted behind me.

I ducked to the side, and the bullet grazed a furrow over my shoulder instead of burying itself in the back of my neck. I was deafened for an instant by the report, but it did not stop me from drawing the Luger and firing twice at the mouth of the alley and then putting a bullet in the chest of the man at my feet as he scrambled to draw his own weapon. It clattered against the cobbles as he slumped to his side, and I dropped into a crouch, snatching up his fallen revolver.

I tucked the revolver into the waistband of my trousers as I crept to the end of the alley and knelt before risking a glance around the corner. A bullet bit into the rock above my head, and stone shards pelted my skin before I ducked back. The shot had come from an alley about ten meters west of the one in which I knelt. I retreated to where the dead man lay in a folded heap and fisted my hand in the collar of his shirt, dragging him to the mouth of the alley and propping him against the wall.

I straightened and took a deep breath before nudging the dead man so that his shoulder and side were exposed to fire. Bullets tore into him immediately, and I leaned around the corner and fired the Luger three times in quick succession. One of the bullets found its mark in the shooter's knee, and he cried out as he crumpled into the street. Two men darted from the alley to drag him to safety, and I fired twice more, catching one man in the arm. I squeezed the trigger again only to be met with a click.

I ducked back into the alley. The jointed arm of the Luger was bent and locked, the breech open and empty. I was out of bullets. I holstered the pistol and retrieved the revolver. Four rounds were left in its cylinder. I rolled my shoulders, feeling the flaring burn in the right. The alley was a dead-end, and I had no desire to be trapped like a hunted hare.

The sound of an engine reached me as I prepared to take my chances in the street. It was a rumble I recognized, and as the sound grew louder and closer, gunfire erupted again, this time not directed at me but at the approaching ambulance.

I swung the cylinder back into the frame on the revolver, stepped from my hiding place, and fired two rounds, sending the men ducking back into the alley. I turned and raced down the street, heart thundering in time with my feet hitting the cobbles. The ambulance sped toward me as I sprinted toward it, and bullets punched through the windscreen even as they kicked up dirt and rocks around me. Charlotte slowed the vehicle only enough for me to throw myself within before she slammed the ambulance into reverse with a groan of gears and squeal of tires.

I crouched on the floorboards, chest heaving, shoulder throbbing. "Stay low."

She was hunched so low I was not certain she could even see over the wheel, but she nodded, not taking her gaze from where it darted back and forth between the side mirrors as she sped backward down the street. "Are you hurt?"

"No." I leaned out the side of the ambulance far enough to fire the last two bullets in the revolver at the men shooting at us. "You?"

"No. Hold on." She wrenched the wheel, and only my grip on the doorframe kept me from being tossed into the street as the ambulance swerved to the right, rocking as it came to an abrupt halt. There was a thump in the back, and Otto barked wildly. The vehicle protested once more as Charlotte threw it into gear and accelerated down the street with the engine roaring.

I climbed into the seat and hung my head as I tried to steady my breathing. My vision and stomach remained steady, but blood pounded in my temples. The revolver dangled from my numb fingers, and I tucked it into the waistband of my trousers once again.

Charlotte straightened and glanced at me, eyes widening. "You said you weren't hurt!"

I craned my neck to look at my shoulder. A bright red stain had crept down my shirtfront and sleeve. "It's just a graze, it is. I'll see to it later."

We sped through the streets, heading east out of the city, and I watched the side mirror for the inevitable. It only took minutes for them to appear. "We have company."

Before I could finish the sentence, there was a bang, and the ambulance lurched. Charlotte's hands tightened on the wheel.

"What was that?"

"They shot a tire," she said, voice grim. Her hand left the wheel and disappeared by her side before she reached across her body and offered me her Colt. "You have seven rounds. Wait until they're close."

"Can you lose them?"

"How many?"

I kept an eye on the side mirror. "Three on motorcycles."

She shifted gears and made a sharp turn, then another, taking

102

corners quickly, hands steady on the wheel as she weaved through the streets until we were out of Vichy and speeding into the countryside. "Still behind us?"

"Not at the moment."

"It's only a matter of time." She brought the vehicle to a quick halt as we reached an arched stone bridge and leapt out. She was climbing back into the driver's seat in a matter of seconds. "The tire is losing pressure swiftly."

"How much time do we have?"

"Not enough."

"Then we will go as far as we can. I'll need the rifle." I handed Charlotte her Colt and opened the door into the back of the ambulance. The poodle greeted me with an anxious whine, and I placed a hand on his bent head. "Hush, Otto *bach*. Go and *cwtch* down. All will be well." I looked at Wilhelm. "I may have need of the rifle."

"We are being pursued?"

Charlotte froze in the act of putting the ambulance in gear at the words spoken in accented English and darted a glance at me over her shoulder.

"Aye."

He fumbled in the pocket of his trousers and handed me a loaded box magazine. "For the Luger. I always carry a spare."

I nodded my thanks and inserted the magazine into the hand grip of the Luger, pulling the jointed arm until it unlocked and snapped straight, chambering a round. I holstered the pistol and reached for the rifle, but he clung to it.

"Allow me to gain you time." I hesitated. "I owe you a debt. Allow me to repay it."

"They will kill you once you run out of bullets."

"I am already dead, you know this." The putrid odor emanating from him echoed his words. He reached up and caught Otto's muzzle, bringing the dog's head down until their foreheads rested against one another. Otto licked the man's cheek, and the laugh that escaped

103

Wilhelm sounded waterlogged. He murmured to the animal in German, and then he tilted his head back to look at Charlotte. "Do not allow Otto out. He will try to return to me. Tell him *bleib* for stay, *fuss* for heel, *platz* for down." The poodle dropped onto his belly at the last command.

Charlotte swallowed. "I'll take care of him."

The German smiled. "I know."

She held onto the dog as I carried Wilhelm from the ambulance and, at his direction, leaned him against the stone balustrade at the end of the bridge. He grimaced, and the seated position made dark, foul smelling blood ooze from his abdomen. Otto began to bark, high pitched and frantic, as Charlotte closed him in the back of the ambulance and approached with the rifle.

I reached for the firearm, but she knelt before Wilhelm and handed it to him. "Thank you."

The water flowing under the bridge sighed and sang, and a bird warbled in the trees. A breeze swept over us, and Wilhelm closed his eyes and tilted his head back, allowing the sun to caress his face. His eyes snapped open at the rumble of approaching engines.

"Go!" he barked.

I clasped his shoulder, and then I caught Charlotte's elbow and pulled her to her feet. We ran, and I tossed Charlotte up into the ambulance and scrambled in after her. She hesitated for a brief moment, glancing back to where we had left Wilhelm, and then she put the ambulance in gear. We rumbled over the bridge, picked up speed on the other side, and were out of sight when we heard the first gunshots and then the cacophony of a firefight. Otto howled in the back of the ambulance.

1 February 1941

Dear Nhad,
Some acquaintances have been arrested.
I do not know what will become of Vildé and the others.
But at this point,
I know it would be naïve to hope to even see them again.
-Owain

viii

Henri

There were advantages to wearing the garb of a Frenchman and having become so ingrained in the Resistance movement over the years. I was trusted, even revered. And when I pointed these hapless boys in the direction I wanted as if they were a weapon and pulled the trigger, they fired. But they were boys, French at that, uncouth and ill-trained and prone to fuck things up, so I observed and then took matters into my own hands.

My bullet pierced the ambulance's tire, but the woman was a daring driver, and she managed to lose me in the labyrinth of narrow streets. I smiled to myself. When I returned to my vineyards and my brushes, I would have to paint more women. I had always found it a challenge to capture both the ferocity and the gentle softness inherent in the female mind and form. So often they were underestimated, but they were so capable. And they had the most ruthless and devious minds.

I eased off the throttle and motioned for the others to do the same. When the rumble of the motorcycles died, I closed my eyes and listened. "There." I pointed. I could hear the ambulance's engine still traveling east out of Vichy.

I thought we had caught up with them when we reached the outskirts of town and a bullet took out my front tire. Before the motorcycle could flip out of control, I laid it down on its side and slid after it in the dirt. The two Frenchmen with me were not so skilled. Their shots went wild as they were catapulted from their motorcycles when the front tires were compromised by a precisely fired bullet.

I stood and dusted myself off. The man propped against the stone balustrade leveled his rifle at me and pulled the trigger, but there was only a fruitless *click*. The rifle was out of bullets. I looked past him over the bridge. The ambulance was nowhere in sight. He was alone, and the man who so closely resembled Owain had slipped out of my reach. I knew where he was going now, though.

I drew my pistol and walked over to the Frenchmen groaning as they sat up. One's arm was broken. He looked up at me as I approached. "Henri—" I shot him, and the other man's eyes went wide before my bullet snuffed out the fear and pain building in his gaze. They were both useless to me now.

I turned back to the man on the bridge to find him watching me.

"You are not French." He spoke in German.

"*Nein.*" It was such a relief to speak in my mother tongue I felt my knees weaken as I approached him. "Tell me about the man you were traveling with."

He was too weak for much movement, but he lifted a hand in a dismissive gesture. "He is merely a father, seeking his son. He is no one to concern yourself with."

"That is for me to decide, sir."

He tilted his head and studied me. "I can tell you no more than that."

I drew a cigarette and lighter from my pocket and offered it to him. When he nodded, I tucked the cigarette into the corner of his mouth and cupped my hand around the lighter as I flicked the flame to life and lit the end.

He closed his eyes and drew in a deep drag, coughing a little as he did so. "*Danke.*"

"*Bitte,*" I said as I shot him in the head.

The cigarette tumbled from his lips, and I retrieved it from the dirt and took a drag myself as I studied the road leading east.

10 August 1941

Dear Nhad,
I have met a girl. Her name is Sévèrin.
Perhaps one day, when this is over, I can bring her home.
-Owain

ix

All was suddenly quiet, even the poodle, and Charlotte veered off the road into the trees. She stopped the vehicle, allowing the engine to idle quietly as if it were catching its breath after its own sprint. A single gunshot pierced the quiet, and Charlotte flinched. I hung my head and rubbed the back of my neck.

We waited long moments, out of sight from the road but ears pricked. The quiet was all-encompassing; no engines rumbled in approach.

Charlotte put the ambulance in gear, and we limped further into the shelter of the woods. When she parked, she turned to me, gaze on my shoulder.

"The tire first," I said.

We changed out the rear right tire with the spare in silence, and then Charlotte bandaged the flesh wound on my shoulder in much the same fashion, both of us lost in thought. Otto whined in the back of the ambulance.

"I want to take a look around," I said, voice low.

Hers was equally quiet. "No fires tonight."

I trekked back through the woods until I had a clear view of the road. I crouched in the undergrowth and watched and waited while the shadows lengthened. As the sun began to set, I stood, knees protesting, shoulder hot and throbbing, and walked the tree line for several kilometers in either direction. No one followed or searched for us.

A purple and orange stain was left on the sky with the passing sun, and the shadows were a deep, cool blue within the trees as I made my way back to the ambulance. I saw the large square shadow first, and then I heard the soft murmur of Charlotte's voice. I drew closer and finally distinguished her shape.

She sat leaning against the replaced tire, Otto's inky form appearing poured over her. Her legs were stretched out in front of her, and the poodle lay draped over them, his head tucked against her stomach. She drew her comb through his hair with tender care and spoke softly to him, her voice so gentle when the mourning dog whimpered that it made my throat tight.

I knelt beside her and placed a hand on the dog's side. His tail thumped.

We did not bother with a meal, and when we climbed into the back of the ambulance, Otto settled onto the stretcher his master had occupied. Charlotte retrieved a long line of rope and tied one end to a looped protrusion of metal on the stretcher bearer before securing the other end around the dog's neck. She adjusted the fit so it was loose enough for comfort but not so loose he would be able to slip his head free.

"I hate to do this to him," she said, though the poodle made no protest.

"It's for the best, it is."

She nodded and then leaned over and kissed the long muzzle before she climbed onto the top stretcher. I settled into the one across from Otto, the events of the day making my eyelids heavy even as my mind raced.

"Where is La Balme-les-Grottes?"

"I looked at the map, and it is less than a day's drive east of Lyon."

"Is the area controlled by the Nazis or have the Allies made it that far east yet?"

"I do not know. But either way, with the ambulance we should be allowed through."

Silence settled around us once more. We had left the ambulance doors open, and I watched the forest grow dark. The battlefield awaited me in dreams.

Machine guns spit bullets in a ferocious line that ripped bloody seams across men's torsos and cut them down like a scythe swept across a crop. I was uncertain which was louder: the guns or the screams.

I crawled on, pulling myself with my elbows, propelling myself with my knees, scrambling through the hot holes left by shells and dragging myself over the sprawled and shredded bodies. Arthur crept after me, and I could hear the ragged sawing of his breath.

I was almost at the tree line when the soldier burst from the cover of the woods and raced toward me with a roar. His rifle was held like a spear, the sun gleaming off the blade at the end. I scrambled to my knees and swung my rifle up to meet him. His bayonet glanced over my shoulder, but his forward momentum drove him straight into mine. After the brief resistance of uniform and flesh, the bayonet sank into his belly with the ease of a sharpened shovel piercing through wet soil.

The soldier grunted, a soft, animal-like noise, and leaned frozen above me. The butt of my rifle dug into my stomach, and I braced it there as I staggered to my feet. The German appeared even younger than I, and he stared at me, eyes a pale, blank blue. Blood spilled from the corner of his mouth and dripped down his chin.

He leaned more heavily into my bayonet as I gained my feet, and I braced my hand against his shoulder. His eyes closed, and I wrenched the blade from his abdomen, then moved aside and let him fall.

I stepped over his legs and met the next soldier with a roar of my own exploding from my chest.

"Rhys." A hand on my shoulder wrenched me from Mametz Wood, and I latched onto the wrist in a bruising grip. "Easy. It's me. It's Charlotte. You were dreaming."

Her voice and the pulse under my fingers were both steady and gentle. A canine whine and nudge brought me to full awareness, and

113

I immediately released the punishing grip on the delicate bones. "I apologize. Did I hurt you?"

"No. I did not mean to startle you, but you didn't respond when I called your name."

I sat up, rubbing my hands over my face, and was startled by the ache in my shoulder before I recalled that this wound had been inflicted by a bullet rather than a bayonet. "I am sorry," I said again.

"There's no need to be. Are you well now?"

"Aye."

She stood and placed a hand on my uninjured shoulder before she climbed back onto the stretcher bearer.

Otto nudged his head against my chest, and when I reclined again, he followed me onto my bedroll. There was barely room for me on the stretcher, but the dog squeezed himself into the remaining space and settled his head on my chest. He sighed as I rubbed his ears, and under his muzzle I felt my heart begin to slow. This time as I slipped into slumber, the dreams were held at bay.

————

We left our hiding place before dawn, and before we exited the shelter of the trees, I walked along the road in either direction until I was satisfied no trap awaited us. My head, jaw, and back felt better than they had since the attack in Paris, and though my shoulder burned, it was just as I told Charlotte: a flesh wound, more nuisance than injury.

The land soon began to undulate, and the tree growth thickened into forest. We stayed away from the main routes and traversed narrow country lanes.

I had awakened with Otto still curled against me, and when I untied him and allowed him to walk with me as I patrolled the area, he had not made any attempts to run. When I told him, "*Fuss*," he fell into step at my left side, his shoulders staying perfectly aligned with my left leg as we moved. Now the poodle sat between us, tongue lolling, gaze and nose vigilant.

We reached Roanne by late morning and crossed the Loire once more. On the eastern side of town, we risked the chance of driving the N-7, and by mid-afternoon we reached the outskirts of Lyon.

As we drew closer to the city center, we passed increasing numbers of people in the street. They pressed in the same direction we did, ever-widening streams flowing toward an unseen confluence. We were forced into a slower and slower pace until we were crawling along in the midst of a mass of people.

Unease gripped me as the crowd milled around us.

Charlotte leaned her head out of the ambulance and asked a passerby, "*Qu'est-ce que c'est?*"

"*Les Américains sont ici!*"

She settled back into her seat. "This could—"

Pounding on the back doors of the ambulance interrupted her, and Otto growled low in his throat, lips curling back from his teeth.

"We need to get out of this crowd." I grabbed the doorframe and held onto Otto as people began to converge on the ambulance, beating on the sides, rocking the vehicle back and forth. Hands grabbed at my legs, and I shook them off.

"Rhys!" Charlotte was pulled to the edge of her seat by a rough hand on her forearm and another wrapped around her thigh.

Before I could even move in her direction, Otto lunged across her snarling, teeth snapping. The man trying to drag her out of the vehicle yelped and fell back, narrowly avoiding having his face ripped apart by canine teeth.

Charlotte lurched back into her seat and spun the wheel to the left, veering through the crowd, narrowly missing a farmer pushing an empty cart. Otto stayed draped over her lap, baring his teeth at anyone close as she maneuvered us through alleys and side streets until we were away from the mob.

"Stop the ambulance," I said once we had reached a quiet side street.

When she slowed the ambulance to a halt, I caught her right

115

hand, hushing Otto when he emitted a protective rumble. I drew her arm across her body and examined the slight limb. A red handprint marred the pale skin of her forearm, close to the juncture of her elbow, the outline of fingers already turning purple at the edges.

"It's fine," she said, though there was a tremor in her voice. "I was more startled than anything. It's fine, Rhys, I promise. I bruise easily."

I relinquished my hold on her arm with some reluctance, and she put the ambulance in motion. "The Americans are here? Is that what they said?"

She nodded. "I think we have interrupted a liberation."

We pressed on toward the city center, detouring around the gaunt masses gathering in the streets. We reached the river at its oxbow, where the Saône and the Rhône curved in parallel arcs through the heart of the city.

"What…"

Charlotte slowed the vehicle, and I jumped down before the ambulance had fully stopped. The river appeared green in the midday sun, and the trees were thick on the opposite bank, girding the lower half of the buildings in such a way that it made the structures appear clad in verdant skirts. I picked my way carefully across the bridge until I was forced to come to a halt.

I felt a hand on my back as Charlotte reached me, Otto at her heels. She stared downriver. "They are all destroyed," she whispered.

I followed her gaze and took in the destruction of the bridges along the Saône. They appeared like a row of cracked and splintered ribs, the center of each buckled into rubble half swallowed by the river. They were all impassable.

"The Germans would have destroyed them as they retreated," I said.

"There must be a way across." Otto followed her as she retreated from the broken bridge and approached a woman pushing a cart down the street.

I walked to the edge of the jagged rent in the bridge and stared down at the river. The water was white where it flowed over the drowning sections of the dynamited central arch as if in an effort to sooth the gaping wound. Nausea churned in my stomach.

I dragged my gaze away and retreated from the precipice when Charlotte called my name. "She said that downriver the Americans have been working on a bridge since they arrived this morning."

We took the quai south, following the curve of the Saône around the city center's peninsula until it converged with the Rhône. The meeting of the rivers marked the confluence of the crowds. The quai was inundated up to the barricades erected in a large half circle around the American troops on the shore. We pressed through the crowd, the milling masses giving way to the ambulance like winter wool parting around sharpened shears. Even so, it took us an hour to reach the makeshift barrier to keep the crowd from pressing the troops into the river.

A soldier spotted the ambulance and raised his hand.

"We were sent down from Paris," Charlotte called to him.

He waved for us to continue and opened the barricade wide enough to permit us entry. He closed it immediately after us and then approached Charlotte's side of the vehicle. "Private Cole, miss, of the 36th Infantry Division." He was young, and his voice was a slow drawl that held a note that reminded me of a plucked string on a fiddle.

"Will we be able to cross the river, Private?"

"Yes, miss." He pointed toward the men working in the middle of the Rhône. "They're finishing the bridge now."

I exited the ambulance to watch the process, and Charlotte joined me, shading her eyes against the sun. A powerboat guided the last raft of three pontoons into place. Once it was lined up with the rest of the floating bridge, men set to work locking the timbers in place on the gunnels.

"And it will be strong enough for a vehicle to cross?"

The private answered me as he leaned over to pet Otto. "Yes, sir. The M4 can bear the weight of a tank."

A short, stocky man stood on the bridge overseeing the construction. When the last balk was in place, he walked the length of the bridge, inspecting each pontoon. He turned back toward the western bank, and the private raised his hand. The man strode toward us, his boots echoing hollowly over the bridge as he approached.

The private snapped a sharp salute. "Colonel, this ambulance team has been sent down from Paris."

A sharp patter of gunfire erupted across the river, and my hand went to the Luger hidden beneath my shirt.

The colonel shook his head. "We'll need more than one ambulance. It's like a revolution in the streets here."

"Is it the Germans?" Charlotte asked.

"No, ma'am. The damn FFI are quick on their triggers and shooting at everything that moves. Best have a care."

"Colonel!"

The shout drew our attention to the man racing across the bridge.

"What is it, Sergeant?" the colonel called.

"They fired a tracer into a hospital, sir, claiming there were Germans inside," he said in the midst of a salute. "The building is burning, and there are still wounded within."

"Goddamn frogs." The colonel bit out the words. "Sergeant, you and the private stay here with the others and control the flow of traffic over the bridge."

Charlotte was already climbing behind the wheel of the ambulance. "The back is empty. We can grab men as we go."

The colonel opened the rear doors of the ambulance and rode standing on the fold-out steps as we crossed the bridge. Charlotte drove cautiously over the planks, and I kept an eye on the water as we crossed. As the private had promised, it held and did not buckle beneath our weight, though the slight undulation under the tires made me uneasy. I released the breath I did not realize I held when we reached the other side.

Gunfire echoed through the heart of Lyon, and as Charlotte navigated the streets, the colonel barked orders to the soldiers we passed. They jumped into the back of the ambulance when Charlotte slowed.

I leaned forward and peered at the skyline through the bullet-hole riddled windscreen. "There!" I pointed toward the billows of smoke rising from the city center.

When we reached the hospital, the upper story was already engulfed. Nurses raced in and out of the building alongside soldiers to evacuate the remaining wounded.

"My god," Charlotte breathed, and Otto whined.

I leapt down as soon as the vehicle came to a halt. "The both of you stay outside and help."

Charlotte buried her fingers in Otto's hair. "If you don't come out, we'll come in after you."

"I'll come back." I retrieved the letter from my pocket and held it out to her. "Keep this safe for me. Please."

She accepted it, handling it carefully, and nodded. I stripped off my shirt and tied the garment over my mouth and nose. "We need a water truck here!" I shouted to the colonel. I did not wait for his response but ran into the burning building.

A nurse staggered in front of me, coughing violently. I grasped her arm and turned her back toward the doors. "Upstairs! Are there men upstairs?" I gestured above me.

She nodded frantically and pointed toward the stairs. A group of soldiers ran in, and I pushed her toward one. "Get her outside. The rest of you men, with me."

We raced up the stairs, and I directed half of the men to cover the second floor. The rest followed me to the third. The fire was already eating through the roof, and the conflagration roared like a wild animal. The smoke was thick and black, choking and blinding.

The soldiers and I shouted, but there was no response.

"Back downstairs," I ordered. "This building is going to come

119

down. Get everyone out!"

The soldiers preceded me down the stairs, and as I started to follow, a sound reached me. "Is anyone here?" I yelled again, and coughed as the acrid smoke fingered the makeshift scarf I had tied around my face.

"*Aidez...aidez-moi!*"

The voice was faint, and I could barely hear it over the thunder of the fire. "Keep talking! Where are you?"

"*S'il vous plaît! Aidez-moi!*"

I crouched and made my way toward the voice, keeping an eye on the ceiling. "I'm coming for you!"

It took me long moments of blind searching to find him. And it was not one man, I realized, but two. A man with both legs gone from the knees down dragged himself across the floor, leading the man crawling behind him. The man he struggled to lead to safety had thick bandages wound round his head, covering his eyes.

I knelt beside them and caught the bandaged man's arm. "Get on my back." I looked at the other man and motioned to my back. "He has to get on my back."

The man spoke quickly to his blinded friend who obeyed the instructions in frantic fumbles. I caught the other man up in my arms and groaned with the effort to stand under both their weights. I staggered in the direction I thought the stairs were, but the smoke was so thick now I could not see even a meter before me. A shower of cinders rained down on our heads, and the beast ate its way across the ceiling toward us.

There was a groan like a wounded animal, and then the floor collapsed below my feet as a burning beam from the roof fell toward us.

Screaming joined the howl of the blaze, and I could not be certain my own voice did not join in before I hit the floor of the story below. I landed hard enough to force the air from my lungs and draw blackness over my gaze for an instant.

I scrambled upright, and my lungs felt as if I were inhaling the fire within me. My eyes streamed, and I wiped at them to no avail. My shirt had been torn away from my face in the fall.

Screaming interrupted the ringing in my head, and I turned. I had been knocked aside in the fall through the ceiling, as had the man I carried. But the blinded man had taken the full brunt of the burning beam. He was trapped beneath its weight, and the flames were already too high to try to drag him free. The fire bit into his flesh and latched on like a rabid creature. He writhed and shrieked in agony.

I drew my Luger and with a well-aimed bullet ended his torment.

I grabbed the other man and slung him over my shoulder. He was limp and heavy, and my legs almost collapsed beneath me. I caught a glimpse of the stairwell and stumbled toward it, forcing my legs into a run as I heard the ceiling creaking and moaning above us. I dove for the stairwell just as the third floor fell entirely, and we tumbled down the stairs in a tangle of limbs.

There was smoke all around, as thick as fog, and for a moment I thought it was yellow and thought the shriek of the inferno was the wail of shells overhead. "Take cover!" I tried to scream to the men beside me in the trenches, fumbling for my gas mask, but my throat was so raw no sound escaped.

Pain ripped through my arm, startling me back to the present. When the pain came again, I realized it was teeth piercing my skin, gripping and trying to pull me. *Otto.*

I struggled to my knees, my head feeling oddly light, and twisted my fist into the other man's shirt collar. I dragged him behind me as I crawled through the smoke. Otto nudged me in the right direction, barking in my ear, and a tendril of fresh air pierced my lungs as painfully as the smoke. And then hands latched onto me, lifting me and carrying me from the destroyed hospital.

"Let me through! Let me through!" a woman's voice shouted as I was carried away from the building and placed on the grass under a tree.

Gentle, strong hands rolled me onto my side and pounded on my back as I coughed so violently I choked. When I could gasp in air once more, those capable hands eased me onto my back, and a soft, damp cloth bathed the soot from my face. Otto licked my arms and hands.

I squinted, eyes swollen and streaming. The face above mine was blurred, but I recognized the honey-colored hair that was coming unbound and the delicate curve of jaw. I wanted to reach up and sooth away the furrow in her brow, but my hand fell before it reached its destination and I lost my grip on consciousness.

24 August 1941

Dear Nhad,
People were dragged off the streets today and taken as hostages.
A communist shot a German officer
at a metro station the other day.
It seems they have decided to lend their guns to the resistance
efforts. But it is not without cost.
The Germans are threatening to execute
the hostages if there are any more assassinations.
The streets of Paris grow increasingly dangerous.
-Owain

X

Henri

I found him easily enough in the makeshift hospital. He was a tall man, noticeable even prone, and the poodle I had seen drag him from the inferno was draped over his legs.

It was chaotic within the cathedral as the American soldiers and French nurses scrambled to care for the wounded and comfort those confused and frightened by the fire. I wove through the cots until I reached his side. The poodle eyed me, and I spoke softly to him. He was a fine German dog. Not as sturdy and powerfully built as my schnauzer had been, but athletic and intelligent. Gerhardt's collar and the cigar box rested heavily in my pockets.

I extended my hand to the poodle, but he made no move to sniff my fingers. He continued to watch me, and I realized my plan to take the man from this place hinged not on going unnoticed by the soldiers and nurses but on the poodle's diligent, guarding presence. I had waited until I saw the woman leave, but I had not counted on the poodle. Only a brute would hurt an animal, so I swiftly reevaluated my options and took a moment to study the man.

The likeness was startling. From a distance, they could be mistaken for brothers, if not for one another. At this proximity, though, I could see the weathered quality of this man's face, the silver streaking the hair at his temples, the lines bracketing his eyes. His face held far more character and wear than his son's, putting him closer to my age, perhaps a decade younger than my fifty-five years.

"Are you a doctor?"

I turned. It was the woman. I studied her, noting the symmetry and brightness of her face, the changeful eyes. She was not beautiful, not exactly, but there was an undeniable appeal about her that would make a man want to study the way the light played in her eyes. Those eyes would be impossible to paint, but I knew I would have to attempt the challenge.

And her face was startlingly familiar. Her head tilted, brow wrinkling as she looked at me, and I knew a sense of recognition needled her as well. I tensed as I realized why she struck me as so familiar.

She repeated her question in French, and I responded in kind. "I am. He is doing better than expected. I was worried about the amount of smoke he may have inhaled, but his lungs are sound. I am not concerned about his recovery."

The relief was plain in her face, and I relaxed when she looked away from me. She placed a bundled assortment of clothing at the foot of the cot and rested her hand on the poodle's head. His eyes closed briefly under her touch, and his tail thumped. "Thank you, Doctor."

I inclined my head to her and moved to the next bed to keep up appearances. When I glanced at the woman from the corner of my eye, she was perched on the edge of the man's cot. She spoke softly to the poodle, stroking a hand along his back, but her gaze was on the man's face. I wondered what was between the pair and if I could use it against him to get the answers I needed.

I left before she could recall the sense of recognition and before I drew the notice of the soldiers and picked a place down the street where I could wait and watch without being seen.

3 October 1941

Dear Nhad,
I met an artist today. His name is Picasso.
He gave me a postcard of one of his paintings. Guernica.
You would hate it.
-Owain

xi

The sound of laughter woke me, and still drifting in the ebbing tide of sleep, I stretched my hand across the bed. I was met only with emptiness and a cold, barren space where once a soft, warm woman had curled. I rolled to my back, fully awake now, and tasted the acrid poison of bitterness at the back of my tongue.

The light was tepid and pale through the window, weakened by the gray sky and sharpened by the blanket of snow on the ground. I rested my hand on my chest, and for a moment I imagined there was no heartbeat within, only a raging hollowness. But then I felt the thump of blood flowing through its chambers. Sourness churned in my gut, and I slung off the quilts, gaining my feet.

Dressing was mechanical, until I heard the laughter again. I paused in threading the braces over my shoulders and glanced out the window, but saw nothing from my room's vantage.

My mother was humming softly in the kitchen when I entered. Puccini, I thought, though her humming was off-key and bordered on tuneless. I kissed the top of her head and accepted the mug of tea she pressed into my hands.

"Mam."

"You should eat, cariad."

Tea was the only thing my stomach did not revolt against lately. I felt weak, and in the fields, my strength was waning. I knew I could not allow myself to waste away, but the sourness in my gut refused to abate. I finished the tea quickly. "Perhaps later. Where are Owain and

Ffaddyr?"

She smiled. "Outside. It snowed again last night."

The snow made a soft murmur of sound as I stepped into it and sank to my ankles. I followed the sound of laughter around the side of the house to find my father and son engaged in battle. My father gently pelted my son with small snowballs. Owain slung snow at my father, but it did not stay in form and merely showered him with powder. Rhiannon ran in circles around the pair, barking, springing into the air to bite at the falling crystals.

Focused on my son, I did not see the snowball coming until it caught me in the face. The laughter and barking went silent, and I wiped the snow from my face with the sleeve of my coat. My father wore a careful expression of innocence, and Owain stared at me, mouth agape, eyes round.

The pleasure on his face had been replaced by hesitation, and I suddenly recalled the tugging at my arm this morning and the whispered, "Dadi, Dadi, come outside and play." I had shaken him off and rolled over.

No more, I told myself, galvanized. No more of this wallowing. I knelt and packed the snow between my hands, tight enough to form a ball but loose enough it would not pain my intended victim on impact. I launched it as I stood, and it hit Owain in the center of his chest, exploding white froth over him.

He sat down hard in the snow, blinking as he wiped his face. And then he let out a war cry that would do any Celt proud as he sprang to his feet and raced toward me. I let him tackle me to the ground and dump handfuls of snow over me. He howled with laughter, and Rhiannon ran in circles around us, barking.

It pained me at first, when a laugh erupted from my chest. It felt as if it lanced my heart, and the bitterness bled away as I lay in the snow laughing with my son.

I startled into wakefulness with a jolt that set off a violent round of coughing.

Charlotte appeared at my side and helped me upright. She handed me a canteen, and I drank eagerly. The cool water soothed my raw throat, and I glanced around as I drank. My eyes burned, bleary and scratchy. She thrust a handkerchief my way, and I doused it with water before bathing my face and wiping my eyes.

"They have set up a cathedral as a makeshift hospital," she explained. Cots lined either side of the nave and the center, leaving just enough space for the doctors and nurses to move between beds. "You were not burnt, merely singed and blistered. But the doctors were concerned about your lungs. I could have sworn I knew the doctor..." I tried to speak, but only a rough croak emerged. "Drink some more," she urged, and sat at the foot of the cot. "You frightened me. When the building began to collapse..." She turned her face away and was quiet for a moment. A deep breath moved through her chest like a bellows. With a tilt of her chin, she directed my gaze across the nave. "I believe our dog is more suited to healing than to war. He's made rounds through the entire place, visiting each patient."

Otto was currently draped over a patient's lap, and the man stroked the poodle's ears. The sheets drawn over the man's legs flattened after the knob of his knees. He must have sensed my eyes on him for he looked up, met my gaze, and inclined his head.

"How many were lost?" My voice was a hoarse whisper that scraped my throat.

Charlotte turned back to me. "Two. A patient and a doctor, both last seen on the third floor." I nodded. I knew what had become of the patient. "Almost one hundred fifty were saved, though."

"Did they find..." A cough rattled in my lungs, and I took another drink from the canteen. "Did they find who fired the tracer into the hospital?"

"No. The Resistance is out of control. The colonel was right. It is like a revolution in the streets."

My voice was a ragged whisper, but the violent coughing had abated. "How long have I been here?"

131

awaiting the crispness of autumn and winter. A roughly hewn ladder leaned against a tree. A basket of cut flowers, now wilted and brown, lay on the back stoop, and no one answered my knocks.

"This place seems…idyllic. Untouched by the war," Charlotte said when she joined me. Her brow furrowed as she looked around. "It feels as if everyone has just stepped out of sight for the moment."

"It is eerie, but the entire town cannot be empty. There must be someone about."

But we found not a soul as we walked south and searched the western side of the village lane by lane. No one responded to our knocks. Several doors stood ajar, and Otto pushed them open with his nose and wandered within. Charlotte waited uneasily in the doorway each time the dog and I searched the empty shops and homes.

There was evidence of abruptly interrupted life everywhere. Bowls of porridge were left to spoil on a table. A child's bicycle lay on its side like a metal carcass in the street. In a shop, a sack of potatoes lay spilled across the floor.

We followed winding paths through the outlying farms and crossed small canals all the way to the river and encountered no one.

The sun had set and dusk was darkening when we reached the main lane upon which we had arrived. A twilight breeze eddied the hem of Charlotte's dress. Otto's attention caught on something fluttering along the cobbles like a wounded bird, and he gave chase. Charlotte followed him, kneeling to inspect his find. She stood as I reached them and offered it to me.

It was a fine handkerchief, delicate and painstakingly embroidered with tiny flowers and the initials *SMC*. The white scrap of femininity was stained with dirt and three smeared russet droplets. Blood.

"What has happened here?" Charlotte whispered.

I had no answer.

———

The farmhouse was likewise empty, though clean and well-

134

worn from living. The stone floors of the lower level were swept, and the large hearth was cold and free from ash. There were no cobwebs clinging to the exposed wooden beams of the ceiling.

The stairs creaked as I ascended them, but the railing was polished. The wooden floors of the second floor were smooth and rolling underfoot. The walls were papered with white and blue pinstripes in the bedroom. The bed was still unmade, and a woman's wrap, all silk and lace, was draped over the end of the bed. The second bedroom was pristine with not a coat of dust on the mantle nor a wrinkle in the quilts on the bed, though the room did not appear to be in use. The other room on the upper level served as a study. Papers were neatly stacked on the desk, and heavy leather-bound tomes lined the shelves. A delicate teacup perched on a saucer beside one pile of papers, and when I dipped my finger into the tea, it was cool. The window was ajar, and I crossed to it, pushing it further open.

The window looked down upon the orchard, and I caught sight of Charlotte and Otto wandering amongst the trees in the pale light of the gloaming. She had the hem of her dress clutched in one hand, and she filled the skirt of her garment with summer-heavy peaches. She glanced up as they made their way under the boughs back to the house and raised a hand when she caught sight of me.

I met her in the kitchen as she placed the picked bounty on the long table in the center of the room.

"I did not think whoever lives here would mind if I picked the ripest," she said. She had also picked two tomatoes, a pepper, and a courgette.

"If they return, I doubt they will miss this slight harvest."

She glanced at the ceiling. "Is it the same here as elsewhere?"

"Aye. We will search the eastern side of the village tomorrow, but I doubt it will be to any avail."

"We can at least find the caves. They should be nearby." She took down a copper pot from where it hung from the ceiling. "Will you check the larder?"

It was tucked away under the stairs, and within I found a modest storehouse of provisions. I cut four thick slices of cured ham and a wedge of cheese but left the rest.

As Charlotte prepared the meal, I lit the lamps in the kitchen and then sat on the front steps and fed Otto two of the slices of ham. He took each morsel from my fingers delicately and seemed to savor each bite before turning to me for the next.

I sat at an angle on the steps, watching over the stone wall that girded the front lawn, but no lights flickered to life in the village. I thought I heard a rumble of an engine from the opposite side of town, but it went silent suddenly. I unclasped two of the buttons of my shirt for easier access to the Luger and waited, but all was quiet and I heard nothing more. As full dark settled about La Balme-les-Grottes, Otto and I retreated within the farmhouse.

Our meal—the flavors, eating from a plate using cutlery while seated at a table—seemed luxurious. I glanced at Charlotte and caught her closing her eyes as her lips closed around the tines of the fork. The peach was weighty in my palm, and the taste so sweet and bright I savored three of them. I set the pits aside to dry, of a mind to take them home and try to plant them.

The lantern guttered as we cleaned up after the meal and returned everything to its place. After Charlotte returned from filling a bucket at the pump, I bolted the doors and led the way upstairs with the lantern. Otto bounded up the steps ahead of us. Charlotte distributed the bucket of water into the basins in the two bedrooms while I lit the lamp in the room with the white and blue pinstripe walls.

Otto leapt onto the bed and curled up in the center of the mattress with a deep sigh. Charlotte fingered the silk of the dressing gown and then folded the garment and placed it on the padded stool before the vanity.

"I cannot imagine why anyone would abandon this place," she said as she gazed around the elegant room.

"They may have had no choice."

136

She nodded, face troubled. "I hope we find answers tomorrow."

"I do as well."

"And your son."

"Aye. *Nos da*, Charlotte."

"Good night," she whispered, eyes dark in the low gleam of light.

I retreated to the bedroom across the hall, placed the lantern on the night stand, and sat down heavily on the edge of the bed. My chest was tight as I pulled the letter from my pocket. I unfolded the worn, creased paper with care.

Dear Nhad,

I found a way to fight that I believe in.

I do not do it to make you proud, but I hope you are.

-Owain

I swallowed around the lump in my throat and stared at the words until they blurred before my eyes. I brought the paper to my face and inhaled. If there had ever been a lingering scent from the moment my son had scrawled those words in his slanted, quick hand, it had long faded. All I smelled now was the acrid hint of smoke that clung to me. I refolded the letter, tucking it into the safety of my pocket.

I scrubbed my hands over my face, grimacing at the beard that scraped my palms, and blew out an uneven breath.

A cake of soap and a cloth lay next to the basin Charlotte had filled on the washstand, and it was a relief to bathe away the grit of the fire and the grime of travel. The swelling in my jaw and at my temple had abated, and now both bore a faint tint of green and yellow. The gash at my temple was healing, but my shoulder and the blisters on my arms were raw and sore.

I found a shaving kit in the top drawer of the dresser and relieved my face of the weight and heat of beard growth. As I drew the razor down my throat, a tremulous sound quavered through the farmhouse. I paused and glanced toward the closed door. It came again, melodic and resonate, but hesitant and tuneless. I finished shaving and pulled my shirt back over my shoulders, leaving my braces hanging and the shirt

137

unbuttoned over my undershirt. The Luger still rested in the holster at my side. That faint rumble of an engine had left me uneasy.

I opened the door silently as the music began to take shape, a haunting, solemn series of notes underpinned softly and steadily by low chords. I followed the refrain down the hall to the study. The door was ajar, the edges gilded in light, and I pushed it further open.

Charlotte sat at the upright piano in the far corner of the room. The lamp from the bedroom sat atop the piano, and the light spilled over the black and ivory keys and over Charlotte's bent head and agile fingers.

Otto was sprawled behind the piano bench, and he lifted his head when I opened the door and then settled back on the floor. Charlotte's back was to me, and her hair was damp and loose about her shoulders. The narrow line of her back followed a gentle curve reminiscent of a fiddle, and she swayed into the piano as her fingers coaxed the notes from the worn keys.

I leaned in the doorway and closed my eyes as the melancholy piece crept in reverberations between my ribs, twining around emotion and memory.

"Where's Mam, Dadi?"

I could not answer him as I stared at the simple stone marking where she lay. Nausea churned in my gut at the thought of her sweet, soft body buried beneath the cold, wet earth, slowly rotting away to dust. A shout or a sob, I knew not which, rattled in my chest, and the urge to claw at the ground to reach her in the depths bore at me. Rage rode me, and despair nipped closely at its heels.

"Dadi." The voice was small and confused, and a tiny hand gripped my fingers, shaking my arm to gain my attention. "Dadi, where's Mam?"

I looked blankly down at the small child by my side. Rain fell on his upturned face, and what had once been a source of pride and humor suddenly pierced me. My son looked exactly like me, the same dark hair and green eyes, the same stubborn jaw. I studied him with a sense of desperation, searching for a hint of Aelwyd's beauty in him, heart clenching when I found only remnants of myself in his features.

"She is gone," I whispered, voice raw.

"She will not be for long," he said, innocent and certain. He was incapable of understanding the weight and tragedy that lay under a mound of rain-washed earth before us. "Mam always returns. But she always tells me while she's gone, I should look after you." He beamed up at me and broke into a peal of laughter. "I tell her she is so silly! You're the dadi, not me!"

I knelt and clutched him to me, clinging to his small body, to the echo of Aelwyd's laughter in his.

"I hope I did not wake you."

I blinked at Charlotte and straightened away from the doorjamb, rubbing a hand over my burning eyes. "Not at all." The last notes still hung in the air. "What was that?"

She had turned on the piano bench, studying me, but she made no mention of the dampness I felt on my face. "A transcription of Rachmaninoff's *Vocalise*. I'm afraid I am sorely out of practice."

"It was beautiful, it was," I said, voice hoarse. I moved further into the study and pulled the chair away from the desk. I angled it to face the piano, and Charlotte turned on the bench to look at me as I took a seat. "How did you become involved in smuggling art?"

Her gaze shot to mine, and then she looked away, tucking a lock of hair behind her ear. "It was not something I set out to become involved in."

"But you did."

"At first, it was simply a matter of helping move the collections from the Louvre to a number of châteaux outside of the city at the first rumors of an eventual invasion."

"To keep them safe from the Nazis."

She nodded. "And from bombing. We began in 1938, and we had ensured all of the most precious works were hidden by early September of '39. The art was safe, hidden away in the countryside. I thought that would be the end of it." She was silent a moment. "The Nazis ordered the reopening of the museum in September of 1940, but most of the galleries were empty. The itineraries were in German, and the opening was merely symbolic. I was not going to be party to that farce, so I joined the American Hospital's Ambulance Field Service." She folded her hands in her lap and studied them, brow furrowed. "I told you of how the Nazis plundered the collections of prominent Jewish families and dealers."

"You did."

"What I did not tell you is that they used the Louvre to store the collections they had stolen. The Nazis requisitioned the galleries devoted to Near Eastern antiquities, closing it off to museum staff, and used the rooms for storage and a showcase for the higher-ups to come pick over." Bitterness and disgust laced her voice. "Monsieur Jaujard knew I had my own ambulance, and when he approached me and told me of the sequestration, I could not refuse." She took a deep breath, and her face tightened. "I...maneuvered myself into a...position of trust and worked with the Nazi officials at the museum, cataloging every stolen piece of art that was transported to Germany." She ran a hand over the keys but added no weight, leaving the gesture soundless. "And when I was able, I worked with a number of the museum staff and the Resistance to secret pieces out of the Nazi's plunder and back into hiding in France."

The haunted tension in her face stayed my questions. "That was courageous of you."

"For four years, I transported prisoners of war to the hospital from the camps. And when they were recovered, I had to take them back to those hell holes, knowing they would rot and starve and die." She swallowed. "And until the autumn of '42, I hid paintings and small sculptures under a false floor in the back of the ambulance. En route, I would meet a..." Her gaze slid away from mine. "I would meet a contact to make the exchange, and he and a partner would transport the art to safety."

I braced my elbows on my knees and rubbed my jaw. The connection struck me in her careful tone and the way she avoided my gaze. Owain was her contact. "What happened in '42?" I asked carefully.

"My contacts did not make our rendezvous one day. It was too dangerous by then to continue the subterfuge and smuggling. There were others braver than I who continued the work. But I know myself well enough to know that I would not have held up under torture if captured. So I did not risk it further."

We sat silently for several long moments, the quiet broken only by Otto's snuffling snores. "I have a request to make of you."

The faraway look in her dark eyes faded as she arched a questioning brow.

"Will you play for me?"

A smile bloomed across her face like a flower opening to the first warmth of the sun. "Of course."

She turned back to the keys, and I closed my eyes as her fingers began to coax forth the notes.

———

Steep cliffs abutted the eastern side of the village, and when we turned down a narrow lane that branched off from the main track, Charlotte touched my arm.

"Rhys, there."

I followed the direction of her extended arm, squinting in the morning light. The cave was a towering dark shadow against the cliff face, cathedral in its size. A chapel was built at the entrance to the cave, constructed against the rock wall in such a way that it appeared monolithic.

"This is magnificent," Charlotte breathed as we approached, neck craned to take in the scope of the cave and chapel.

The chapel sat atop a tall flight of stone steps. The stairs were narrow and steep, and we climbed them well away from the edge. The chapel was small within, and I shone the torch around the room. The tapestries were tattered, and the paintings on the walls were so faded I

141

could not discern if they depicted saints, madonnas, or messiahs. The prayer benches were covered in a fine layer of dust. The room was empty and had been for some time.

When I exited the chapel, I directed the beam of my torch into the cave to little avail. The light was too weak to penetrate the depths, even from this elevated vantage point.

"I have never seen anything like this," Charlotte said. "Do you think it is very deep?"

I looked up and studied the arch of the ceiling above us. The rock was solid, sloping toward the back of the cave. "I think we should find out."

We descended the steps and ventured deeper into the cave. A semblance of a path led us further into the dark heart of the cliffs. In the evening, with the sun in the west, the daylight would illuminate the depths of the cave. As it was, the torch I carried was imperative once we reached the rock fall at the back of the large cavern.

Crude steps were cut into the ancient fall, and Charlotte held up a hand toward Otto. "Stay, boy. I do not want you getting separated from us down here. *Bleib.*"

He whined his disapproval of the command but remained in place as we climbed the roughhewn steps. The ceiling sloped lower and the walls of the chamber narrowed toward us as we climbed, funneling us onto a high overhang in the next chamber.

It was cooler in the second chamber, and the sound of dripping water echoed in the darkness. The black was absolute save the weak light behind us and the fragile beam of the torch.

I closed my eyes against the oppressiveness of it, and my heart began to knock against my breastbone. Sweat beaded on my brow.

"Rhys?"

Charlotte's voice grounded me, and I opened my eyes, breathing slowly through my nose. I played my light over the second cave, and Charlotte sucked in a breath. We stood at the pinnacle of the chamber. The cavern sloped down from the precipice on which

142

we stood and branched into a number of twisted labyrinths. A fluttering disturbed the air above us, and Charlotte ducked, pressing her head against my arm.

I swept the light over the ceiling. It was closer above our heads than I realized, and my fingers clenched. I swallowed around the growing vice encircling my throat. "Bats. They are merely—"

Something swept past our legs, and Charlotte cried out and lunged after it. "Otto!"

I grabbed her arm to keep her from falling as she tried to follow the poodle. I tracked him with the light as he nimbly descended from the ledge and darted down one of the tunnel offshoots.

"Rhys, he'll get lost."

I waited and kept the light trained on the mouth of the tunnel down which Otto had disappeared. After a moment, his dark shape separated from the shadows. He barked, and the sound bounced off the cave walls. "No, he is trying to lead us. Come along, but carefully. And stay close."

It was a slow climb down, but Otto waited, and once we reached the damp cave floor, he raced ahead of us. The tunnel was wide at its opening, narrowing the deeper we forged. I could feel Charlotte at my back, and I fought to keep my breathing steady. The sound of dripping water grew louder, competing with the pulse hammering in my ears.

The tunnel opened up at the top of a terrace-like structure. Water pooled along the pale ledges and spilled down the rock. In the light of my torch, the stone appeared white.

We skirted the edge of the cave, where the way was precariously slick but the water was no more than a few centimeters deep.

The chamber split into two tunnels. The shallow underground river flowed into the one with a ceiling so low I could only have traversed it at a crawl. Otto disappeared down the other. I would be able to walk upright through the second tunnel, but the way was so narrow I would have to turn sideways to pass.

I could hear my own breath as it sawed and wheezed from my

tight chest, and my palm was slick where it gripped the torch.

The fire-step made for a narrow, uncomfortable bed, but I shut my ears to the mutters of conversation around me and closed my eyes against the murky midday sun. Arthur played his pibgorn nearby, and with my eyes shut, I could almost imagine we were home in the hills, the sheep grazing nearby. I drifted between wakefulness and slumber. I could not remember the last time I had properly slept. It seemed a luxury now, exhaustion as constant a companion as the boredom and fear.

I filled my mind with home, breathing slowly, struggling to force the tension from my limbs. I recalled the smell of my mother's bread as it cooled; the sound of my father playing the fiddle, the firelight gleaming on the wood of instrument and bow; the feel of air so clean and pure it pained the lungs; the hills a rolling, open expanse that stretched past my vision's limit; the softness of Aelwyd's skin and the sweetness of her smile.

"Incoming!"

The shout was a whisper against the whining shriek of an incoming shell. I rolled off the fire-step onto my hands and knees. The duck-boards had long since disappeared beneath the mire. I buried my face in the mud and covered my head with my arms just as the shell struck.

The earth lurched, bellowed, and erupted with a violence that felt as if the world were ending. The side of the trench buckled, and chunks of soil rained down on me. A sandbag hit me between the shoulder blades and drove me flat, knocking the wind from my chest. And then the bodies piled into the dug-out shelter fell over me like a rank tide released from a bursting dam.

I screamed, choking and drowning in the mud as the weight of earth and the dead threatened to bury me.

"Rhys?"

Charlotte's soft query made me realize my feet were rooted to the floor, and I locked my knees to keep them from buckling. The ceiling seemed to sink lower, and when Otto barked somewhere ahead in the darkness, it reverberated through the air like a drumbeat.

"Rhys." Charlotte's fingers closed around my wrist, stilling the trembling beam of light. "Do you need to return to the surface?"

My mouth was parched, and I had to swallow several times before I could speak. "No. We have already come this far."

She coaxed my fingers from their clenched grip and relieved me of the torch. "I will lead the way and let you know when the going is tight."

She ventured ahead of me, close enough to reach out and touch her, warning me of the labyrinth's tight twists and turns. The trek seemed to last a century before she said, "Careful here. I think it widens ahead, but this spot is especially close."

The rock was pressed against my back, and as I slid through the narrow opening, the curved wall at my front brushed against my chest.

"Do you smell that?" Charlotte whispered.

Aye, I did. The rank odor of rotting flesh and putrid wounds, of gunpowder and hot metal. Between one blink and the next, the wall before me turned from solid rock to dank mud writhing with lice and rats, stratified with blood.

"Rhys, do you smell that?"

I shook my head, and the memories of the trenches faded. I squeezed after Charlotte, and the passageway began to widen. Otto's frantic barking suddenly stretched into a haunting bay, and on my next breath, I caught the scent Charlotte had smelled earlier.

She picked up her pace. "Otto! Here, boy!"

"Wait, Charlotte," I said, mind clearing abruptly, jarred by the smell. "Do not—"

She yelped as she turned the corner and fell, tripping over an obstruction at the entry of the next chamber. She was scrambling backward when I reached her, a strange whimper coming from her as she crashed against my legs. I caught her about the elbow and hauled her to her feet. She clung to me, turning her face into my chest.

145

She had lost her grip on the torch when she fell, and it was wedged with the light pointing upward, illuminating the sprawled bodies blanketing the cave floor.

13 January 1942

Dear Nhad,
My path has crossed with a man who is much admired.
He is brilliant and passionate about art.
But I sense all is not as it seems with him.
He calls himself Henri.
-Owain

xii

The bodies lay where they had fallen in a tangled interweaving of limbs that told me they had been herded into the cavern like livestock and systematically executed. Men, women, and children alike had been mown down with ruthless precision. Blood had seeped across the floor and saturated every article of clothing and lock of hair it touched, drying into blackened pools beneath the bodies.

The slack, graying body of an infant was draped over her mother's bullet-riddled chest. An old man and woman had been murdered even as they held onto each other, falling wrapped around one another.

Charlotte had tripped over the slight body of a child who had been shot in the head and who was tangled with his father's sprawled legs. Still holding her to me, I leaned over and retrieved the torch from where it was wedged between limbs.

I played the light over the cavern. The dead numbered well over a hundred, forming a grisly carpet that covered the floor of the cave. We had found the villagers.

Charlotte moaned, pressing her hands over her mouth.

"Do not look," I said roughly, focusing the light on where Otto stood in the midst of the dead. He tilted his head back, and the mournful howl he emitted raised the hair at the nape of my neck. "Come, *bach.* Come here."

His howl tapered off, and he nosed at the bodies around him.

"Otto, *come.*" He looked at me and whined. "Wait here," I told Charlotte, and she nodded wordlessly, eyes closed.

I had to nudge aside arms and legs, wedging my feet between

149

torsos, to make my way to Otto. The cave floor was tacky beneath my boots. I avoided looking into the sightless eyes that caught the beam of my torch, but I could not miss the look of terror frozen onto the features of young and old. The poodle waited for me in the midst of a group of school children. Three nuns were sprawled with the children, and Otto whined again, prodding one of the nuns with his nose.

I rested a hand on his back as I crouched beside him. "Easy, Otto *bach*." I could see no reason for him to be frantic over this body. Her habit was stained with a diaspora of blood originating from a bullet wound high in the left side of her chest. I brushed her veil aside and rest my hand along her throat.

Her eyes flew open, and she latched onto my wrist. I started, heart lurching into my own throat. Her gaze darted around frantically before locking onto my face. "Owain," she breathed.

"You are safe now. You're safe," I assured her.

Her eyes were sunken, lips colorless, and her throat worked as she tried to speak. I leaned closer to make out the words.

"*Les enfants*," she whispered brokenly. "*Les en—*" She fainted, eyes rolling back in her head, hand slipping from my wrist.

I lifted her carefully into my arms and picked my way back across the cave. Otto followed.

"She's alive?" Charlotte knelt next to her when I placed the nun on the floor of the tunnel.

"For now." I shone the light over the cave and looked at Otto. He was panting, and though he sat, he edged closer and closer to Charlotte. "From his reaction, it seems she is the only survivor."

Charlotte wrapped an arm around the dog.

"She said my son's name. She called me Owain." I pulled in a deep breath through my mouth. "I cannot...I have to know."

Charlotte looked out over the cave's profusion of death and blanched. "I will help you."

"No, you do not need—"

"It will be quicker this way," she said, voice brisk.

We moved through the cave, wading through the grim sea of bodies and picking through it as if searching the shores at low tide. We peered at faces one after the other, turning the bodies over if they had fallen facedown. Some faces had been obliterated by a bullet, but none of their bodies matched my son's tall build.

"Stop," I said finally when we reached the far side of the cave where Otto had found the nun. "There is no need to search further. The rest are children. Owain is not here."

It was a challenge to get the gravely wounded nun out of the grottos, but Charlotte and I managed it together. It was midday when we emerged from the labyrinth of caves. The sun was blinding after the depth of darkness from which we climbed, and I had to squint against the brightness of the clear noon day as I carried the woman to the farmhouse. Her breathing was shallow as I placed her on the settee in the parlor, her pulse a mere flutter.

"Charlotte, do you—"

She strode past me, Otto trotting at her heels. Her face had taken on a careful blank mask in the cave, but now her movements were hurried. I followed her as she dropped her Colt onto the table in the kitchen and snatched up a bristle brush and cake of soap. She rushed out the back door.

I paused in the doorway as she stripped off her dress and cast it aside, letting it flutter to the ground as she headed to the pump. She untied the holster from about her waist and thigh and dropped it into the grass before levering the handle almost frantically until the bucket was overflowing. She picked it up and dumped the water over her head.

I grimaced, knowing the water sluicing over her was frigid. She tossed the bucket aside and took the soap and brush to her skin with a vigor that turned her flesh red. I approached and righted the bucket, filling it again with water for her and setting it in the sun to alleviate some of the chill.

"Give me your shoes," I said, voice soft. "I will clean them for you."

Her chin trembled as she unlaced her battered Oxfords and handed them to me, leaving her shivering in her brassiere, girdle, and anklets.

I retreated to the back step and used a dusting of dirt and a handful of leaves to remove all traces of blood from her shoes. I set them aside when they were cleaned and removed my boots, repeating the process.

"How long ago were they killed?"

I glanced up to find Charlotte kneeling beside Otto, rinsing his legs and scrubbing his feet. She was gentler with the poodle than she had been with herself, and I could see her skin was raw in places.

"Less than a week," I said, recalling the grotesque bloating and putrefaction of the bodies left strewn where they had fallen at Mametz Wood and Ypres.

"They spared no one. Not even…" She looked away and dragged the back of her wrist over her eyes. "Why? I have never even heard of this village. Everyone here must have been farmers and not much more. Why a…a massacre?"

I stood and unbuttoned my shirt, feeling the need to wash the taint from the grim tomb from my skin as well. "To make a point."

———

When the nun opened her eyes, Charlotte leaned forward into her line of vision and spoke gently in French. The nun's face was tight with anxiety until she glanced past Charlotte and caught sight of me. The tension about her eased, and she responded to Charlotte's queries. She faded quickly, though, slipping out of consciousness within moments.

Charlotte sat back and sighed. "She is from a convent in Grenoble. Once she met Owain here, their plan was to travel to the abbey at Dingy-Saint-Clair."

"Where is Dingy-Saint-Clair?"

"I don't know. I do not recognize the name." She looked up at me. "The village's executioners were German."

"I suspected as much."

"And, Rhys," she said, voice soft, "they were here looking for Owain."

"And did they find him here?"

She shook her head. "She lost consciousness before she could say more."

I turned away, rubbing the back of my neck.

"What do you want to do from here?"

I stared into the empty, cold hearth. I followed the same path as my son, but a dawning, heavy feeling that he would always be just out of my reach settled over me. I hung my head, squeezing my neck. "Let's look at the map. The only thing we know for certain is he was supposed to make for this abbey next."

Charlotte retrieved the map from the ambulance and spread it over the table in the kitchen. We peered at it closely, searching in quadrants, to no avail. Dingy-Saint-Clair was not listed on the paper.

"He has been moving east this entire time," Charlotte mused.

"Is he headed toward Italy or Switzerland?"

Her brow wrinkled. "If he were going to Italy, why would she come so far north from Grenoble?"

I studied the map and finally pointed to a speck of blue in a pool of green. "Here. I think we should make our way to Annecy."

———

The nun never reawakened, and as the day faded, she faintly breathed her last.

Charlotte and I met again in the study after we had turned in to our borrowed rooms. She coaxed haunting melodies from the piano well into the night.

We left at first light, taking provisions from the larder and baskets of fruit and vegetables from the garden and orchard. We found cans of petrol stashed away and added those to our loot. Charlotte checked the ambulance's petrol, oil, and water after replacing the distributor cap, and then we left the empty village behind.

Charlotte drove east, and when we reached the cerulean waters of the Rhône, we crossed the river at the first bridge we found. The narrow track led us through a small village nestled in the river basin at the foot of stone-faced cliffs. A towering monolith stood in the center square, gilded in the early morning light. The village was just beginning to stir and waken.

We traversed the foothills of the mountains to the north, following winding paths through the undulating terrain. It was midday before we reached the Rhône where it curved back toward its headwaters in the glaciers of the Swiss Alps. Where we crossed, the Rhône ran parallel to the Savoie. We drove north between the rivers before finding a place to cross the eastern Savoie.

The roads we had traveled through the foothills had been rough, crude paths, but now the gravel was smoothed and maintained. The road circumvented the northern curve of a long lake, and then it continued its northeast amble, leading us along the edge of the mountains to the south.

We reached Annecy as the sun was sinking at our back. The city cradled the northern reaches of a pristine lake, the hills we had traversed to the east, mountains to the west. This was the France Aelwyd would have loved. The city's rustic charm was evident even as it sought to recover from the occupation. Profusions of flowers spilled from window boxes. On a street corner, a café overflowed onto the walk. Some of the men and women had rifles propped against their chairs, but no gunfire echoed through the streets. Glances were still wary, but the tension that had gripped Paris, Vichy, and Lyon seemed to be loosening its grip here.

"Someone in this crowd may know of Dingy-Saint-Clair," Charlotte said, studying the lively café. "Wait here, and I will inquire."

I rested a hand on Otto's back when he would have followed her, and the poodle whined his displeasure.

"She won't be but a moment," I reassured him, and watched as Charlotte spoke to a table populated with old men. One nodded, and when he spoke, he gesticulated with gnarled hands.

Otto's tail thumped when Charlotte returned, and she stroked his head before putting the ambulance in gear. "You made the right choice with Annecy. Dingy-Saint-Clair is only about fifteen kilometers from here. The man said to take the road on the eastern side of the lake up into the mountains. When it branches in Bluffy, we are to take the left road." She glanced at me. "At the next branch, we take the left road. At the next, the right. The next, take the left, and that road will lead us to the village."

"Well. I do not see how we could become lost with those directions."

Her laughter was infectious, and I joined in, the chuckle seeming to relieve some of the weighted pressure that had taken up residence in my chest overnight.

After a moment, though, she sobered. "He warned me to have a care. There are still Germans up in the mountains."

We traversed the cobbled streets of the Old Town, which had been spared from bombs, and then took a narrow, tree-lined street that led us through the city along the northern bank of the lake. Annecy curved around the northeast edge of the lake, and the road followed the curve, hugging the water, soon leaving the town behind. The lake was stunning as the sun set over the western slopes in colors akin to a conflagration. The deep evening light gleamed emerald off the water, so still as to appear solid, not even a ripple to crack the surface.

The road meandered south along the lake before venturing west, ascending into the mountainous terrain. The ambulance took up the width of the road, and the forest was dense on either side. We climbed into the Alps as the moon climbed into the sky from its dimmet cradle.

Charlotte did not bother with the lights; the moon provided enough illumination as we followed the old man's directions higher and deeper into the mountains. The hamlet of Digny-Saint-Clair was nestled in a valley amidst towering peaks. The moon gleamed white off the limestone cliffs to the east. The village was quiet, shutters drawn to hide

155

any glint of light from within.

"No one is going to open their door to direct us to the abbey," Charlotte said softly, glancing around as she drove through the village.

"There." I pointed into the hills to the west. A stone structure stood out from the forest like a beacon in the moonlight. "If that is not it, we will at least have a vantage over the area."

We followed a lane that led east from the heart of the mountain hamlet and drove into the hills. The way was dark, the trees leaning in to create a canopy over the path. The clearing came suddenly around a curve, the woodland giving way to the grand stone structure and grounds. The lane had wound around the hill to the back of the structure I had glimpsed from below. A stone wall girded the grounds.

Charlotte brought the ambulance to a halt at the edge of the trees. The bell tower and apse were unmistakable, even in the dark. "This is at least a church."

"Aye. Now to learn whether it is the abbey of which the nun spoke."

Charlotte parked the ambulance at the iron gate, which was locked. After instructing Otto to remain with the vehicle, I boosted Charlotte to the top of the stone wall and then followed her over.

Neat hedges lined either side of the path leading to the abbey, and when I used the brass knocker, I could hear the echo within. Silence was the only answer for several long minutes. I stepped back and scanned the stone facade. The door creaked open, and a nun appeared in the thin gap, haloed by the lamp she carried.

Her query was in French, but she lifted the lamp and peered past Charlotte as she began to respond. The nun's eyes widened, and she opened the door further.

"Owain?" She glanced behind me. "Did you bring them? We heard you had been—" She broke off as she looked at me more closely and backed away. "You are not Owain."

I placed my hand on the door, fearing she would close and

bolt it. "He is my son. Please. I need to find him."

She studied me, gaze searching my face. "You best come inside. Did you walk?"

"We drove," Charlotte said.

The nun pulled a ring of keys from the folds of her habit. "I will unlock the gate. You may park in the barn." Her worn face softened at the sight of Otto when she unlocked the gate, and when he leapt from the vehicle and approached her, she leaned over to cup his muzzle in her hand and speak softly to him.

When the gate was once more secured and the ambulance was parked in the bay and hidden from view, the nun led us into the abbey. It was dark within, the sconces on the walls giving off the weakest of light that created more shadow than illumination. The interior was vast and cavernous, the ceiling lost to the dark, our footfall a soft echo.

"I hoped I would never again have to see the day when I had to lock the gate and bolt the door to the church," she said as she slid the bar into place across the towering arched door. "I am Mother Clémence." Her eyes widened as she glanced behind where Charlotte and I stood, and she held her hands out to us before we could turn. "Please, do not be alarmed and do not retaliate. She will mean you no harm once I explain."

I turned as a young nun separated from the shadows. A rifle was clutched in her trembling hands and leveled at my chest. I raised my own hands and held them up before me. Charlotte reached for where her Colt was hidden, but I nudged her shoulder with my elbow. "Wait."

The abbess stepped past me, her hands extended. "*Tout va bien, mon enfant*," she said, voice gentle. She continued to speak soothingly as she placed herself in the line of fire and approached the other woman. The younger woman's eyes darted from the abbess to me, haunted confusion etched into the fragile lines of her face.

"*Il veut nous blesser*," she whispered.

Charlotte tensed beside me. "*Non. Non, il ne le fait pas. C'est un homme bon, un homme gentil. Et il ne vous blessera pas.*"

157

"*C'est vrai, mon cher,*" the abbess said. "*Rappelez-vous Owain? C'est son père.*"

"*Son père?*" The young woman studied me, face working, and when the abbess placed a hand on the barrel of the rifle, she did not resist as it was relieved from her grasp. She blinked at me, and then her gaze fell to the side and caught on something beside me.

I glanced down to find Otto observing the woman with his head tilted and ears pricked. He padded forward, and his tail wagged as he nudged the young woman's now empty hands. A smile trembled across her lips.

The abbess set the rifle aside and released an uneven breath. "May she take your dog to the kitchens and feed him? She responds best to animals. I promise you, she will not harm him."

Charlotte glanced at me, and when I nodded, she said, "*Il s'appelle Otto.*"

As the young nun turned away, her belly, swollen and heavy with child, was unmistakable beneath her habit. The abbess sighed as she gazed after her. "That is Sister Angelique. You must forgive her. Her mind is not what it once was."

"We were warned there are Germans still in the mountains."

Mother Clémence's mouth tightened. "*Oui.*" The word was clipped, and she offered no more as she gestured for us to follow and led us through the church. A nave led us into an open courtyard, and the abbess directed us through the cloister to what appeared to be the old rectory. The room she invited us into was a simple study, unadorned aside from the rustic desk, three chairs, and a crucifix on the wall. "*S'il vous plaît,* be seated."

She sat behind the desk as Charlotte and I took the two chairs opposite. The abbess set her lamp to the side of the desk and adjusted the wick to brighten the light. She peered at me. "The resemblance is uncanny."

"Aye."

"I wish I had better tidings for you, but if you have come

seeking your son, he is not here."

"You said you had heard something, though, of his whereabouts?"

She folded her hands as if in prayer. "We received word that he was captured and held by the Gestapo."

My chair scraped across the floor as I stood and paced away. I rubbed the back of my neck. "Where? When did you receive word?"

"Five days ago. Our radio contact said that he is in Lyon."

I met Charlotte's gaze, frustration simmering in my chest. "We know of his work."

Mother Clémence stood and collected the lamp. "Then there is something I must show you."

She directed us through the inner cloister into a different section of the church. "There is a hidden room below the crypt," she said as she led the way down a winding flight of stone steps. "That is where we keep them while we wait for Owain and Sévèrin to provide safe transport."

The mausoleum was cool and dark, the only light the pool from the abbess's lamp, and our footsteps echoed in the heavy quiet. Arches were cut into the walls, some serving as enclosed tombs, others with human bones either stacked or placed on careful display. She led us to the last sepulcher, which was deep and housed a dozen human skulls. When she reached within and began to gather them in her arms, Charlotte took a step back, unease clear on her face.

"I think they would not mind, *oui*?" Mother Clémence said as she set the skulls aside and then climbed within the newly emptied space. What appeared to be a solid stone wall at the back, she pushed aside and then dropped out of sight. "Have a care here. It is a slight drop onto the steps and the footing is uneven."

Charlotte glanced at me. "Will you manage?"

"I must." I handed her up into the opening, leaning in and keeping hold of her wrist as she dropped off the back edge of the sepulcher.

"I have my footing now," she said.

I followed her, the stone scraping against my shoulders as I crawled through. My stomach and lungs tightened, and sweat beaded my forehead.

The sepulcher had been built to seal off—or conceal—a narrow spiral staircase that led down into the darkness. The abbess was already descending when I dropped off the meter-high ledge onto the steps. Charlotte waited several steps below me, and she reached back and caught my hand as we followed Mother Clémence. I had to turn sideways to navigate the steps, the walls were so narrow, and only Charlotte's certain grip on my hand kept my heart from thundering from my chest.

It was a relief when the steps leveled abruptly and led us into what appeared to have once been a chapel. I stumbled to a halt at the scene before me. I could not seem to draw air into my lungs, and it had nothing to do with the cramped space from which we had emerged. Charlotte's fingers clutched mine, and her face was colorless.

"My god," she whispered, and when she looked up at me, her eyes were wide and dark.

The abbess looked back and forth between us, a line forming between her brow. "You said you know of Owain's network?"

I opened my mouth, but no sound emerged. I thought I knew of my son's network, but what was before me were not pieces of art or trunks of family heirlooms.

Instead, nine children stared back at me.

8 April 1942

Dear Nhad,
We are now all required to carry an identity card.
Every one of us over the age of sixteen.
I think no good will come of this.
-Owain

xiii

Henri

I knew from their faces what the man and woman found in the caves. The woman's eyes were wide and dark, her face colorless; the man's features were grim and set. The nun he carried in his arms would not last the night.

Once they were out of sight, retreating to the farmhouse where they had made camp the night before, I searched the caves myself. It would be a terrible place to store paintings with the dampness of the underground river. Owain dabbled at drawing, and though he was not talentless, he knew nothing of art. He simply wanted to make a difference in the war effort on the side of the Jews.

I chuckled to myself as I followed the labyrinths deeper. *Make a difference.* Individuals were but a drop of rain compared to the ocean of existence. The arrogance of those eager to lend their lives, believing they could make a grand contribution to some effort never ceased to amuse me.

I had never fooled myself. My name would be forgotten, and I would fade from memory. Perhaps even before I was gone. Nothing survived but art.

I did not mind so much that Göring confiscated the majority of the ownerless collections I retrieved for the Paris *Hauptarbeitsgruppen.* He did not have a love for it. The fat, shrewd bastard collected it because he thought it made him appear cultured. But that was more acceptable than Hitler getting his small weasel hands on it. That *dummkopf* would not know Rococo from Baroque from the paper he used to wipe his ass.

I kept the best for myself, of course. It had been my downfall. I had been arrogant enough to think my purloining would go unnoticed. It had cost my loyal, faithful Gerhardt his life. My stomach churned at the thought of those bastards in my home, drinking my best vintage, lounging on my furnishings. Touching, hurting my wife.

I followed each narrow tunnel deeper into the belly of the earth, searching the caverns for the paintings. *You must find them, Heinrich,* Göring had said. *His work is part of the heart of Blut und Boden. It would not do to have the pieces left in those filthy hands.* I had found them two years ago, though I had not bothered to tell Göring. I had found them in a tiny attic in Paris and had immediately imagined how the paintings would look hanging together in my library.

Now, they may very well cost my Mila her life. I closed my eyes. Years I had been away from home now, but I could remember every detail. Which board would creak underfoot, how the breeze carried the scent of the ripening vines, the fine texture of Mila's hair between my fingers, the depth of Gerhardt's bark and the weight of his warm bulk draped over my feet. I would not be returning to the same home, I knew that now. My own greed had ensured it.

I did not find the paintings. If Owain had hidden them, they were in depths I did not dare venture without risking losing my way back to the surface. The grotto did not frighten me, though. There was a tranquility here in the bowels of the land, a quiet closeness that reminded me of the trenches. I had drawn some of my best portraits there. Each stroke of charcoal had felt heightened and important, *essential*, in that setting. Suffering and sorrow always made for better art.

I did find what had so disturbed Owain's father and the woman traveling with him. I grimaced at the scene stretched before me and knew immediately who was responsible. Some men sought any excuse for gross, unnecessary excess. Some had no understanding of artfulness and subtlety. Some only appreciated heavy-handedness and blatant displays of power. The Butcher was certainly one of those men, and I knew where to find him.

I retreated from the caves and raided the farmhouses on the western side of town for food. I checked the walls and cellars for art but found nothing worth the effort of carrying it with me, so I turned the motorcycle back to Lyon.

11 May 1942

Dear Nhad,
Five students have been arrested
after an anti-German demonstration at a boys'
secondary school in the 15th arrondissement.
Little more than children,
and I fear they will face the firing squad.
-Owain

xiv

The cathedral was silent, more shadowed than not, for the only light came from the fulgurating flames of votive candles near the altar. I rested my elbows on my knees and rubbed the back of my neck.

"Tell me it is not true."

"Nhad, I can explain—"

"What is there to explain? What possible excuse could you have?"

"Rhys, please," my mother began.

"You knew?"

"I did, and I knew you would—"

"I had to find out from Gareth Driscoll that my son is a goddamned conchie!" My voice had risen to a shout, and I turned away, rubbing my forehead and pinching the bridge of my nose.

"I am not a soldier, Nhad."

"It matters naught what you think you are in times of war. You will go back and—"

"I will not."

I rounded on him, and his chair scraped back as he stood. He almost stood eye to eye with me now, and he did not flinch as he met my gaze.

"There are ways to fight in this war without a gun."

"You are a naïve fool."

"I want no part in the killing!"

I pointed a finger at him and noted absently that a tremor shook the appendage. *"I will not call a coward my son."*

He sucked in a breath, face paling, shoulders hunching.

"Get out. I do not want to see your face again until you have

169

learned to be a man who accepts his duties and responsibilities."

"Rhys, no—"

It was Owain who held up his hand to silence my mother's protests. He held my gaze, shoulders straightening, and then he pushed past me to retreat into his room.

In the morning, he was gone.

The soft tread of approaching footsteps brought me back to the present. I knew by the light, crisp fragrance of peppermint it was Charlotte who sought me out before she settled on the bench beside me. She did not attempt to make conversation but sat with me quietly, her presence a soothing balm.

"Where is Otto?" I finally asked.

"In the crypt with the children. They seemed comforted by him, and he is basking in the attention."

I raked my hands through my hair. "*Esgob annwyl. Children,* Charlotte."

Her hand came to rest on my shoulder. "I know."

"And held by the Gestapo in Lyon…" My stomach churned at the thought. "He was right there."

"There is no way you could have known."

My throat was so tight I could scarcely force the words out. "I found out from a neighbor that Owain was a conscientious objector. I was livid, I was, and…" I swallowed. "And ashamed. Embarrassed by my own son." I scrubbed my hands over my face, dragging my palms over the fading bruises at my temple and jaw. "War would have destroyed him. My son always was a…a gentle soul, and war has shredded many a harder man. I knew this. I dreaded it for him. But a man does what needs to be done, what duty calls for him to do." I turned my head and met Charlotte's gaze. "I called him a coward, told him I could not call him my son." I thumped my chest with my fist. "*I* was the coward. I allowed my embarrassment to overtake my love for my son." My voice broke, and the tears that blurred my vision prevented me from discerning any expression on Charlotte's face.

She slid closer to me and caught my hand where it was pressing against my breastbone to prevent my heart from cracking apart. She wrapped her hands around mine, voice soft but firm and insistent. "You were angry. You lashed out in the moment and said something you regret. You were *human*. Everyone is fallible. *Everyone*. Sons *and* fathers. But you are *here*. In a strange, torn country in the grip of war, searching tirelessly for him. You can tell me of your wrongs 'til the cows come home, but *that*…that tells me more about you as a man, as a father, than words you spoke years ago that haunt you still."

"I have to find him," I whispered. "I must."

She squeezed my fingers. "We will. We can leave tonight and return to Lyon. We can leave now."

"No." The whispered word startled us both, and I blinked to clear my vision. The abbess approached us silently but swiftly, her face tense. "Right now, you must hide. The Germans are at the gate."

———

We hid in the concealed stairwell in the crypt. Mother Clémence replaced the relic bones after us, and before I slid the door that served as a false wall into place, she caught my eye.

"*S'il vous plaît*, no matter what you may hear, do not reveal yourselves. The children depend upon it. With Owain and Sévèrin gone, their safety depends on hiding here." There was fear in her eyes, but the set of her jaw was resolute.

"I do not like this," Charlotte whispered as I sealed us into the stairwell.

Nor did I, but I followed her down into the old subterranean chapel. Otto stood and padded to Charlotte.

A single candle lit the room, and though all the children were tucked into their pallets, all save the infant were tense. The pounding on the church door and shouting reverberated even here in this hidden sanctum. The children's wide-eyed, fixed stares reminded me of the dazed expressions I had seen so often in the trenches.

When Charlotte moved to snuff the flame, I caught her arm.

"The scent of smoke will carry."

We stood in the center of the chapel, attention on the ceiling. A tug on my wrist brought my gaze down. A young boy stood at my side, and he held up his hands. I leaned down and lifted him into my arms. His body was compact, and once I held him where we could peer eye to eye, I studied him in the low light.

His face was round and cherubic with a snub of a nose and eyes that slanted upward at the outer corners. His small mouth held a downward tilt, and his tongue was wedged against his lower lip. His eyes were bright, face a study of innocence, and he perused my features as curiously as I did his.

Something shifted within me when he leaned down and rested his head on my shoulder. I glanced at Charlotte to find her head tilted as she listened for any sounds above. One hand was buried in Otto's hair, the other hidden in the folds of her skirt, concealing, I knew, her grip on her Colt.

I looked around the room. The oldest girl, no more than ten or eleven, held the sleeping infant against her thin chest. Two boys, obviously twins, shared a pallet, and a girl who had to be their older sister had given the pair her blanket. A young boy no older than seven or eight sat leaning in the corner as his two younger sisters curled against his legs. Their gazes were wary and resigned.

My decision was made even before I heard the screams.

The child in my arms flinched, and a shudder coursed through him. I rubbed his back as I crossed the room and knelt to place him on the empty pallet. I covered him with a blanket and summoned Otto. The poodle settled next to the boy, curling against him and resting his muzzle on the child's shoulder.

I straightened and turned to Charlotte.

"I am going with you," she whispered.

"We have the element of surprise on our side. We need to keep it as long as possible."

The crypt was empty as I climbed from the sepulcher. I leaned back in and gave Charlotte a hand up, and then moved to the foot of the stairs as she slid the door back into place behind her and rearranged the skulls I had pushed aside.

Light gleamed around the curve of the steps, and I could hear voices echoing in the church above.

"There must be another way out," I whispered.

Charlotte led the way deeper into the crypt. The air was still and held a dank chill. The darkness deepened as we ventured further until it was absolute.

I stopped, blind, and reached for Charlotte, catching her hair with my fingers before I found her shoulder. Her chin brushed the back of my hand, and her breath was warm against my wrist. "Are you well?"

"Aye." The darkness cloaked any tightening of the space and made the mausoleum feel cavernous.

"I think I feel a draft, but I—" She went rigid beneath my hand as German voices interrupted her and heavy footfall echoed behind us. The soldiers were descending into the crypt.

I nudged Charlotte forward. *"Go!"*

We moved as quickly and silently as possible in the darkness, shuffling to avoid falling, groping at the wall to avoid being lost in the black.

Light pierced the dark just as Charlotte made a sudden turn to the left and yanked me after her. I tripped over the sudden elevation in the floor but regained my footing and pressed into the recesses of the staircase as the light bounced off the crypt's stone walls.

My heart raced as I watched the light dart into corners. Charlotte was pressed against me, and I could feel the rapid rise and fall of her chest at my back. Her fingers tightened on my arm as the light and voices drew closer. I fumbled in the dark, unclasped two of the buttons on my shirt, and carefully drew the Luger from the concealed holster. The slide of metal against leather seemed cacophonous, and the voices paused. When they resumed, though, they were in retreat rather than advance. After several long moments, the crypt was once more a dark, silent tomb.

I let out the breath I had not realized I held and returned the Luger to the holster.

"This way," Charlotte whispered.

I followed her up the winding staircase. The brief beams of light made the darkness even more impenetrable, and I found my way with my hands on either wall of the narrow shaft. The black dimmed to gray the higher we climbed, and the stairwell curved once more and then leveled.

"Where are we?"

The moonlight edging through the high round window lingered over the rows of laden shelves. "A muniment room," I said, voice low. I wound through the stacks and found the iron latticed door at the far side of the room. I eased it open, bracing for a metallic groan, but the hinges were well-oiled. The door opened silently and led us into an empty chapter house.

The door at the far side of the room stood open. It led out into the night, framing a moonlit courtyard. Charlotte started toward the opening.

The scuff of a boot on stone and the murmur of movement reached my ears, and I placed a staying hand on Charlotte's elbow.

We both froze as a German soldier stepped into the doorway. Charlotte stood at the fringes of deeper shadow, visible to anyone peering within. I waited, tense, for the shout, the scramble for his weapon. But neither came.

The soldier stood with his back to the room, facing out into the night as he lit a cigarette. He hummed as he shook out the match and drew a long drag into his lungs before exhaling the smoke.

As the German began to sing under his breath, I drew the Luger from its holster and handed it to Charlotte. She glanced at me, eyes wide, her own pistol in hand, but I shook my head and motioned for silence. I undid my belt as I crept across the room, the whisper of leather sliding across fabric masked by the off-key singing. I slid the end of the belt back through the buckle and wrapped the tail around my fist.

The soldier was shorter than I but solidly built. A stirring of movement or perhaps some sudden sense of no longer being alone must have alerted the German, for he turned his head as I reached him. His face was round and pock-marked, and his eyes went wide when he saw me.

I dropped the loop of the belt over his head and yanked the noose tight, cutting off his shout before it could leave his throat. His cigarette burned my arm as it fell.

I dragged him backward into the chamber, pulling the belt taut. He flailed, reaching over his head to claw at my face. He threw his weight against me, and I staggered into the wall. When he fumbled for his gun, I wrapped the belt around my left forearm and caught his wrist with my free hand. He had managed to get the pistol clear of the holster, and though I squeezed his wrist hard enough to feel the bones contract beneath my grasp, he did not relinquish his grip.

My arm shook with the effort to hold onto the belt one-handed as he struggled. The leather burned as it dug into and dragged against my skin. My palm dampened with sweat, and the belt slid in my hand.

I brought my knee up as I drove his arm down, catching his forearm across my thigh.

The bone snapped with an audible crack. The pistol clattered to the floor, and I felt the soundless scream vibrating through his chest.

He threw himself forward, the movement catching me off balance, and we fell in a tangle of limbs. Desperation lent him strength, and he fought wildly. I took an elbow to the ribs and to the jaw, the last hitting me in the same place as the healing bruise from the attack in Paris. It sent a shard of pain through me and set my head to ringing, disorienting me for a moment.

A moment was all the German needed to land a knee in my gut and scramble away, clawing at the leather garroted around his neck. He got his knees under him and turned toward me, drawing his knife as I righted myself.

"Rhys!"

"Get *back*," I snapped at Charlotte, and launched myself at the German.

I tackled him, and the knife slid across the floor. I reared over him and drove my fist into his stomach in a quick succession of blows. He rolled to his side, curling into a fetal position, his broken arm cradled to his chest. I sat and yanked him upright and back against me. I pulled the belt tight around his throat and felt his chest work helplessly to draw in air.

His legs kicked, arms flailing, and I leaned backward to avoid his fingers curled like claws, pulling on the belt so tightly my arms shook. The flails reduced to limpness and then to the occasional twitch until the German lay heavy and boneless over me.

"Rhys." Charlotte's voice seemed to reach me through a dense fog. "He…he is dead."

I let myself fall back against the floor. I was winded, heart thrumming, and it took me a moment to gather the strength to roll the soldier off of me. He fell aside in a limp sprawl. I pushed upright, and my hands trembled as I loosened the belt from about the other man's neck and pulled it away.

I stood, letting my head hang for a moment when the room spun, and once I was steady, I methodically fed the belt through the loops in my trousers. I secured the buckle and then held my hand out for the Luger I had shed. Charlotte approached me slowly and handed it to me wordlessly, eyes large in a face that appeared even paler in the moonlight.

I replaced the Luger in its holster and leaned over to retrieve the fallen knife and pistol. I handed Charlotte the pistol and watched as she inspected the weapon and checked the round in the chamber. Finally, she nodded and tucked it away, keeping the Colt in hand. When she looked up at me, her face was once again composed.

"Wait as long as possible to shoot?"

"Aye. There should only be a few soldiers posted as lookouts. When you hear gunfire from within, take that as your signal." I peered cautiously out into the night, but the only sight that greeted me was the empty courtyard and the neat, well-tended rows of a vegetable garden.

Charlotte caught my arm. "Rhys." She searched my face but said no more.

"I will see you momentarily," I said, and slipped from her grasp and into the night.

I crept through the shadows cast by the stone structure and followed the sound of screaming around the northeast corner of the abbey. There were no sentries standing watch on the north side of the abbey, and the reason became apparent as I stole closer to the light that spilled from an open doorway.

The screams from within were wild and animalistic, raising the hair at the nape of my neck. Punctuating the cries were male voices and raucous laughter. I did not need to understand German to understand the tone.

I knelt and peered around the doorjamb. A soldier stood just within, blocking my view. His trousers sagged around his thighs, and he worked himself in frantic motions while calling encouragement to his comrades.

I ducked out of sight, stomach turning, and tested the knife I had lifted from the other soldier. It slid easily against the pad of my thumb, honed to a razor's edge. I felt no pain, but in the dimness a drop of blood welled black in the wake of the blade.

I took a deep breath and wiped my hand on my trousers, adjusting my feet into a wider stance. Then I leaned around the doorframe and clapped a hand over the soldier's mouth. I used my grip on his face to wrench his head back and with a quick, weighted motion, I sliced the knife across the exposed, vulnerable column of his throat.

The warmth of his blood hit my arm in a spray before I had even finished the motion. He jerked as I dragged him outside and into the shadows, but when I released my hold over his mouth, he crumpled silently to the ground.

I clasped the knife in a slick hand and whirled toward the door, but it remained empty.

The two Germans within were too preoccupied to notice their companion's abrupt and violent departure, or my presence in the kitchen. One stood at the entry of the larder, waiting his turn. He was hurriedly unbuckling his belt when I grabbed him from behind. He abandoned his task to wrench at my arm, but I had already laid open his throat with the knife.

He hit the ground gurgling and thrashing, and the noise was enough to distract the third from his rutting. He staggered to his feet.

"*Was ist das?*" His voice held the commanding bark of rank and medals glinted on his chest. He struggled to get his trousers up from about his knees.

I did not give him the chance. The scream that tore from his lips when I drove the knife into his groin was high and wailing. It cut silent, though, when I wrenched the knife out, clasped his shoulder when he would have reeled backward, and slipped the blade up between his ribs, piercing his heart. It was as if a candle had been snuffed. He went silent and limp in an instant. I pulled the knife free and stepped aside to let him fall.

It was the young nun swollen with child who lay whimpering on the stone floor of the larder. I did not attempt to approach her as she struggled to draw the torn habit about her. I knelt in the doorway. The sounds escaping her throat sounded like those of a wounded, frightened animal.

"Shh. Shh, now. You're safe, you are. They'll not harm you any longer."

The bullet that bit into the wall over my head belied my assurances, and I dove into the larder with a curse. A hailstorm of bullets chipped at stone and wood and shattered crockery. I shoved the nun deeper into the larder and with a hand on her shoulder forced her flat to the floor. She fought against me, keening, and I struggled to keep her head covered as debris rained over us.

A lull came in the barrage. I tucked the wet knife into my boot and drew the Luger as I gained my feet.

The two soldiers had ducked to either side of the inner doorway into the kitchen. They scrambled to reload their weapons.

I strode toward the door, firing at either side as I advanced. One soldier's knee was exposed, and the second bullet I fired at him found flesh. He fell into sight with a shriek of pain, hands clutching the maimed joint, but I focused on his companion. The second soldier lunged around the doorframe, gun raised. I fired in swift succession, and two of the three bullets found their mark in his torso. He fell in a sprawl, his gun clattering to the floor.

I turned the Luger back to the first soldier just as he chambered a round and turned his on me. We stared at one another over the barrels. His face was a tight grimace of pain.

Shouts and the ringing of boot heels against stone snagged the soldier's attention. His head turned, and the barrel of his gun dipped infinitesimally.

I moved to the side and fired. His finger reflexively squeezed the trigger in response, but the bullet passed harmlessly by. He slumped against the wall, dead, and I grabbed his gun and the other soldier's. I pulled their holsters, gleaming with 9mm ammunition, from about their hips.

I stepped over their bodies and realized I was back in the inner cloister. Light spilled from the church across the open courtyard, the braziers within lit and burning brightly. I ducked behind an arch as shadows passed before the doorways on the other side of the cloister. Voices barked inquiries, and I glanced at the bodies I had left in my wake. When no response came, the confusion was evident in the voices and quick, furtive movements.

Hidden from view for the moment, I crouched and tucked the two guns into my trousers at the small of my back. I ejected the magazine from my Luger and kept an eye on the arches across the way as I collected eight bullets from one of the pilfered holsters and fed them into the box. A shadow separated from deeper shadow and crept from arch to arch across the courtyard. A scuff of movement behind me gave away the approach of another on this side of the cloister. At least two flanked me at an eight points approach, and I could not risk being completely surrounded.

Gunfire from within the church ripped through the night.

"*Scheisse!*" The shadow in the arch across from me straightened and pointed back toward the church in sharp motions. I slid the magazine home and pulled the jointed arm to chamber a round. "*Zurückbekommen! Komme—*"

Two bullets from my gun piercing his chest interrupted his command. I leaned around the stone arch and fired three times at the soldier standing in the moonlight, looking back and forth in confusion. He grunted at the impact and crumbled.

I ran in a crouch along the wall where the shadows were deepest. As I approached the church, the gunfire within fell silent. I peered around the corner and slumped with relief at the sight before me.

Charlotte spun from where she knelt to help the abbess upright, her Colt level with my chest, as soon as I darkened the entry. She let out a breath and slipped the gun into her hidden holster. "Rhys." Her eyes widened as I stepped into the light. "You are hurt." She stood and hurried toward me.

I held up a hand to stay her. My fingers trembled slightly, and my skin was stained russet with blood. Weariness settled about my shoulders like a weighty cloak. "None of the blood is mine. Did you take care of the lookouts?"

"There were two outside." She nodded at the men sprawled dead amidst the pews. "And three in here."

"There were four, *Fräulein*."

She whirled toward the German who stepped from the nave, but his gun was already leveled at her head. He looked to me and met my gaze over the barrel of my own raised Luger.

"Do not attempt anything foolish. I will put a bullet in her head before you manage to kill me. Put your weapon down."

Charlotte glanced at me, her jaw tight. "Don't do it."

He squeezed the trigger, and the report of the bullet was drowned out by my helpless shout. Charlotte flinched, but she did not fall. I moved toward her.

"Halt! I will not miss her again. Drop the gun."

Charlotte's eyes were wide as she met my gaze. The bullet had gone over her head, but her face was leeched of color.

"I will not ask again."

"Do not shoot her." I bent and placed the Luger at my feet and then straightened. I raised my hands.

"Now, both of you, on your knees." We glanced at one another, and he strode toward us. "On your knees *now*! Put your hands behind your head."

"Do it," I said, voice low.

Charlotte's lips tightened, but she obeyed, lacing her fingers behind her head and lowering to kneel on the stone floor. I followed suit, but I did not lace my fingers together. I stacked my hands behind my head and watched the German closely.

He stopped within a meter from where I knelt, but then he wisely took several steps back out of range. "I will not—"

The blast of a rifle interrupted him. I dove for Charlotte, pressing her flat to the floor as I drew one of the pistols from where it was tucked at my back. The German's gun dropped as his hands came up to cover the gaping hole in his chest. He stared at me, face frozen in shock.

He dropped to his knees and then slumped to the side, revealing the abbess standing behind him with a rifle clutched in her hands.

30 May 1942

Dear Nhad,
I saw a child today, no older than eight or nine years of age,
wearing a yellow badge upon her sleeve. A Star of David.
Already Jews are barred from restaurants and other public places.
Their synagogues attacked and vandalized.
Now they are branded...I grow more and more uneasy.
-Owain

XV

The abbess's face was blank, blood spilling over her chin from a split lip, a knot welling over her left eye. The mask slipped, though, and her face crumbled in horror.

I gained my feet and lifted Charlotte to hers. "Are you well?" I passed a hand over her hair to reassure myself the bullet had left her unscathed.

She nodded, but I felt a fine tremor pass through her. She approached Mother Clémence slowly, and the abbess allowed Charlotte to relieve the rifle from her shaking hands.

"What have I done?" She crossed herself, voice desolate. "What have you done?" Charlotte and I met one another's gaze. "More will come now. The children…"

"Where does Owain take the children from here?" I looked to Charlotte.

She spoke before I could say more. "We can take the children to safety."

Mother Clémence shook her head. "You do not understand. I…I do not know. Only Owain and Sévèrin knew."

"There must be a map."

"There is no map. Only a note Owain left for Sévèrin."

"A note?"

"*Oui.* They rarely traveled together. Only within the last months had they begun doing so. The abbey was their meeting place, but Owain left instructions for Sévèrin should he be…delayed. It was never needed. Until now. And we cannot read it."

"Why not?"

She shrugged, spreading her hands in a helpless gesture in response to Charlotte's query. "The language is strange. It is neither French nor English. We do not—"

"Let me see it."

Both women were startled by the abruptness of my tone, but the abbess nodded. "Permit me to see to Sister Angelique. Then I will meet you in my study."

———

He had written the note in Welsh.

"Can you read this?"

"Aye." I ran my finger over the scrawl of letters, feeling where his pen had dug uneven furrows into the paper. While Mother Clémence had seen to the wounded young woman in the larder and settled her into bed, I had washed at the well. My shirt was stained irreparably, and I absently noted the brown blood caked around the nail of my thumb. "*Take the mountain road 'round the school of clocks to the horseshoe. Cross the white horse and look to the water at dawn.* Does that mean anything to you?"

The abbess paced away. "Read it once more to me." I did so and her brow wrinkled. "There is a school in Cluses. *L'École d'horlogerie.*"

"Watchmaking?" Charlotte translated.

"*Oui.* And you said horseshoe? What is this in French?"

"*Fer à cheval,*" Charlotte said.

"*Fer à cheval,*" she whispered. "Sixt-fer-à-Cheval. It is a village, and the white horse. *Le Cheval Blanc.* It is a mountain on the border in the Chablais Alps."

I folded the paper and tucked it into my pocket alongside the worn letter. "How many are there of you?"

"*Quelle?*"

"How many? You, the young nun. Who else?"

"It is only the two. Myself and Sister Angelique. The others are gone. I sent them away. I had to stay for the children, and Sister Angelique…" She looked away. "This is her only home now."

"Pack up what you do not want left behind. You may seek shelter in the village, or you may come with us. But we all leave tonight."

———

We left the dead where they lay.

Charlotte pulled the ambulance from the barn and backed it close to the entrance of the church. As she and the abbess gathered the children from the hidden chapel, I stripped the bodies of weapons and ammunitions.

Otto raced out of the dark, wary of the strewn bodies, and followed close at my side as I loaded the cache into the ambulance, stowing the arsenal out of easy reach of the children. I kept three guns on me and reloaded the magazines as I turned and peered out into the night.

The front gate listed on its hinges. The two vehicles the Germans had driven through the gate sat crippled in the courtyard by Charlotte's mechanical knowledge.

The surrounding woods were deep but alive with the sounds of darkling creatures. I patted my pocket, seeking my cigarette, before I recalled its loss. The burn on my forearm was a quiet throb.

Footsteps and whispers alerted me to the approach, and I turned to find Charlotte and Mother Clémence hurrying the small band of children through the church. Their eyes were wide, faces colorless and frightened, and I cursed the lack of foresight in not hiding the bodies from them. Their small faces were already haunted enough.

"*Rapidement maintenant, mes infants,*" Charlotte whispered, touching their shoulders when several stopped to stare at the fallen Germans.

Two of the younger girls began to cry, and the infant whimpered. The abbess shifted the infant to the crook of one arm and lifted the smallest girl to her hip, doing her best to soothe them.

187

The young boy I had held earlier spotted me and broke away from the group. He greeted Otto first, sticking his face in the poodle's to kiss the canine's narrow muzzle. The dog made no protest, and his tail wagged as he licked the boy across his cherubic face.

The child turned to me and raised his arms. I picked him up, and he leaned forward to wrap his arms around my neck. I held him for a moment, the weight of him taking me back years, before I patted his back and placed him in the rear of the ambulance. Otto leapt in after him, and I pointed to the far end of the stretcher. Boy and dog obeyed.

Charlotte climbed in after them, and I handed the children up to her one after the other. Each carried a blanket and little else, and she settled them on our bedrolls.

I turned to the abbess and lifted the older child from her arms.

"We will come with you. I would see the children to safety." She glanced back into the church. "And be away from this place." She took a deep breath and touched the swelling on her forehead. "Will you assist me with Sister Angelique?"

"Aye."

"I gave her medicine to aid her sleep. I think it best this way." She handed the infant up to Charlotte. "Come."

She directed me back through the church and rectory and up a flight of stairs. The room she led me to was spartan, bare save for the narrow bed and a bedside table. The nun slept curled on her side, hands fisted under her chin. Her eyelids flickered in sleep, and she flinched when the abbess tucked the worn blanket closer about her. I could not imagine her sleep was peaceful.

"You did not know your son was smuggling children to safety."

I rubbed the back of my neck and answered her honestly. "No. Are they all Jews?"

She folded several garments and blankets into a satchel. "The oldest child and the youngest are Romani. And you have met Hugo."

I lifted the woman into my arms. Even with the additional

weight of her unborn child, she was painfully light, and her head lolled against my shoulder. She whimpered in her drug-induced sleep. "The boy with the curious features."

"*Oui.*" She placed the bible on the night stand in the satchel and led the way back through the dormitory. "He is a Mongoloid."

I was not familiar with the term. "And the children's parents?"

"Gone on the trains or dead, I am certain. I do not know the details. Only that your son was their only hope for safety."

———

We drove into the night, winding through valleys shadowed by ever-taller peaks.

"Left here." I turned off the torch and re-folded the map. Thônes slept as we passed over its cobbled lanes, and moonlight rippled over the stream that ran parallel to the gravel track we followed. "This road will lead us all the way to Cluses."

"I have been lying to you."

I turned to study Charlotte's profile. She had been silent since we left Digny-Saint-Clair, silent save for the chattering of her teeth and her soft, "No," when I asked if she was cold. "Owain was your contact."

She glanced at me, and a glimmer of a smile crossed her drawn face. "I thought you must have known."

"You said his name in Paris before I could tell you it was Owain."

She nodded. "You are right. He was my contact. I knew no more than his name, but when I saw you, I knew you had to be his father. I mistook you for Owain himself when I first saw them drag you into the alley."

"Why do you seek him?"

"In September of '42, he failed to make a rendezvous, and he simply…disappeared. There was no talk of him being captured or killed. He was simply gone. As were a number of the paintings he had been tasked with smuggling out of Paris."

I glanced at her sharply. "You think he stole the paintings."

189

She hesitated, tapping a finger against the steering wheel. "I was a cataloguer at the Louvre. Records, bibliographies, numbers. Those are what I am most familiar with. And I kept a log of everything, on both ends."

"And the numbers did not add up."

"No. Eleven paintings went missing between my handling and the receiving at the other end of the channel. Owain was not my only contact. We had half a dozen people tasked with transporting art out of Paris. But in all the shipments where the numbers did not add up, Owain was the constant."

"You want answers from him, then."

"I do. I spent a year scouring Paris for him to no avail. Three of those paintings were from my great-aunt's collection. Dionne's grandmother. She married a Jewish man, though thankfully both were gone long before the war began and my cousin has been able to keep her heritage a secret. Dionne had no interest in art, but Tatie knew of my love. They were my favorite paintings from her collection, and she left them to me when she died."

"I am sorry."

"I am as well. I had given up finding them. Until I saw you in the alley in Paris."

"He would not have taken those paintings for himself."

"I believe you. But that is what my records show. He and his partner—" Her voice cut off abruptly, and she slowed the ambulance. "His partner."

"You mentioned one before. Did you know him?"

"No, not even his name. I only saw him a few times, I mainly dealt with Owain. But…"

"But?"

"The doctor in Lyon after the fire. I thought I recognized him, but I could not place him at the time."

"And now?"

"Now, I…I am certain it was Owain's partner. But that is

impossible."

"Why?"

She shifted gears, and the moon raced with us along the dark ribbon of the mountain road. "Because there was rumor that Owain had killed his partner before disappearing."

———————

I did not risk sleep when we pulled into an abandoned barn in a quiet valley in the hours before dawn. I knew what awaited me in slumber, and I did not care to revisit the battlefields with the closing of my eyes.

The stalls were all empty, and I spread fresh hay in the deepest pen furthest from the doors. While the others slept, I kept watch.

The children had remained silent as we bedded them down, exhaustion and fright rendering them hollowed phantoms of young innocence. The abbess leaned against the wood plank wall in the midst of their tightly curled bodies with the nun's head cradled in her lap. The young woman had not stirred as I carried her from the ambulance, and she slept on now, though I knew from the rigid stillness of her shadow that the abbess sat sleepless.

Charlotte slept on her side with her knees drawn up around the infant and Otto lying at her back. When she flinched and murmured in sleep, I place a hand on her shoulder. She eased at my touch, a slight sigh escaping her, and it was a temptation to allow my hand to linger.

I withdrew, rubbing Otto's ears when he lifted his head, and turned back to watch the entrance of the barn from where I sat leaning in the doorway of the stall. The open entrance remained dark and empty.

A rustle of movement drew my attention into the stall, and the boy named Hugo approached me with his blanket trailing after him. Since I was seated, we were eye to eye, and he met my gaze for a moment before he blinked owlishly and yawned.

I sat unmoving as he knelt and climbed into my lap, leaning against my chest. The sensation was so hauntingly familiar a lump rose in my throat as I shook out the blanket and settled it around him. I rested my hand on his back. He soon grew limp and heavy against me, and when I closed my eyes, it was not the Somme or Ypres that met me but Owain.

"Get out. I will not call a coward my son."

The small face looking up at me crumbled. He reached for my hand, but I turned and strode away.

"Dadi!" His voice was frightened and plaintive. "Dadi, please! Wait for me!"

I glanced back to find him struggling to follow me. His short legs, even as sturdy as they were, no match for my stride.

He held his arms out to me. "Os gwelwch yn dda, Dadi."

I ignored him, and his sobs and cries followed me as I climbed our hills. The sky was dark and foreboding overhead.

Owain's calls suddenly fell silent. I turned back, but the hills around me were empty.

"Owain?"

A mist crept over the hills, and with it came the sound of weeping as it curled around my ankles. The heather grew thorns and caught at my legs as I ventured downhill, and rocks rolled underfoot.

"Owain? Where are you, machgen i? Owain!"

Wind swept over the land, and it drowned my shouts.

When I finally heard his voice, it was a whisper directly at my ear. "Dadi, help me."

I lurched awake so abruptly I floundered in finding my bearings. For a moment, I thought the child sleeping against my chest was Owain, and I clung to him before the boy in my arms shifted and murmured in French.

I released an unsteady breath and glanced around. Dawn was encroaching upon the night, and the darkness was beginning to lighten. The children, Charlotte, and Otto still lay sleeping. The nun's rest was troubled, for she shuddered and whimpered in sleep. The abbess was not there to soothe her.

I eased Hugo off my lap and placed him in the hay at Otto's

side. Moving through the shadows of the barn, I checked each stall and the rear of the ambulance to no avail. As I approached the entrance of the barn, though, I heard the sound of retching. I stopped and listened as the heaving soon turned to the sound of quiet weeping.

The murmur of voices drew my attention back to the stall, and the tone of the exchange had me crossing the distance quickly. A beam of torchlight sliced the dark recesses.

"Rhys? *Rhys!*"

The panic in Charlotte's voice made me break into a run, and when I reached the stall, I drew short at the scene before me.

Charlotte knelt beside the nun, who lay curled on her side moaning. Sister Angelique's face was twisted in pain, her arms clutched around her stomach. A growing pool of blood spread under her.

Charlotte rested her hand on the woman's hip, and when she looked up at me, the fear was evident on her face in the harsh gleam of torchlight. "She's bleeding," she said needlessly.

"Get the children in the ambulance."

She hurried to do so as I gently lifted the nun in my arms. She was too wracked by pain to flinch away from me.

The abbess was wiping her eyes when she came into view, and her face creased in worry. "*Que s'est-il passé?*"

"We must get her to a hospital immediately."

The nun cried out, grasping her stomach with one hand, the fingers of her other hand digging into my shoulder. I felt the graze from the bullet in Vichy begin to bleed under her grip.

The abbess crossed herself and hurried to help usher the children into the ambulance. "There is a hospital in Cluses. My nephew is a doctor there."

I climbed into the back of the ambulance. "Sit and allow her to lean against you," I told Mother Clémence, and then turned to Charlotte. "Get us to Cluses as quickly as you can."

She nodded and whistled to Otto, who leapt into the back before she closed the doors. The poodle settled on the opposite stretcher bearer, and the children huddled around him, faces etched in fear and confusion.

I placed the nun gently on the bedroll and sat on the floor beside the stretcher. She curled on her side, groaning, and when I placed my hand on her back, the spasming muscles felt as hard as stone. "Ask her if she is in constant pain or if it is in fits and starts."

The abbess repeated my query in French, and the response was laced with tears. "She says the pain is sharp constantly, but there is also pressure that comes and goes rapidly."

I rested my hand on her stomach and felt it go hard, then relax, and then hard in a constant wave. "She is in labor, but the pains are too fast."

"In labor? But it is too early?"

We rocked backward as the engine leapt to life and into gear.

"Are you a doctor?"

"No," I said, rolling up my shirtsleeves. "A sheep farmer."

"*Que Dieu nous aide,*" she whispered.

"Tell her I am not going to hurt her. Just breathe and try not to push."

Time was measured in the slow breaths I encouraged the nun to take, but all too soon I could see the feet. The color of those tiny appendages made my heart sink.

"Give me her wimple." The fabric was pressed into my hand. "Push now, Angelique. You are almost finished, you are."

Within a few pushes, I was able to guide the infant free from the young woman. The afterbirth came out with the baby.

It was a boy, and I wrapped him in the nun's wimple, cleaning him with gentle strokes of the cloth. I did not slap his rump to make him cry. I knew it was no use.

He was small and thin, fully formed but undersized. Fragile and limp and blue. I swaddled him securely in his mother's wimple. His head was heavy in my palm, and the damp tuft of dark hair on his head was as soft as down. My eyes burned, and my vision wavered.

"Let me see the baby. Why is he not crying? Please, let me see him."

"It is a little girl, Aelwyd." I took the silent, still infant from my mother. "A beautiful little girl."

"I need to see her." My wife's voice broke, and the despair on her face said she knew before I even placed our child against her chest.

Her sobs tore my heart the rest of the way apart. "I failed you," she wept. "I failed."

I eased onto the bed beside her and brushed her hair back from her damp brow. "No, cariad aur. No. Never."

She grabbed my arm as her face blanched white. "Something is wrong." She gasped and clutched her stomach. "Esgod annwyl, it hurts."

My mother met my gaze over Aelwyd's bent knees. "You were right. There is another baby."

Aelwyd shook her head frantically, and her face was filled with fear and sorrow as she looked up at me. "Hold me, Rhys. Please. Something is wrong."

"Something is wrong."

I blinked and was once more in the back of the ambulance.

The nun's head lolled against Mother Clémence's legs, and she did not respond to shaking or pats on her cheek. Her face was devoid of color.

We were climbing, rounding curves with enough speed that I swayed.

"Charlotte?" I raised my voice to a shout to be heard.

"Not yet!"

It seemed an eternity before the ambulance ground to a halt, and by then, Sister Angelique's face was gray in tone. The bleeding had slowed, but I feared she had lost too much already.

I placed her still son on her chest and lifted her into my arms. Charlotte threw open the back door, and I leapt down. Her face flinched when she caught sight of the infant.

195

"Keep the children hidden." I did not wait for a response but ran into the hospital. "A doctor!" I shouted. "I need a doctor!"

We were surrounded immediately, hands lifting the unconscious woman from my arms and placing her on a gurney. The abbess was right at my heels, and she spoke rapidly, her voice breaking. One of the nurses handed the infant to a passing orderly with a hushed word, and then they were gone, hurrying down a long hall with Mother Clémence clinging to the nun's limp hand.

I let out a breath and rubbed my forehead before pinching the bridge of my nose. When I turned, the orderly was about to disappear down another hall, and I followed her. "Wait. Please." I caught her arm and held out my hands. "Please. I will take the babe."

She may not have understood my words, but she understood the gesture and tone, and she placed the small bundle in my arms.

"*Je suis désolée.*" She tucked the loose end of the wimple back into the swaddling.

My feet felt weighted as I exited the hospital. Charlotte had parked across the town square, and she lift a hand to catch my attention.

The morning light fell over the valley-ensconced town in gentle fingers of soft gold as the sun rose over the surrounding peaks. I crossed the cobbled square, a shadow slipping over me as I passed a battered but stalwart monument in the center. I felt that brush of cool darkness like a physical touch and shivered even as the sun fell once more across my back.

Charlotte sat in the driver's seat, and she remained silent as I approached. I sat heavily on the floor of the cab beside her perch, my back to her. The breath I took was ragged, and it rattled in my chest.

"I could not bear to let him be thrown out like rubbish." My voice sounded hollow to my own ears. I rubbed my face wearily with one hand and held the dead infant cradled to my chest with the other.

Charlotte rested a hand on my shoulder. "Then we will find a good place to bury him."

196

I buried the infant in the cemetery at the edge of Cluses. I chose a quiet far corner shaded by trees and used a shovel I took from the caretaker's shed. Charlotte had placed the infant in a round wooden cheese box taken from the farmhouse in La Balme-les-Grottes and laid him gently in the ground.

There were family plots nearby, and mountain peaks looked over the spot. Beyond the leaning iron fence near him, a few alpine flowers stubbornly refused to yet give up their bloom.

When I shoveled the last mound of dirt over him and built a small cairn to mark where he rested, I was satisfied. It was a peaceful place. I took a deep breath and patted the mound of dirt softly before I stood and walked away.

20 July 1942

Dear Nhad,
Thousands have been rounded up by the French
police and have disappeared.
They are simply gone. Men, women, and children.
I cannot sit idly by.
-Owain

Meghan Holloway

XVI

The kilometers between Cluses and Sixt-fer-à-Cheval led us deeper into the forests and higher into the mountainous terrain. Small villages became sparser and further apart after we crossed a river, and the way became wilder, rougher.

The air was crisp and carried with it the scent of pine and spruce. The river flowed white beside the track we followed, and clouds slunk low over the peaks to curtain the climbing sun.

The river cleaved Sixt-fer-à-Cheval in two, and we stayed on the northern banks as we passed through. The roofs were tall and steeply sloped, and smoke curled above the chimneys.

"There is already a chill in the air." Charlotte downshifted, glancing around the quiet village before turning her gaze to the veiled mountains above us. "It will only grow colder the higher we go."

"How is your sewing?"

"Decent. And yours?"

"Passable. We will have to spare a day or two in order to gather provisions." I eyed the narrow, rough track that continued along the river. "This road will likely end soon."

We followed it as it traced the undulating curve of the river deeper into the valley. We passed a small stone shrine by the roadside and then the outlying homes on the western side of the village. We slowed to a crawl behind a wagon. The horse plodded at a steady pace, but the driver soon steered the mare off to the side. He eyed us as we passed, suspicion etched into the lines of his face.

The road became narrower and more rutted. A rickety wooden bridge spanned the river, and it groaned under the wheels of the ambulance.

We rounded a sharp curve, and Charlotte gasped, slowing the vehicle to a halt. We both leaned forward to peer through the windscreen at the vista before us.

"It is stunning. I have never seen anything so magnificent."

The semicircular cliffs towered high above, forming an amphitheater above a rolling meadow. The clouds seemed to catch in the crags, and with the gleam of the sun hidden, the sheer limestone faces appeared blue, trimmed with verdant forest, seamed by the white waterfalls that cascaded from the enormous heights. I counted five spouts, but I imagined that in the spring there were numerous more from the snowmelt.

I removed Owain's scrawled note from my pocket and read his words once more. "This is the horseshoe."

The road ended at the far side of the meadow as the land rose into the foothills below the cliffs. At the edge of the trees sat a lodge of stone and timber. No smoke wafted over the chimney, and the windows were all tightly shuttered. Scatterings of outbuildings were closed up as well.

"Wait here with the children," I said when Charlotte pulled the ambulance around the back of the building. Firewood was stacked under a lean-to, but all seemed quiet and deserted.

The small lodge was boarded up for winter. No one responded to my knocks. The door was easy enough to force open, but all remained still and silent within. I felt for a switch along the wall but found none so I pried the shutters from a window and swung the panes open. The light was pale and weak but enough to lessen the darkness of the shadowed interior.

The lodge was sparsely furnished with benches, chairs, and a table all roughly hewn. The stone fireplace in the center of the room was cold and swept clean. The stove was in the same condition.

The loft was just as clean and barren. No mattresses cushioned the bed frames, but at the foot of all four beds stood storage trunks. When I investigated, I found each held bedrolls, blankets, and a number of sweaters and trousers. The scent of cedar permeated the room as I looked through each trunk and dislodged the layering of shavings.

I retreated outside and met Charlotte at the back of the ambulance. "We can stay here while we make preparations for the trek. We will just have to be vigilant."

She lifted her gaze to the soaring peaks. "Is it necessary, do you think? The journey will be risky, and they are so young. Perhaps we could find them homes…"

"Who can we trust? And how can we be certain the Allied advance will hold?"

She nodded. "I know."

"You do not have to cross the mountain with me. I know this is not what brought you across France."

She was silent for a long moment. "When I transported prisoners of war from the hospital back to the camps, some begged me the entire way not to return them. But I think the ones who did not beg were the ones who haunt me the most, the ones who just looked at me." She took a deep breath. "I want to help you get the children to safety." She gestured toward the towering mountains. "That just seems… impassable."

It did. Once the children were inside and the ambulance hidden within the trees and disabled, Charlotte set about measuring each child in turn to alter the cloaks the abbess had bundled into a pack. I searched the shelves and found what I was looking for on the highest shelf: a topographical map.

I dragged the table under an open window for light and then unrolled the map and spread it across the surface. Otto nudged against my legs as he retreated under the table and settled in a sprawl with a heavy sigh.

I studied the map closely and found Sixt-fer-à-Cheval in the Haute-Savoie department at the end of the Giffre Valley. The horseshoe formation was close to skirting the border of Switzerland.

I felt a presence at my side and glanced down to find Hugo

peering up at me. I tousled his hair and was rewarded with a beaming smile. He stood on his toes to look at the map alongside me for several moments before he lost interest. He dropped to his hands and knees and joined Otto under the table.

"The white horse. What is the French term?"

"*Le cheval blanc.*"

I leaned over the map and scanned the surrounding mountains. I found the mountain my son alluded to in his note straddling the border southeast of the horseshoe. An alpine lake was nestled to the northeast. As the crow flew, the mountain appeared to only be five kilometers or so away, but I knew in this terrain, distance was deceptive. It was marked at almost three thousand meters in elevation; where we sheltered now sat at only just over nine hundred fifty meters.

I rubbed the back of my neck and ran my fingertips over the surface of the map.

I turned to Charlotte. "Will you and the children be well here for a time?"

"I would think so." She straightened from pinning a hem on a cloak that swallowed one of the younger girls. When she stood, she placed her hands on her hips and arched her back with a grimace. "If you are finished with the table, I will use it as a pedestal. That will be easier on my back and knees."

"It is yours." I rolled the map and placed it back on the shelf.

"Did you not have any luck?"

"I did. I found the mountain, and a lake is marked nearby within Switzerland. But I can find a way better on foot than studying paper."

She smiled. "Of course." Hugo scrambled from beneath the table and hurried to my side with Otto close at his heels. "If you take him with you, he may be a good judge of whether the way is feasible for the children."

I held my hand out to him, and he grasped my fingers in a

warm, two-handed grip. "We will be back…" I took in the boy's short legs. "Before nightfall. Board the door behind me."

Hugo set our pace. He was one of the three youngest, and I could see immediately that the girl a year or two younger than he would have to be carried. He was dogged, though, traipsing along at my side, releasing his grip on my hand to squat and inspect the stones in the dry creek bed we crossed. Otto nudged against him, snuffling the ground, investigating what intrigued the boy. The poodle's movements upset the child's balance, knocking him over, and Hugo fell on his side laughing. Seeing a game at hand, Otto rooted under him and licked his face.

I smiled at their antics before I turned and followed the creek bed with my gaze. On the slopes above us, it branched into four fingers and stretched toward the base of the sheer cliffs. I studied the creek bed's ascent and then turned to boy and dog. Chuckling, I rubbed Otto's ears before lifting Hugo and setting him on his feet. I adjusted my stride to accommodate his and headed south.

The rolling hills we roamed were densely forested, fragrant and cool with shadow. The next creek bed we came upon was wider, and a shallow stream of mountain runoff flowed through the center.

Otto sniffed the water and then lapped his fill. I crouched and dipped a hand in the water, feeling the icy current curl around my fingers. I made a shallow bowl of my hand, allowed water to pool in my palm, and then bent my head and drank. The water was bracing, and when Hugo moved to follow suit, he gasped.

"*Il fait fraud!*" He jerked his hand back and wiped it dry on his trousers.

I rested a hand on his head before I straightened. "*Mae 'n oer.*"

He repeated the words, his pronunciation perfect on the first attempt. He beamed when I smiled at him.

We followed the creek bed south. Water would be an asset as we climbed in elevation, and if the waters had carved their path over the rock long enough, I hoped they had worn the way enough for us to climb.

That was not the case when we traced a confluence up to the base of a cliff. It was too steep to ascend.

I backtracked, boy and dog at my heels, and followed the creek deeper and higher into the hills. The canyon it led us through was cool and shadowed, and though the rocky walls were steep, they were not sheer.

We found the source of the creek when we reached the deepest point of the canyon. The water tumbled in a small cascade from an overhang above. The overhang guarded a narrow gorge that climbed sharply into the mountain's heights. In the spring, a deluge would sweep through the precipitous gouge in the rock. But for now, as autumn settled over the land and winter swiftly approached, it was dry.

I turned from studying the chasm to find Hugo with his hand outstretched to catch the falling water in his palm. His face had taken on a ruddy tone, but though our pace was slow, he had trekked thus far with no mishaps. The way would be challenging, if he could manage it at all.

"Hugo, Otto. Come along, lads."

They both followed me eagerly into the gorge. Otto darted ahead, nimble and agile on four paws.

The gorge was so narrow I could brace both palms on either side, and I warily eyed the walls above us. The danger of a rock slide here was great. Even the rocks underfoot were precariously situated.

"Easy now," I said softly to both the poodle ahead of me and the boy behind me.

I placed one foot carefully in front of the other, judging the sureness of the next rock before I let it take my full weight. It was akin to climbing an unsteady, declivitous staircase. The steps of rock were uneven, some tall enough that I had to lift Hugo over the hurdle.

He was soon breathing heavily, and twin flags of color darkened his cheeks. My own breath was coming faster, and the air felt rationed the higher we climbed. I paused often to allow Hugo a chance to rest. The way grew steeper and more arduous.

Hugo climbed using his legs and arms, and when a rock shifted under him, he fell to his hands and knees. He grunted, the sound high and panicked, as he began to slide backward.

I lunged and caught him before he fell far. He clung to me as I climbed to a more stable spot.

Otto joined us, sniffing at Hugo's damp cheeks when I placed him on a boulder and inspected the scrapes on his palms and knees. He would be fine, but I could tell he was growing tired and the fall had frightened him.

We were not quite halfway up the gorge, and I needed to see if we could cross the mountain taking this route. I did not care to lead nine young children so far only to find the way impassable and be forced to turn back.

I rubbed the back of my neck and looked at the pair perched on the boulder. Hugo dragged the back of his hand over his damp eyes. "I want the pair of you to stay here." I held up my hand to indicate what I was requesting and pointed at the rock upon which they sat. "Stay. I will be back."

When I turned to continue the climb, Hugo scrambled after me. "*Non, non!*" He fisted a hand in the leg of my trousers. "*Ne me quitte pas.*"

"Easy now, *cariad bach*. Easy." I could see there was no use coaxing him, though, so I lifted him onto the rock above me and turned so he could climb onto my back. I patted my shoulder, and he slung his arms around my neck and wrapped his legs around my torso. I adjusted his arms so that he was not gripping over the gouge the bullet had left in my shoulder. "Hold tightly now."

I was cautious as I climbed, aware of the weight on my back and how it affected my balance. Otto's progress became slower and more careful as well. The last half kilometer was a near-vertical climb up a ladder of boulders.

The gorge opened up into an alpine bowl. If the range we

sought to traverse were a four-step staircase, we had reached the pinnacle of the first step.

I braced my hands on my hips and paused to catch my breath. I turned back to survey the valley we had climbed from and stood in awe at the vista below me. The valley was deep and verdant. Mist curled down the ridges and clung to the treetops like the white, eddying crest of a green wave. It was a rugged, breathtaking sprawl that loosened something tight within me as I took it in.

The weight on my back reminded me of my responsibility, though, and I turned from the view to study the bowl into which we had emerged.

We could not make it up to the next ridge by direct approach. This was avalanche territory, and though the snow that skirted the bowl was gray and frozen into ice, the loose scree would be as deadly in a slide as a fall of snow.

The only way to traverse this dangerous section to reach the tundra was to follow a ridge that led north before curving back to the east. From the tundra, we would have to cross a glacier field, but the White Horse was visible above us.

Before we began our descent, I surveyed the view once more and noted the valley branched to the north from where Charlotte and the rest of the children sheltered. I would explore the adjacent valley tomorrow and see if there were an easier path, but this one would see us over the mountain and to safety if not.

The descent was more challenging than the climb. By the time we made it to the base of the gorge, my knees and shoulder ached and my back was damp with sweat.

I set Hugo on his feet, and the three of us drank greedily from the cascade. The water was cold enough to make my teeth ache, but it was a relief after the climb. I dipped my head under the stream, and an icy sluice flowed over the back of my neck and under my shirt. Hugo mimicked my actions and yelped at the cold.

"*Mae'n oer*," he said.

I chuckled. "*Ydy.*"

The afternoon was sliding into evening when we reached the lodge. Hugo and Otto returned to their sprawl under the table, and both were asleep almost immediately.

"We can make it over the mountain."

Charlotte's shoulders slumped in relief. "You're certain? Even the littlest ones?"

"We will have to go slowly, and we will not be able to make it in a day. But I found a way that is passable. Challenging but not impossible."

She stared at the children, her brow furrowed. "We have plenty of food from the farmhouse."

"What of the clothing? It will be cold on the mountain at night."

"Between the sweaters in the chests and the cloaks from the abbey, I think we will be well outfitted."

While the valley was still well-lit, I searched the outbuildings. I found three coils of rope hanging in the shed, two ice pick axes, and a pair of crampons. On a shelf, I saw a hammer and a box of pitons. I did not think we would need to climb, but I collected them just in case. An ax was stored across the beams of the lean-to.

Back in the lodge, I climbed into the loft and retrieved the four rucksacks hanging from hooks on the wall. They appeared to be Swiss-made, durable combinations of tough leather and thick canvas. I carried them from the loft and placed the largest on the floor.

"Simone." I gestured for the young girl around three years of age to come closer, but she ducked her head and hid behind her older brother.

Charlotte set her sewing aside. "Will we need to carry her?"

"Aye. She will not be able to make the climb up the gorge. She will be more secure riding in this, and I will not be concerned about her losing her grip."

She led the child closer, speaking softly in French, and helped

with his head on Otto's side.

Charlotte caught my eye and smiled as she readjusted the blankets. I waited until she was settled as well before I extinguished the lantern.

I lay back with my hands folded over my chest, and a deep, dreamless sleep crept over me.

———————

My breath created white wisps of fog as I trekked through the north spur of the valley. Water had scoured either wall of the canyon, and the creek beds that had their confluence on the valley floor were like tangled threads, overlapping and snarled together.

The way was easier through the depths of this valley, though it narrowed the further I ventured. The western walls would be far easier to climb, but the route would take us days to circle to the north and east, if it were even passable at the higher elevations. The eastern walls were steep and rugged. When I tried to climb, the ground crumbled and rolled beneath my feet, sending me sliding back down to the valley floor.

I stepped back and peered upward. Even if we managed to climb out of the valley to the ridge above, the peaks looming over this northern gorge were nearly sheer and covered in snow that would either give way in an avalanche underfoot or be a precarious frozen ice slick.

The sound of voices was as galvanizing as if it were the sound of a gunshot. There was little tree growth on this side of the valley, only low-lying shrub for coverage. The sound came from deeper in the valley, around the next bend, but drew closer.

I dropped to my stomach and crawled beneath the sparse shrub, knowing that anyone looking closely would discern my hiding spot. I lay unmoving, breathing shallowly, face pressed into the cold dirt.

The voices drew near after a few moments and three pairs of boots soon entered my field of vision. I did not dare to lift my head to see more, but their voices confirmed my suspicion: they were German.

I did not dare to even breathe as the Germans walked along the edge of the woods. The limp, lifeless weight of a dead soldier over me was both crushing and scant protection. I struggled to remain motionless. The flies that nipped at the corners of my mouth and eyes made me want to shove the body aside and claw at my face.

I had buried Arthur under a pile of bodies nearby. His lips had trembled, his eyes wide with terror as I hid his limp body with the dead. "Do...not...leave me, Rhys."

"I will not," I whispered to him as I dragged a fallen man over him. "I promise."

The Germans were silent as they picked over the dead save for one who laughed raucously.

The toe of a boot connected with my ribs in a rough kick, and the breath I had been holding left me in a wheeze. I froze, heart lurching in my chest when I felt the soldier pause beside the pile of bodies under which I lay. After a long moment of stillness, there was a sudden slicing sound of metal on cloth and flesh. The body jostled above me, and I bit the coarse fabric of his uniform. It was the only thing that kept me from screaming when the bayonet pierced my arm.

Shouting erupted nearby, and I was certain Arthur or I had been discovered. But someone else had been found alive, and he cried out before gunshots pierced the air.

I was breathing hard, shaking, hot and chilled at once, straining to hear the soldiers as they moved on across the field of the slain.

The voices around me went silent, and I jolted into the present, afraid that I had made a noise while lost to memories and alerted the three Germans to my presence. I tensed, sliding my hand inside my shirt to rest against the butt of the Luger. There was a shuffle of noise, and then a sigh and the spatter of urine streaming into the dirt.

I kept my hand on the pistol as the German finished and readjusted his uniform. When he rejoined the other two, the three began

213

their conversation once more and ventured back in the direction from which they had come.

I cautiously lifted my head but did not move from my hiding place. I searched the opposite ridge for any sign of movement indicating a lookout. Long minutes passed, and I saw nothing. If there were a lookout perched up the canyon wall, I would likely already be dead.

I slid from my hiding place and drew the Luger as I crept after the three Germans. I stayed well behind them, never venturing into sight and keeping close to the canyon wall. The morning sun was far from reaching its zenith, and the shadows along the eastern wall were deep.

As I approached one sharp bend in the valley, I could hear the murmur of voices and movement. I backtracked, not wanting to get too close, and knelt in the shadows to watch. No one rounded the bend, and the sounds drew no closer.

Here, the shrub was taller, denser, skirting the canyon's sloping walls in a green thicket. I ventured into the growth, climbing higher, careful not to create any rockslides. When I reached a ridge, I dropped into a crouch and crawled to the precipice.

The valley came to an abrupt end in a level bowl deep in the heart of the mountains. A small cascade tumbled down the cliff and curved along the edge of the meadow. It was quiet, isolated, far from where anyone would wander in their day to day goings.

It was the perfect hideout for the twenty to thirty German soldiers camped there.

22 September 1942

Dear Nhad,
I killed a man today.
-Owain

XVII

Henri

When I arrived at the military health school, I found the
façade lying in rubble. I climbed over the bomb-stricken debris into the
remnants of the school, descended a crumbling staircase, and found the
entrance to the hidden tunnels in the basement.

I was accosted immediately, shoved against the wall of the
tunnel. I held up my hands and assented to the brusque search.

"I am here to see the *Hauptsturmführer*." It was a relief to
speak in German, and the pair searching me paused. "I am part of the
Sonderstab Bildende Kunst."

They led me through the labyrinth of passages to a series of
hidden rooms. One knocked on a door and snapped a smart salute when
it opened.

My path had crossed with the man before me in '43. He was
everything that had gone wrong with the National Socialist Party. I had
disliked him instantly, and I was certain the feeling was mutual.

"Heinrich Jäger," he said, sweeping his hand out in a grand
gesture to admit me into the room. "A pleasant surprise. Join us."
His broad smile made me suspicious, and the reason why was apparent
as soon as I entered. The metallic smell of blood and the sharp ammonic
of urine filled the room. My stomach turned in disgust, and when I met
Klaus's gaze, his lips quirked knowingly.

His smirk made me want to wipe it from his face with a swift
blow from the back of my hand. He was little more than a boy, full of

217

undeserved self-import, puffed up with the power allotted him. He relished the pain he could inflict on others, and the evidence was clear from the tenting of his trousers. Watching the *Gueule Tordue* beat the girl with a spiked ball hanging from a cosh excited him. Francis André's broken face, though, remained impassive as he delivered blow after blow.

I looked away, disgusted, and hid a flinch when I heard the girl's spine crack. She was too weak and beaten to even scream, but her agonized groan went abruptly silent when she fainted.

Klaus laughed like a delighted child. "That will be all, Francis." The *Gueule Tordue*'s mouth appeared even more twisted than usual as he left the room.

I forced a smile when Klaus turned to me and inclined my head. "Well done, *Hauptsturmführer*."

"Indeed. Would you care for a drink?"

"*Nein.*"

He paused to stroke his hand over the girl's bloody, wrecked flesh before he crossed to his desk and poured a glass of amber liquid. He left a smear of blood on the decanter. "I miss our beer. But you are more of a wine drinker yourself, are you not?"

"My vineyards are the best in the country."

"Perhaps after this mess is finished I shall come visit you and partake of your wine."

"I would be honored." I smiled, even as I imagined killing him deep in the rows of my vines. It would have to be bloodless. I did not care to imagine being able to taste him in the year's harvest.

"Now, what is it that has brought you here?"

"I am looking for a man I believe you have captured."

"And what makes you believe I have him?"

I would have to tread carefully. I could tell from the tone of his voice he was looking for an opportunity to play one of his malicious games. "The ingenuity in the way the situation was handled in La Balme-les-Grottes could only be at your orders."

His chest expanded. "You are speaking of the Englishman."

"Welshman."

He shrugged. "I have both he and his wife."

I kept my surprise carefully veiled. I had not realized he was married. "I have a debt to settle with the pair."

"So this is personal, a favor to you?"

I could not back up the request with orders, so I adopted an acquiescent mien. "*Ja.*"

He stroked his chin. "This will inconvenience me. I have information I need from him." He was too distracted by the thrill of torture to care about prying answers from some poor soul. The girl tied to the overturned chair moaned. "I have heard your art collection rivals even Göring's."

It did, it had, but he would be the last person to whom I would admit it. And how much was left now, I did not know. I shrugged. "Göring's collection is admirable. I doubt anything could compare to it."

"I want one of the Degas paintings you took from Paris. One of the nudes." He leaned over and traced the bare curve of the wounded girl's buttocks. She flinched away from him. "No, two. Since I am handing two over to you."

"Very well. But they are at my home. I cannot get the paintings for you immediately." I would sooner burn them than see Degas's work in his hands.

He met my gaze. "Perhaps next time I am in Germany I will visit your wife and retrieve them then. I have heard she has had some visitors while you have been away. One more cannot hurt, *ja?*"

My smile felt thin on my face, and I forced my jaw to relax. "She is a fine hostess." I would strangle him, I decided. I would wrap my hands tight around his throat, watch his face turn purple and blood fill his eyes, and feel his life seep away beneath my palms.

"It is settled, then. Wait here while I retrieve them. And please—" he offered the cosh to me "—be my guest."

I accepted it and imagined cracking his head open with the

spiked ball. *"Bitte, Hauptsturmführer."*

When he left, I tossed the cosh aside and approached the girl. She whimpered as I drew near. "Shh, *mademoiselle.*"

"S'il vous plaît, ne me blessez pas." Her voice cracked.

"I will not." My voice was low and soothing, and I stroked her hair and spoke to her in tones as gentle as I would a dog. She wept, head hanging in the awkward, upside down position Klaus and his fools had tied her. Her hair brushed the ground, the tresses dragging in her own pooling blood. Her spine was shattered. The white slivers of bone were visible beneath the broken skin. I would not even allow a dog who bit me to suffer so much. "Shh, now. He will not hurt you any longer."

She let out a shuddering breath, her sobs quavering in her chest. *"Merci, monsieur."*

"You are welcome, my dear," I said, and then I broke her neck.

The gunshots startled me, and I stood, cursing my foolishness. I threw open the door, shouldered past the guards, and raced down the tunnel toward the sound of shouting. Of course he would kill the pair before handing them over to me.

16 November 1942

Dear Nhad,
I found a way to fight that I believe in.
I do not do it to make you proud, but I hope you are.
-Owain

xviii

"Get the children ready. We need to leave." I strove to keep my voice even lest I frighten the children, but I was winded from running.

Charlotte's eyes widened when she turned to me. "What has happened?"

I glanced around the young faces sitting about her. The tone of my voice had the tension and fear creeping back into their visages. "Come outside a moment."

She set her sewing aside and followed me. "What's wrong, Rhys?" She brushed at the dirt clinging to my shirt. "Are you hurt?"

"There are Germans only a few kilometers from here."

Her head snapped up, and she searched my face. "In the northern valley?"

"Aye. As many as thirty perhaps, camped at the far end of the gorge."

"Did they see you?"

"No. None whom I saw. But there may be more posted as lookouts at higher vantage points."

"So they may know we are here."

"Aye. I wager they are in retreat, simply trying to hide and escape the advance. But we are greatly outnumbered. And with the children—"

"We cannot risk it." She gazed toward the north valley, her brow furrowed. "I will ready the children while you pack the rucksacks."

The children were uneasy, huddling close together around Otto as Charlotte helped them don their cloaks and tie scarves about their necks. They would grow warm as they climbed, but the morning air held a crisp chill that the sun had not yet burned away. Charlotte traded her

Oxfords for woolen socks and the pair of boots she had brought with her from Paris.

We had six bedrolls and eight blankets, the supplies I had taken from the shed, the weapons and ammunition taken from the soldiers at the abbey, the first aid kit from the ambulance, and food to last a week. I used the smallest rucksack for the blankets and first aid kit, keeping it light enough for the oldest child to carry. The food, supplies, weapons, and bedrolls I dispersed evenly through the other two packs.

Charlotte bundled Simone in a blanket and helped her into the rucksack. When I had the child secured against my back, Charlotte hoisted one of the packs up, and I slipped into the shoulder straps, adjusting it over the rucksack holding Simone.

"Is she well?" I cinched the outer pack around my hips to keep it secure. It sat lower on my back, but the combined weight was not enough to upset my balance. I had carried sheep heavier than my current load.

When Charlotte spoke to the child, I heard a muffled "*Oui,*" at my back.

We used a blanket to secure Anne-Marie to Charlotte in a sling about her torso. I tied the ends around her waist under the babe's bottom and at Charlotte's back between her shoulder blades. Only the top of the six-month-old's downy head resting against Charlotte's chest was visible.

I lifted the last rucksack and held it while Charlotte adjusted the straps over her shoulders and tightened them. She shifted, shrugging her shoulders to settle the weight.

"You will be able to carry both? I can—"

She touched my arm. "I will be fine."

I searched her face. In the low light, her eyes were dark and gray, and she met my gaze evenly. "Let's be away, then."

We boarded the windows and door once more. The ambulance was concealed within the trees, hidden at first glance, disabled if found. Both of us had added an additional holster about our hips to carry an extra pistol and ammunition.

I pointed toward the far end of the horseshoe rock formation. "Lead the way south, toward that ridge. I will follow shortly."

Charlotte nodded and whistled for Otto. He trotted ahead of her while the children fell into step behind her. Hugo paused and started toward me, but Charlotte caught his hand and spoke softly to him as she led him away.

I watched until they disappeared into the shelter of the forest. Then I found a hiding place in the trees behind the lodge and crouched to wait and watch.

———

I caught up with Charlotte and the children deep in the canyon.

"Is anyone following us?"

"No, but we'll not light any fires, just to be safe."

I traded places with Charlotte, and she took up the tail as I led the way deeper and higher into the hills.

Leading a group of children was much like herding sheep: once they were in motion, they tended to cluster together and follow one after the other. The key was to keep them in motion and keep them going the right direction. With a well-trained dog, it was merely an issue of communication and patience. Otto did not have the training my Bess and Bracken did, but he performed admirably.

We reached the overhang at midday and took a break for the children to rest before the climb. Simone had ridden in the pack soundlessly and motionlessly, and when Charlotte helped me ease the rucksack from my shoulders, we discovered her sleeping inside.

I filled the four canteens we had while Charlotte doled out food for the children. She took only a peach for herself and ducked under the overhang to peer up the steep gorge that ascended into the mountains like a staircase.

"How far of a climb is it?"

"A few kilometers. The way is precarious, but if we are slow and cautious, we can manage it."

She smiled up at me suddenly, that smile that was so like the sudden light of dawn piercing the gray morning mist. "I believe you could manage anything, Rhys."

I chuckled. "It helps to have someone capable alongside me."

Her smile softened, even as color came to her cheeks. "I am thankful our paths crossed in Paris."

"Only days ago, it was."

"It seems like a lifetime."

"Aye."

After eating, the children shed their cloaks, and we bundled them into a tight roll and tied the ends crossways over their thin chests. Simone climbed back into her rucksack, and once all the packs were donned and secured, we set off.

The climb was challenging for the children, and we paused often to rest. Scraped palms and bruised shins occurred regularly. But none complained, and though our progress was slow, we gradually gained higher and higher elevation.

Otto proved to offer better encouragement than Charlotte or I could provide. Whenever one child began to lag or chins trembled over torn knees, he was right there to comfort with licks and nudges. The poodle seemed more suited to being a nanny than a war dog, and he and the children both basked in the attention they gave one another.

The gorge flattened onto a deep ledge like a landing on a staircase before the climb became nearly vertical. The brief plateau was about four meters deep and two meters wide. The rock was stable here, smooth and level.

I eyed the climb ahead of us and then looked to the sky. The light was dying as the sun sank toward the western horizon, and I recalled the barren landscape that awaited us at the top of the gorge.

We would not make it over the peak before nightfall. The temperature was dropping, and the wind was picking up. If we made the rest of the climb today, we would be sleeping exposed to the elements on the side of the mountain.

I leaned down and lifted the children one after the other onto the ledge and then offered my hand to Charlotte. We clasped wrists, and I noted my fingers met and overlapped around her slim joint.

"We'll set up camp here for the night."

Her eyes widened. She gripped my sleeve as she glanced over the edge down at the steep rockfall we had climbed. "I hope no one tends to wander in their sleep."

"We will alternate keeping watch. For anyone following us and to make certain no one gets too close to the edge."

She nodded. Her face was as pink as the children's, and my back was damp under the rucksacks. Charlotte shrugged out of her pack and handed the baby to the oldest girl before helping me unload the weight of the two rucksacks I carried. Simone smiled at me readily when I lifted her free of the pack.

Once we stopped moving, the cold set in quickly, and we unrolled coats and helped the children don them before they caught a chill. I spread the bedrolls along the ledge, keeping well away from the precipice, while Charlotte portioned out food. The children ate hungrily, and both Otto and the children wanted additional portions.

I rationed the water, hoping that we would have enough to withhold from necessitating a fire to boil snow or lake water. Everyone received a cupful, and Otto drank from my palm before hurrying back to ensure each child had left no crumb uneaten.

The light dimmed quickly here at this elevation tucked deep into the undulations of the mountain range. We were protected from the wind, but the shadows held a crispness that felt like a chill touch.

The children's eyes were heavy, and Charlotte suppressed a yawn with her fingers against her lips.

"I will take the first watch." I knew she was tired when she did not argue.

The ledge was deep and wide enough for everyone to sleep laid out closely side by side from the innermost recesses to where

Charlotte lay as the outer barrier. Otto took up his place lying across the children's feet, and Charlotte spread the blankets over him as well. Hugo once more repositioned himself to use the poodle as a pillow. This time he kept his head buried under the shelter of the blankets.

"You'll wake me so you can get some sleep as well?" Charlotte curled on her side facing where I sat leaning against the side of the gorge and folded her hands under her cheek.

"Aye. Rest now. I will wake you."

She closed her eyes, and a sigh slipped from her. "And you will not let me roll over the edge."

I smiled. She was almost two meters from the precipice. "Of course not."

Her lips quirked, and I watched as her body slowly settled into the weighted bonelessness of sleep and her face went slack.

Darkness gathered and deepened, and the temperature dropped further. I drew on my own coat, the thick sheepskin I wore in the winter when snow dusted my hills and the wind cut straight to the bone. I pulled the lapel across my face and could imagine there was still a clinging scent of home caught in the shearling.

I tucked my hands into the warm hollows under my arms and tilted my head back against the rock to watch the stars prick through the black blanket of the night sky. As the hours progressed, the display grew to be as impressive as the one I could see from the hills at home. I sought the brightness of Capella, and then found the rest of Auriga.

"Show me the shepherd in the sky again, Dadi."

I crouched beside Owain, resting one hand on his shoulder while I used the other to point out the constellation. "Just there. Do you see?" I traced the outline of the main stars with my finger.

"I want him to hold sheep instead of goats."

I chuckled. "Then we shall say he is holding lambs in his arms instead of kids."

He was silent for a moment. "When Mam has the babies, will you be able to hold all of us, Dadi?"

228

I lifted him into my arms. "Aye, machgen i. There will be room in my arms to hold all of you, always."

I smiled at the memory and glanced at my charges. The children and Charlotte slept deeply. When a tendril of wind drifted into our rock corridor, I drew the heavy wool blankets up over their heads. Not even Otto stirred.

I knew Charlotte would not appreciate me allowing her to sleep through the night, so I woke her a few hours before dawn. When I rested my hand on her shoulder, she burrowed deeper beneath the blankets before rolling to her back with a sigh and stretching.

"Your watch." I kept my voice at a whisper so as not to disturb the children.

She scrubbed both hands over her face and pulled her scarf from the pocket of her coat as she sat upright. "Is all well?"

"Aye. It is a beautiful, quiet night, it is."

I traded places with her, settling into the residual pool of heat her body had left behind. She took much the same position I had. Once she wrapped her scarf about her neck, she tucked her hands under her arms and tilted her head back to the night sky.

I did not expect to sleep, but I did. I woke at first light, when the sky was the color of a bruise and the world was cast in shades of gray.

The children were difficult to rouse, and the baby began to cry. The sound was cacophonous in the morning quiet, and Charlotte rushed to soothe her. Her wails grew louder as Charlotte changed her napkin. I kept an eye on the gorge's depths.

Her shrieks devolved to whimpers once she was dry, and Charlotte lifted Anne-Marie into her arms and patted her back. When she looked to me, her face was tense. "Anyone?"

"Not that I saw. But that does not mean she was not heard."

Charlotte fed the children and Otto while I packed the bedrolls and blankets. Once the youngest two children were secured in sling and rucksack, we began the grueling climb.

229

"Go on, *bach*," I said to Otto. "I will follow you."

He picked his way up the steep ascent, and I followed cautiously after him. The dawn was spreading over the sky like a blush, but the shadows here were cool and deep. The light was low, but not so low I needed to make use of the torch.

"Tell the children to step exactly as I do."

The half kilometer climb was rigorous. The oldest three children managed it with my assistance. The wind buffeted us when we reached the alpine bowl, and I directed them well away from the edge.

I shrugged out of the rucksacks I carried and placed them on the ground. Simone had fallen asleep in the pack on my back. She stirred when I checked on her and peaked her head out of the sack, but she ducked back into her warm cocoon when the wind slapped her dark hair across her face.

"Stay here. I am going back for the others." I held up my hand. "Stay."

The oldest girl nodded and wrapped on arm around Otto's neck. The children sat on the leeward side of the rucksacks, but they provided little barrier.

I left them and climbed down to Charlotte and the other children. They were struggling with the climb, and Charlotte had to lift each one to the next crag.

"Is it much further?"

I reached down and lifted the child she was assisting. "I will carry them the rest of the way."

I repeated the ascent with the four younger children, carrying one on my back to the temporary summit, leaving her with Otto and the other children, and then climbing down for the next.

Hugo was the last, and he smiled and held out his arms to me. I chuckled. "We have done this already, have we not, *cariad*?"

Charlotte climbed close at my heels. I glanced back when I heard rocks tumble and saw that she had one arm braced tight across the baby strapped to her chest.

I paused. "Are you hurt?"

"No, merely lost my footing for a moment."

We reached the top of the gorge without further mishap and rested only for a moment before we continued our trek. We followed the ridge that led north before curving back to the east.

The wind was a torment, howling over the mountains and tearing at hair and clothing. I walked with my head down, the wind whipping tears from my eyes.

The sun soon climbed over the peaks, and when we reached the top of the ridge, the landscape changed dramatically. Gone was the green. The terrain was jagged with rock, and the plant life that clung to the ground was coarse, brown and gray in color. Patches of snow formed dirty white pools of slush. We had crossed into the tundra.

There was a haunting beauty to the tundra. The growth that clung to the crevices was as hardy as it was fragile. Life advanced tenaciously even in the starkness.

I stopped and glanced behind me. The children huddled together, their heads down against the wind, red hands buried in Otto's curls. Charlotte's hair was whipped from its moorings, and the strands blew like ribbons around her head.

I pointed to the peak looming above us. "The White Horse." I had to raise my voice to a shout to be heard.

We crossed over the tundra in a tight line hunched forward against the driving push of the wind. It was relentless at this height, and I could only hope that once we crossed the mountain, the far side would provide some shelter from its harsh assault.

We reached the glacier field below the peak of the White Horse at midday, and the sun gleamed off the slush of snow that blanketed the ice mass. I shaded my eyes against the glare of daylight and studied the mountainside.

"This way." I led my small band up a rocky ridge adjacent to the glacier. We were south of the mountain's summit now, but if we cut diagonally across the glacier, we could cross over the mountain north of its craggy peak and closer to the lake on the map.

We climbed the length of the ridge until we could go no further without crossing plains of packed snow and ice. I crouched to remove the rucksacks on my back, and Simone crawled from the confines of the pack with a blanket clutched about her. Charlotte knelt beside me.

"Can we cross this?" The wind had leached the color from her face and raked across her cheeks, the tip of her nose, and her lips, leaving them chapped red.

"Not without some preparations. We—" Otto's bark caught my attention and drew my gaze to where Hugo stepped tentatively onto the snow. "*No!*"

It was too late. The thin layer of slick snow gave way under the boy's feet. He fell to his belly, cracking his chin against the ice, and slid.

I yanked the ice pick from where it was tied to the side of my rucksack and shoved Charlotte aside to lunge after him.

Blood smeared across the glacier after him in a red wake, and I could not run quickly enough down the ridge to catch up with his increasing speed. He slid further away from my reach into the steeper drop beneath the mountain peak. He was silent as he plummeted down the mountainside, but the terror on his face was as loud as a scream.

I dove onto the glacier after him. Given my heavier weight, I slid faster and caught up with him in seconds. I snagged his outstretched hand and swung the pick ax as hard as I could.

The edge drove into the glacier and caught, yanking us to a halt so swiftly I was flipped onto my back, and I almost lost my grip on the handle. I gritted my teeth against the wrench in my shoulder.

I adjusted my grip and pulled Hugo to my chest. He clung to me, shaking violently, his back heaving under my arm. "All's well now, *cariad*. All's well." My voice was breathless. "I have you, I do."

Otto had raced down the ridge after us and stood barking off the side of the glacier. We were about twenty-five meters from the edge. Still anchored by my grip on the ice pick, I kicked my heels into the snow and ice until I created a deep enough ridge to brace my weight as I sat up.

Charlotte caught up with Otto and skidded to a halt. "Jesus, Rhys!"

"Stay there!" I yelled to her. Otto stepped out onto the glacier but his paws skidded and he leapt back to safety. "Keep Otto from coming out after us."

She knelt beside the poodle and buried her fingers in his curls.

"Hold onto me now, Hugo. Just hold on." The boy wrapped his arms about my neck and his legs about my hips, pressing his damp face into my throat.

Braced against the small shelf I had scraped into the glacier, I levered the pick free from the ice and then leaned over and jammed it into place a meter to the side. Once it was lodged in place, I stretched out a leg and kicked a foothold ledge into the ice with my boot heel. I scooted us across the ice with my grip on the pick and then braced myself against the new ledge I had created to pry the pick from the glacier and hammer it into place further along. I repeated the process across the expanse of the glacier until we reached the rocky ridge.

Charlotte and Otto both caught hold of me, the poodle locking his teeth into my sleeve, Charlotte gripping fistfuls of my coat at my collar. The pair pulled us over the edge to safety.

I rolled onto my side, breathing heavily.

"Are you hurt? There's blood."

I shook my head and sat up. Otto snuffled at my neck and ears and nudged at Hugo, his whimpers sounding as frantic as the ones escaping the boy. I had to pry Hugo from my chest. Tears slipped down his face, and blood streamed from his split chin.

"You are fine now, *cariad bach*." I ran my hands over his head and limbs, relieved to find no other damage. "You're fine, you are."

Charlotte tugged her scarf from around her neck and wound it

233

over Hugo's head and under his jaw. She spoke softly to him in French as she bandaged the gushing wound, her voice soothing but shaken by a tremor. She grabbed the pick and splintered off a chunk of ice from the glacier, tucking it into the folds of the scarf.

"That should slow the bleeding." She caught the movement as I rolled my right shoulder and grimaced. "Are you certain you are not hurt?"

"Just sore. The other children?"

"Are fine."

I looked up the mountain. We had fallen at least one hundred meters.

"How are we going to make it across this?"

I studied the grooves I had dug into the glacier. "I have an idea."

We ascended the ridge once more. I retrieved the crampons and strapped them over my boots and then tucked the ice pick into my belt and grabbed the ax. It would cut better than the pick.

Charlotte approached and tied the end of one of the ropes around me. "I do not care to repeat that."

"If I slip and you cannot hold my weight, let go."

She did not respond, but her jaw tightened, as did her grip on the rope.

The metal claws of the crampons bit into the snow and ice and held as I stepped onto the glacier. The rope pulled taut about me, and when I glanced back, Charlotte had the length wrapped around her waist, her boots braced wide apart.

"Ease your hold. All's well."

She fed the line as I made my way slowly across the expanse. And with each step, I used the ax and cut a level foothold into the ice. It was a slow process. The glacier was at least two hundred meters across, and the footholds had to be close together for the children to safely make use of them.

The sun had climbed further to the west by the time I made it to the ridge north of the jagged peak of the White Horse. My back ached from my hunched trek across the glacier, and the wind stung my ears and knuckles.

I straightened, stretching my back and rubbing my hands together. It was as if I stood atop the world, and for a moment, as I breathed deeply of the air so pure it made my lungs ache, it seemed as if I existed alone with the world spread beneath my feet and only the wind for company. There was no past, no future. Simply the moment. I closed my eyes and breathed deeply in this world stripped bare.

And then I opened my eyes and turned back. Charlotte, Otto, and the children were mere figures in the distance, and I lifted a hand to indicate I had made it all the way across.

We had run out of rope, and the slack trailed loosely after me. As I wound it around my elbow and palm, I looked to the east. *Look to the water.* It was there, just as Owain had written, a pure blue-green lake that glinted in the sun.

Once More Unto the Breach

16 February 1943

Dear Nhad,
The Germans are demanding that all men between the ages
of twenty and twenty-three work for two years in the war industries
for them, either here in France or in Germany.
They have said it will be an exchange.
Send the young men, and they will return the old
and ill prisoners of war from Germany.
It is little comfort to sacrifice one man to gain another.
-Owain

237

xix

Charlotte and I tied the rope around each child's waist, leaving slack between the knots. The ends we secured about ourselves.

I tightened the straps of the pack holding Simone as Charlotte readjusted the sling cradling the baby. "Ready?"

She nodded.

I whistled for Otto. "Go on, *bach*. Lead the way."

He was hesitant, though, whimpering at the edge of the glacier, placing a paw on the slope but backing away when he could not gain traction. I knelt and lifted the poodle to drape over my shoulders. He shifted uneasily for a moment before settling into place. "Remind the children to only step along the path I have made."

We crossed the glacier with slow care. There were no mishaps, and we summited the White Horse into the safety of Switzerland.

The lake was made up of two large pools that appeared to be divided by a rocky promontory jutting into the water from the north. The lake lay protected by craggy peaks, sheltered in the high valley.

A steep slope of scree separated us from the banks of the upper section of the lake. I kept Otto over my shoulders and left the rope secure about the waists of my small charges.

We crossed the scree field in much the same manner we had crossed the glacier: cutting across the precarious slope at an angle rather than attempting to descend it directly. The children slid several times, crying out in fear when their footing gave way, but the rope strung between us ensured Charlotte and I could halt their fall.

We reached the talus slope banks of the lake as the sun began its descent behind us. I placed Otto on his own four paws, and I removed

239

the rope from about the children's midsections.

We picked our way over the boulders along the lake's edge. The water was low at this time of year, and the ridge that bisected the lakes was cloaked in pines. The wind was not as bitter on this side of the mountain, but as the shadows lengthened, the air chilled.

The trees provided some shelter from the wind. As Charlotte settled the children in for the night, Otto and I followed the faint trail along the curve of the ridge that formed the southern boundary of the lower portion of the lake.

Look to the water. I saw nothing that gave insight into the words my son had written until I had circled to the far side of the lake.

The mountain road was a narrow track of dirt and rock. I knelt alongside it and studied the faint markings left by a vehicle's tires. They were set too wide apart to be anything but a truck, and the markings were faint, made days ago.

Otto and I followed the track downhill until it curved around a bend. From this vantage point, I could see the serpentine route it took down the mountain before it disappeared around the next ridge. I crouched and watched the road below to see if anyone appeared as the sun set, but no dust stirred and the only sounds were those of the wind, mountain, and water.

I pulled the letter I received months ago from my pocket and carefully unfolded the thin paper. The edges were worn and tattered from much handling. The ink was smudged in places, and my son's scrawl was quick and slanted.

Otto returned from his own investigation along the road and lay in the dirt by my side with a sigh. I rested my hand on his back.

I did not need the dying light to read the words. I knew them, had read them countless times, was haunted by them.

"Aye, *machgen i*." Otto's ears perked at my whisper. "Aye. I am proud."

———

"Should I follow the road in the morning and find where it

leads?" Charlotte unwound the makeshift bandage from about Hugo's head and tilted his face toward the moonlight. The gash along his chin was black in the pale gleam of light, but no blood flowed from the cut. She retrieved a plaster from the first aid kit and smoothed it along the curve of his chin, though, to ensure the wound did not open in the night.

"Not yet. The road has been traveled, though I do not know how recently. Since Owain's directions end here at the lake, that leads me to believe this place is significant."

"A rendezvous point, it seems." She settled Hugo in with the other children on the bedrolls, tucking the blankets over them and around the poodle curled up in the center. She shifted onto her side, tucking an arm beneath her head and drawing the lapels of her coat together under her chin. "Should we make camp closer to the road?"

"Here. Lift your head." I sat close enough that I did not need to stand to reach her once I pulled the scarf from about my neck. She obeyed, and I leaned over and threaded the scrap of fabric around the slender column of her throat.

"Thank you." Her face was in shadow. I could not see her smile, but I heard it in her voice.

I leaned back against the pine. "I do not know who may make use of this road. I think it is safer if we camp here and check the road at dawn each morning."

"I do not care to just wait and watch."

"Nor do I. But there is little else we can do."

We waited two days. In the hours before dawn, we led the children to the forest along the road and waited. Once the sun had risen, one of us kept watch while the other led the children back to camp. The mountain track remained empty. No one came.

It was in the middle of our third night sheltered in the trees between the lakes that I heard the sound, like a rock rolling underfoot. I peered at the tree line adjacent to our position, the lake's shoreline between still in the moonlight. I listened but heard and saw nothing more. It could easily have been a night creature prowling nearby, but the

241

edginess and knot of awareness between my shoulder blades would not relent.

I glanced at Otto where he lay at my side. He was alert, ears pricked, his lips curling back from his teeth in a soundless growl. I leaned over and placed a hand lightly over Charlotte's mouth. She woke instantly, hands coming up to latch around my wrist. Her fingers relaxed when she realized it was me, and she tapped the back of my hand to indicate understanding the need for silence. I lifted my hand away from her face, and she pushed herself upright, wrapping the scarf she had used for a pillow around her neck.

I bent close until my mouth brushed the curve of her ear. "We are no longer alone," I whispered, voice barely a breath of sound. "Get the children deeper into the woods."

She nodded and quickly set to rousing the children and keeping them quiet. The baby did not understand, though, and awoke frightened, letting out a mournful wail that reverberated like a haunting animal call through the night.

Charlotte clasped the little girl to her and stood frozen, and even in the darkness I could see how wide her eyes were when she looked to me.

"*Ffyc.*" I caught the muzzle flash from the corner of my eye before I heard the report. "*Get down!*" I barked, yanking the three children closest to me to the ground and hunching over them.

Charlotte staggered, and for an instant, I thought she had been hit, but then she dropped to the ground with Anne-Marie clutched to her chest, pulled her Colt, and fired off two shots in the direction from which the bullet had come.

Gunfire split the night, and in the dark I saw four muzzle flashes at the edge of the trees along the northern shore of the lower lake. I whistled sharply to catch Charlotte's attention, and when her head turned toward me, I motioned for her to hold her fire. A lull in the bullets came shortly after.

The children I hunched over trembled but made no sound. I

nudged them back further into the cover of the trees and held my hand flat against the cold ground to indicate how I wanted them to stay. They scrambled to obey, and I crawled to Charlotte.

"Get the children further back into the trees and stay flat to the ground," I whispered against her ear.

She caught my elbow. "What are you going to do?"

I drew the Luger and moved into a crouch. "I am going hunting."

"I will hide the children and then draw their fire to give you time to get behind them." She handed Anne-Marie to one of the older girls and whispered instructions to the children.

I hesitated, torn, studying the shadows that filled the delicate lines of her face. "Very well. I will flank them from over the ridge."

She hurried the children further away from the line of fire, and I ran hunched over, well within the tree line, climbing along the craggy curve of the ridge. When a silent shadow separated from the dark and attached itself to my side, I startled for a moment, but then dropped into a crouch to wait for Charlotte and rested my hand on Otto's shoulder.

When the crack of Charlotte's pistol split the night and the four others responded, we ran. We skirted the shoreline and headed deeper into the woods, higher along the ridge to circle back.

There were four of them, and they were German. They had moved just beyond the tree line to take cover behind a low rocky outcropping. They shot wildly into the woods where Charlotte and the children hid. There was no return fire from Charlotte now, and I forced my concern aside. Otto crouched at my side, coiled tight, muscles quivering. When two paused to reload, I attacked.

I shot the one with the rifle first, catching him high in the shoulder. He spun even as he slumped sideways, yelping in shock and pain, and lost his grip on the rifle. My second bullet caught him in the chest, driving him back against the rock. He was dead before he hit the ground.

A bullet whipped past me, so close I felt the pressure of the air

243

change and my ears rang. Splinters of wood bit at my face and neck as the bullet buried itself in the tree next to me.

Otto was a streak of shadow as he tore across the short distance and launched himself at the shooter. He left the ground in a flying leap and latched onto the soldier's gun arm. The gun fired, but the bullet kicked up dirt and rock meters to my left. Otto's momentum took both of them to the ground, and the man screamed as canine teeth bit through flesh and sinew.

The two others scrambled to regroup. My third bullet went through the throat of the one who aimed his gun at Otto. He fell, hands futilely attempting to stem the fountain of blood that poured from him. The other soldier dropped the magazine he was fumbling to insert into his pistol, and he met my gaze, eyes wide. He let his pistol fall and was in the midst of lifting his hands, palms out, when my bullet hit his forehead. His head snapped back as if I had punched him.

I did not wait to watch him crumble to the ground, but turned back to Otto and the last soldier. The poodle snarled, shaking the man's arm as the German struggled to regain his footing. Moonlight glinted on the blade he raised high over his head.

I did not pause to aim. I unloaded the three remaining bullets in the direction of his arm. The second found its mark in his forearm before he could plunge the knife into the dog.

I tossed the gun aside, strode over, and kicked the German in the face. He fell back in a limp, loose sprawl, but when I knelt over him, he smiled up at me. His nose was crushed, and his lips and teeth were dark with blood.

"Heil Hitler," he wheezed.

I leaned down until I could whisper in his ear. "Fuck you and Hitler."

He laughed, a gurgling, maniacal sound. He was still laughing when I snapped his neck.

I sat back, hands shaking, heart thrumming at a pace I felt in my ears. I reached out to Otto, whose jaws were still clamped around the man's arm.

"That is a good lad. Well done, Otto. Well done."

At the low, soothing tone of my voice, he slowly released the dead man's arm and came around to me. I ran my hands over him, relieved to find no injuries, though a fine tremor crawled through the muscles beneath flesh and hair. I petted him in long, sweeping strokes down his spine and sides, and the tremors soon faded. "There is my big, soft *cariad*." His tail wagged, and he nudged his head against my chest.

The night had settled back into its natural stillness, and an owl called mournfully for its mate somewhere in the darkness. I gained my feet, found the Luger, and started across the uneven shoreline. Charlotte stepped to the edge of the tree line as soon as I came into view.

Otto loped to meet her, and she rested a hand on his head. "Are you hurt?"

"No. You and the children?"

"They are frightened, but fine." She gazed across the shore. "Who were they?"

"A small band of Germans."

"The same from the north valley?"

"No, I think these men were not the same."

"Are there more?"

"I would rather not find out," I said. "We need to move. I prefer to avoid any predators that may be here. Human or animal."

"I will gather the children."

I reloaded the Luger with the ammunition taken from the abbey, and then we packed the rucksacks once more and set out. I carried Simone on my back, Charlotte held Anne-Marie, and the rest of the children fell in line between us as I picked a different path around the lake, staying away from the trail that gleamed like a stream in the starlight. The moon was bright even in its last quarter as it listed in the sky toward the horizon, but I led my small band through the shadow of the trees. The way was steep along the ridge, and snow was gathered in the recesses of the woods. We reached the mountain track when the

245

night was still swaddled in darkness.

I lifted Simone from the rucksack, placed her on her feet, and waited for Charlotte to reach me. "Let us hope this is the dawn we have been waiting for." I turned from scanning the track when she did not answer. She stood with a hand braced against a tree, bent forward slightly at the waist. "What is it? Are you hurt?"

"No, I am merely winded." She straightened. "I have not done any training for climbing the Alps."

I smiled at the crispness of her tone. "Bed the children down. Let them rest. Dawn will arrive within the hour."

The sky was beginning to lighten in the east when I heard the sound of an approaching engine. I glanced at Charlotte. She sat leaning against the trunk of a tree with four of the children using her outstretched legs as a pillow. Anne-Marie was curled against her chest. She appeared to have fallen asleep, so I grasped the toe of her boot and shook her foot. Charlotte was slow to wake, and I had to shake her foot again to fully rouse her.

"A vehicle approaches."

She nodded and gently woke the children. In the pale light of the approaching morning, their eyes seemed particularly wide and haunted. Hugo leaned against me, and I rested my hand on the back of his head as I watched the road.

The sound of the vehicle laboring up the steep, winding mountain road drew closer until a large, wooden-sided farm truck rounded the bend. The vehicle completed the arduous climb and turned around to face downhill. A smile tugged at my mouth at the sound coming from the back of the truck.

Charlotte glanced at me. "Are those…?"

"Sheep," I confirmed.

The truck idled on the road, and two older women climbed down from the cab and moved to the back on the pretense of checking the bleating sheep. I moved to stand, but Charlotte put a hand on my shoulder and gained her feet.

"I will go. Wait here."

I accepted the weight of the slumbering child as she transferred Anne-Marie to my arms. I tensed as she left the sanctuary of the trees and the taller of the two women grabbed a rifle hidden in the back of the truck and leveled it at Charlotte. She spoke in French and held her hands out by her sides. After a few moments of hushed exchange, the woman lowered the rifle. Charlotte turned and motioned to join her.

Hugo caught hold of my hand, and the rest of the children trailed after me as I led them from hiding.

Up close, I could see the age difference in the women more clearly. They must have been mother and daughter, for they bore a striking resemblance. I could tell from their surprised perusal they recognized me as Owain's father.

"We expected Owain and Séverin weeks ago," the younger woman said in heavily accented English. "We were worried when they did not make the rendezvous. We have come up the mountain every four days since to check, but we did not want to draw attention. The other day was to be our last journey until we heard word from Owain, but... My mother was convinced we needed to come back once more."

How close we had come to having nine children left in our care and no sanctuary to offer them. "I am grateful to your mother, to you both. The children will be safe and cared for?"

The older woman approached me and reached for Anne-Marie. The children hung back, clustered around Otto, whose head tilted back and forth at the sound of the sheep.

The younger woman answered. "They will be. We will protect them with our lives. We have good homes already arranged for them."

I allowed the older woman to take the little girl from me, and then I assisted her in climbing over the back gate of the truck. Black faces crowded close and peered down at me curiously. I recognized the breed: Valais Blacknose. I felt a sudden longing for home and the musty presence of my Balwens.

Charlotte spoke softly with the children, adjusting their cloaks

247

and scarves as the younger woman and I handed them up to her mother. The children were directed to lie down in the midst of the huddle of sheep, and one by one, they disappeared under the white woolen bodies.

Hugo clung to my leg, and I crouched down to look into his slanted eyes. "All will be well, *cariad bach*. You will be looked after. There is no need to be afraid."

His tongue wedged against his lower lip as he looked up at Charlotte as she translated. A tear slid down his rounded cheek, and I caught it with my thumb and wiped it away. "I want you to be brave now, Hugo. Help look after the little ones. Will you do that for me?"

He nodded as Charlotte translated and then threw his arms around my neck. I held him close, and the feel of his small, sturdy body in my arms lanced my heart. I closed my eyes and patted his back before pulling away. I had to clear my throat before I could speak. "Come along now."

He released me and turned to Charlotte, who flinched and hid a grimace when Hugo threw his arms around her waist.

"Are you certain you are well?"

Her smile was strained at the edges. "It is nothing." She addressed the children in French, and her voice was calm and gentle, but when she moved to lift Hugo into the back of the truck, she faltered with the boy's feet only centimeters off the ground.

I took the child from Charlotte and handed him to the older woman. He clung to my neck once more before she drew him deeper into the back of the truck and helped him settle under the sheep.

The younger woman climbed up into the back of the truck and then leaned down and caught my hand. "Bless you. Bless you both."

I squeezed her fingers. "Quickly now." I stepped back and raised a hand in farewell as the truck began its rumbling descent down the narrow mountain road. Otto trotted after it until I called him back to my side.

We watched until the truck disappeared from sight around the bend. I turned to Charlotte. "Tell me what is wrong."

"It is not important. We should not linger."

I could not waste time coaxing an explanation from her, so we set off around the lake, following the trail we had blazed along the ridge. The way seemed steeper in the light, rocks rolling underfoot, and Charlotte quickly fell behind. Otto loped back and forth between us, but when he barked, I looked back. Charlotte had stopped, her head down, hand pressed against her side.

When I reached her, I noted the sweat upon her brow and how pale her skin had become. "What—"

She caught hold of my arm and left a wet, russet smear across the sleeve of my coat. "Rhys. I am afraid you are going to be angry with me."

And then she collapsed.

Meghan Holloway

3 March 1943

Dear Nhad,
I miss home fiercely, I do.
-Owain

XX

I caught her before she fell. She was limp against me. I hooked an arm under her knees and scrambled from the precarious ridge down to the trail along the lake. I knelt and stripped off the rucksack she carried and the extra holster strapped around her waist, tossing both aside and cradling the back of her head in my hand as I lowered her to the ground. Her scalp was warm, her hair like cool, fine silk between my fingers. Otto paced around us whining.

"Quiet, *bach*. Go and *cwtch* down." He obeyed, curling his body around Charlotte's head and resting his muzzle on her shoulder. My hands shook as I unbuttoned her coat and drew the fabric aside. "*Esgob annwyl*, Charlotte. *Cachu hwch.*"

"It is bad, isn't it?" Her voice held a quaver I had not heard before.

Her light blue dress was stained red from under her left breast fanning down to mid-thigh around the dark hole a bullet had left in her side.

I stood. "I will be back. The truck cannot have gone far, and   "

She caught the hem of my trousers, her grip twisting in the fabric. "I would only draw attention to those women and the children. We know there's a hospital nearby in France. And I…I don't want to leave you."

I knelt beside her and drew a hand over my face. "*Cachu. Ffyc.*"

"Are you cursing?"

"Aye, I am." My hands shook. "*Coc oen.*"

She laughed, but the sound cut off with a gasp of pain. "I have never heard you curse before."

"You are right. I am angry. You foolish woman. *Enaid*, why did you not tell me?" She moved to touch her side, but I caught her hand. "Don't." I could not check the motion and drew her hand to my face, pressing her palm hard against my cheek and turning my lips into her wrist.

She swallowed and blinked up at the sky. "There was no point in telling you. I…I think it is too late."

"Do not speak such nonsense." I released her hand and shrugged the pack from my shoulders. The first aid kit seemed woefully ill-prepared for the situation at hand, and the urge to smash the tin against a nearby rock welled within me.

Five buttons adorned her dress from the collar to the wide waist band, and I slipped them from their moorings and then used my knife to open the dress to her navel and across to the side seam.

"You could have ripped it. I do not think I will be able to repair this one."

"Hush." I carefully pulled the saturated cotton back from her skin. The wound was a small, dark hole, ugly and brutal against her flesh. With gentle hands, I rolled her onto her opposite side and checked her back. There was no exit wound.

Blood pulsed in a steady stream from the wound. I felt her eyes upon me as I retrieved the field dressing from the kit, but I avoided meeting her gaze. She looked unbearably fragile. The lattice work of her ribs reminded me of a delicate birdcage. Her skin was pale and smooth and stained with her own blood. Pressure seized my throat, and my eyes burned. I untied the cords around her waist and thigh and tucked her holster and Colt into the rucksack.

I cleared my throat and placed the dressing over the wound. I caught her hand and rested it over the dressing. "Hold this in place, but do not exert any pressure." I wrapped the tails around her narrow torso. "That will do." She moved her hand and I continued the wrapping until there was just enough tail left to tie a knot at her side. I retrieved another field dressing from the kit and repeated the process.

When I finished, I met her gaze in time to see a tear slip from the corner of her eye down her temple. Otto snuffled her throat, and I caught the tear with my thumb before it ventured into the shelter of her hair. "Are you in pain?"

She shook her head. "I'm frightened."

I swallowed. As was I. "There is no need to be. All will be well."

"I do not think I can walk any further, and you cannot carry me over the mountain."

I shrugged the rucksack back over my shoulders and then wrapped her coat about her once more. "Hold on about my neck." I eased her into my arms, carefully regaining my feet on the uneven trail. She rested her head against my shoulder, and I pressed my lips to her hair. "I can, and I will."

The path around the lake seemed twice as long as it had been, and when I reached the ridge, movement near the shoreline caught my gaze. An eagle glided down from the high currents above the mountains, his image mirrored on the lake, wingtips stirring ripples in the water. He landed on the outcropping of rock the four Germans had hid behind, startling an unkindness of ravens into flight. A fox crept along the shoreline.

Within the pine forest of the ridge where we had made camp the last few nights, I stopped and placed Charlotte gently on the ground. Her eyes were closed, and the skin around her lips and eyes was tense with pain. Otto sniffed around her head, nudging her forehead when she did not respond to him as she usually did. I patted her cheek and caught her slim wrist in my hand. The flutter of her pulse against my palm had me closing my own eyes for a moment in relief.

"Charlotte," I whispered, brushing the wisps of hair back from her forehead.

Her eyes opened. "You are the only one who calls me that." She gave a weak chuckle when Otto licked her cheek and ear.

"Enough, *bach*," I said. "Charlie is a boy's name. It is not fit for a beautiful woman."

255

She smiled up at me. "I like it when you call me Charlotte."

I unbuttoned her coat and moved the shorn panel of her dress away from her side. Blood had seeped through the layered bandaging over the wound. I dragged a hand over my face. "You are losing too much blood, you are."

Her throat worked as she swallowed. "I know."

I cleared a stretch of ground down to the dirt just outside the tree line and proceeded to build a fire. Kindling was readily available, and the flames caught and held. I added thicker branches until the fire blossomed into red and orange flares that released sparks to the morning air.

My back was damp with sweat, but Charlotte shivered, her skin pebbling in the cool mountain air. I shrugged out of my coat and covered her and then shook out the heavy blanket rolled into the bottom of the pack and wrapped it around her legs.

She watched me the entire time, eyes large and dark in her wan face.

"Are you warm enough?"

"Aye."

I smiled at her attempt to mimic me.

"I am sorry I lied to you about your son."

"It is already forgiven. I understand why you did not tell me."

"You should leave me," she whispered.

I looked away, studying the fire. "I am not leaving you."

"I have slowed you. You cannot afford to—"

"Enough." My voice was sharper than I intended, and I made an effort to soften it. "Enough. There will be no talk of me leaving you. I will not hear of it."

I used an iodine swab on the knife, and when the fire had burnt down, I placed the blade in the coals. While the metal heated, I broke a stick down to hand's length.

"Are you going to remove the bullet?"

I swallowed. "No. I do not know how much damage it has

256

done, and I won't be prying around in a wound not knowing what I am doing. I am going to stop the bleeding." I met her gaze as I offered her the stick. "Put this between your teeth."

Her breath quavered in her chest and her eyes were dark with fear and pain, but she obeyed.

I lifted the soaked bandages and used another iodine swab to clean the area around the bullet hole. Blood still welled from the wound, and she flinched under my touch.

When I checked the knife in the coals, it was not quite glowing red. I retrieved it from the fire and returned to her side. I met her gaze. "Bite down now."

She clenched her teeth around the stick and turned her face into Otto's side. I took a deep breath and gently pressed the flat side of the hot knife onto the wound.

Her skin hissed and sizzled, and she screamed, the wrenching sound muffled against the makeshift wooden gag. When her scream cut off suddenly and her tense, shaking body went limp, I knew she had fainted and was relieved.

Otto leapt to his feet and whined, pacing around her head. I lifted the knife and pressed it in short increments over the wound until it was sealed and the blood flow ceased.

I tossed the knife aside, gut roiling, and rubbed my shaking hands over my face. It took me several tries to open another iodine swab and clean the now-sealed flesh. My stomach tried to creep into my throat at the sight of the raw, angry wound and the smell of burnt skin that still hung in the air. I swallowed repeatedly as I used the last bandage in the kit, binding it around her waist so her clothing would not chafe against the wound.

I pulled her stained dress back around her and buttoned her coat and mine all the way to her chin before I consolidated the food and supplies into one rucksack. I left behind all of the bedrolls save one and swaddled Charlotte in the blankets.

Infection was imminent, and I dreaded it more than I had dreaded cauterizing the hole the bullet had gouged into her. I tucked the knife back into my boot. I kicked out the fire, donned the rucksack, and lifted her into my arms. Her head lolled against my shoulder, and Otto stood on his hind legs, propping one front paw against her thigh, to nudge his head under Charlotte's elbow. Her arm slid over her side and hung limp.

"She will be fine, Otto *bach*." The conviction in my voice was as much to reassure myself as it was him.

The way was difficult, but I had hauled sheep across treacherous terrain my entire life, and my grip was sure even when I slid several times climbing the scree field. Otto climbed ahead of me, fleet of foot, picking out the way.

We crossed the mountain as the sun reached its zenith overhead.

Charlotte stirred when I placed her on the ground and knelt to tie the crampons around my boots.

"Rhys?"

I leaned over her and cupped her cheek in my hand. "I am here." Her skin was cool to the touch, clammy and colorless.

She smiled at me, but then her eyes slid closed.

I patted her cheek. "Stay with me, *fy nghariad aur*. I need you to stay with me."

"I will." Her voice was a mere murmur, and I had to strain to hear her.

When I started across the glacier, Otto moved to follow me but slid on the snow and ice. He leapt back and paced beside the glacier, whining.

"Come, Otto. Come."

He would not, though, and began to bark frantically.

Charlotte jerked in my arms. "Otto? Where is he? Here, boy."

"He will not follow us onto the glacier."

"Don't leave him. Please don't leave him behind." Her voice was agitated, and she struggled to look over my shoulder.

"Shh. I will not." I turned, careful not to lose traction on the precarious slope, and made my way back to the poodle, whose tail worked frantically as I approached. "You fool animal." My voice was soft. "Willing to take on an armed soldier but afraid to venture onto ice."

Once I had him situated, I started across the glacier again, dog draped over my shoulders, woman cradled to my chest. Across the glacier, I placed Otto back on his feet and put away the crampons before gathering Charlotte in my arms again and beginning the long trek across the tundra down the ridge.

I had to rest when I reached the top of the gorge. There was no way I could carry her down the rockfall in my arms, unable to watch my footing. I shed the rucksack, tucked our identity papers into my pocket, and secured her holster and Colt to my thigh. I tied Charlotte's forearms together, looping her bound arms over my head. I pulled her onto my back and secured her against me with a length of rope.

The climb down the gorge was grueling. Several times, Charlotte roused enough to hold onto me, but the majority of the climb, she was limp against me, saved from slipping off my back by the ropes knotted securely around us.

By the time we reached the overhang and the creek bed, the sun stained the sky red and purple as it descended toward the horizon. Charlotte had begun to tremble.

I cut the ropes binding us together and eased her onto the ground. Otto and I drank deeply from the overhang cascade, and I dampened Charlotte's dry lips but was leery of trying to coax her to drink.

She was in and out of consciousness, and when I checked her wound, she whimpered as I lifted the bandages. The cauterization had held, though, and the hole the bullet had punched through her flesh remained closed.

I wrapped her back in our coats and the blankets. She moaned when I lifted her, and I pressed my lips to her brow. Her skin was warm and damp.

The kilometers passed quickly underfoot, and Otto stayed close at my side. We reached the track leading to the village as the deep blue twilight faded to the black of night. The moon was in its last quarter, waning into its crescent. Its light was enough to illuminate the track at my feet when it climbed high enough in the sky to not be veiled by the forest. The shadows were deep and cool, and they grew deeper when a smattering of clouds crept across the stars.

Spits of snowflakes fell, visible in the tepid moonlight, disappearing before they reached the ground. My shirt grew damp where Charlotte was pressed against me from the heat radiating from her. The craggy mountain path undulated along the river and smoothed into the road leading to Cluses. When we passed through Sixt-fer-à-Cheval, the village slumbered, homes shuttered against the night. I saw no sign for a doctor, no indication of a hospital. And I knew Charlotte required more care than a village physician could provide, so I kept walking.

My shoulders began to ache, but I lengthened my stride and tightened my grip. Charlotte began to moan, murmuring words I could not make out. I clutched her close and spoke to her of home. Of the stone fence in need of repair, of the musty pungency of the Balwens when they were wet, of the cottage my grandfather's great-great-grandfather had built, of how the wind made the hills sing. I told her about Owain as a child, about the time he had tried to milk the neighbor's bull, about when the raft he had built had started sinking in the middle of the cold river and I had to swim out and fetch him.

Hours later, when I passed the cemetery on the edge of Cluses where I had buried the infant, she was burning with fever and delirious.

The approach of the sun was lightening the eastern sky when I reached the hospital. I tried the door only to find it locked, and I pounded the frame with my boot. "Open up! I need a doctor!" I continued to shout until I heard footfall on the other side of the door.

It cracked open to reveal a young woman. *"Monsieur—"*

I shouldered my way into the hospital, and the young woman scrambled after me as I strode down the corridor.

"*Monsieur, vous ne pouvez pas—*"

A dour-faced nurse exited a room into the hallway, and I almost plowed her over. Her eyes rounded, and she caught hold of the blankets wrapped around Charlotte in an effort to right herself. When she caught sight of Charlotte's face, she questioned me in French.

"Please. I need a doctor now."

She nodded and addressed the woman trailing after me before turning back to me. "Come. How was she hurt?"

"She was struck by a bullet in her lower left side. Yesterday morning." I followed her as she led me down the corridor and turned right into another wing. "I cauterized the wound. She would have bled out otherwise."

"Place her here." She led me into the surgery and gestured to the operating table in the room.

I laid Charlotte on the table and cupped her cheek in my hand. Her brows and lashes appeared stark in her colorless face, and she did not respond when I whispered her name.

A group of doctors and nurses hurried in as I was ushered out.

"You will need to wait in the main corridor," the dour-faced nurse said. She glanced down, and her smile was gentle. "Your dog as well."

Otto trotted at my heels as I retreated from the surgery wing. When I slid down the wall to sit on the floor, he curled up beside me and rested his muzzle on my knee. I placed a hand on his head and leaned my own back against the wall to wait.

———

She threaded her fingers through my hair as I rested my cheek on the swelling protrusion of her belly.

"I think I can hear them within."

She shook as she laughed, and I rolled over to see her face. She smiled at me, face tender. "You are daft, you are. And why are you so certain it is 'them'?"

I closed my eyes and pressed my ear to her stomach. The fabric of her dress was soft and worn, her skin beneath warm and fragrant.

261

There was movement within her belly, like a moth's wings beating against the night or the flutter of a curtain in the wind. A breeze swept over us, heavy with the scent of heather and spring-fertile soil. "I can feel it."

She traced my brow with a gentle finger, and I carefully wedged my arms under her to embrace her fully. Peace was an uneasy burden, but it was lighter to bear when touching her, the ground still chilled from winter beneath the blanket upon which we sprawled, the sun picking its way through the branches above to dapple us in light.

"Dadi! Dadi!"

The small voice was tremulous and distraught, and I sat upright. Owain's short, sturdy legs bore him down the hill toward us at a pace that almost tripped him, and Rhiannon darted in front of him, barking, to slow his pace.

I caught him in my arms as he reached us. His face was grimy and streaked with tears. "What is it, machgen i?"

He held his hands cupped to his thin chest, and at my question, he opened them and held them out for me to see. In his square, pink palms lay a delicate bird's egg, broken in half. "I only wanted to see it, Dadi. I did not mean to hurt it." A sob quaked in his chest.

"Hush now." I took the broken egg from him and set it aside. "Some things we have to pay extra care with for they are easily broken."

He burrowed against my chest and wept as I leaned back onto the blanket. Rhiannon settled at our feet with a sigh. Aelwyd rolled to her side and rubbed our son's back until his crying lessened into snuffles and he soon grew heavy and limp against me.

"Promise me something, Rhys," she whispered once Owain was asleep.

"Anything."

"Promise me you will look after Owain."

I turned my head to meet her gaze. "You know I will always look after all of you."

*"I know. But after Owain especially." She gazed at the boy
as she caressed his tousled hair. "His heart is gentle. It is one of those
things that is easily broken."*

*I rested my hand on my son's back, and my palm and fingers
spanned the narrow width of his young frame. As warm and sturdy as
he was, he felt fragile beneath my rough hand. His back rose and fell
in easy rhythm, and Aelwyd placed her hand over mine, interlacing our
fingers. "I promise."*

The hand on my shoulder brought me back to the present and
made me realize I had fallen asleep. I blinked bleary eyes at the woman
crouched before me. It took me several moments to recognize her with
the absence of the habit and veil.

"Mother Clémence."

"Just Berthe. I think that part of my life is over now."

She sat on the other side of Otto, mimicking my pose with her
legs stretched out before her and her ankles crossed.

"The girl? Angelique?"

She had lines etched into the skin around her eyes and mouth, and
they deepened with her slight, bittersweet smile. "She did not make it."

"I am sorry."

With her head bare, her short hair exposed, she appeared fragile
and vulnerable. "I comfort myself with the knowledge that she is no
longer so tormented and her pain is eased. She was a tortured soul
since…" She took a deep breath. "I could not protect her here, and God,
for some reason, chose not to. It is enough to make an old woman bitter
if I did not cling to my faith."

I had not had any faith to cling to for decades now, but I offered
her what comfort I could. "The children are safe."

She met my gaze, and the lines about her face softened. "I am
thankful. They would not have been were it not for you."

"Were it not for Owain."

She dipped her head. "Of course."

263

"How did he become involved in this?"

She searched my face. "He did not become involved. He *created* this network of schools and abbeys to hide and transport children across the country to safety."

I leaned my head back against the wall. "His network."

"*Oui.* The Gravenor Network. That is what we have taken to calling it."

"How did he start it?"

She stroked a hand over Otto's back. "He would never say. It is not safe to do so, and he did not seem to be one who was keen to talk about himself."

"No, he was not."

"But his wife told me that he began with art in Paris. Working with the Rothschilds, the Veil-Picards, the Seligmanns, a man by the name of Kann, and with a group from the Louvre. One day in an attic, he found a group of children. Their parents had hidden them before Vel' d'Hiv."

"And that was the beginning." I rubbed my forehead and pinched the bridge of my nose. "How many children?"

"With the ones you took to safety? Five hundred twenty-seven. That I know of."

I closed my eyes, staggered.

"I am thankful you returned. I have had some news."

I straightened and turned to her, but she avoided my eyes.

"Sévèrin has been found. She is in a hospital in Lyon."

"And Owain?"

I knew her answer even before she met my gaze and shook her head.

4 September 1943

Dear Nhad,
The factories and railroad yards were bombed
yesterday by the Allies.
Hope and horror is a heady mixture.
-Owain

#

Henri

"There was a misunderstanding," Klaus said, though his smile spoke otherwise. "He did not agree with the way we were treating his wife." He kicked the man on the floor. "It seems he killed one of my guards."

I glanced into the room behind Klaus and took in the carnage. The guard was sprawled on the floor, his face a pulp of blood, bone, and tissue. The woman's condition made my gut churn. She was tied to a table, obscenely splayed as if on a butcher's block. Had she been my wife, I would have caved the skull of the guard brutalizing her as well. I knelt beside Owain and rolled him onto his back. He was beaten and maimed almost beyond recognition. He was breathing, though, and the bullet wounds in his arm and leg would need attention but they were not lethal.

"I will need help carrying them up to the street."

"But of course." Klaus was once again the genial host, nodding for the guards to assist me.

The guards helped me carry the pair out of the tunnels but would venture no further than the basements for fear of being discovered. I hid Owain in the boiler room and then climbed from the ruins with his wife cradled in my arms. She was unconscious, limp and startlingly light. Her bare, dirty feet bounced against my thigh as I hurried through the streets.

When I entered the hospital, I needed only to call for help before we were surrounded and the woman was relieved from my arms.

I slipped away before anyone could take too much note of me and returned to where I had left Owain.

He groaned as I carried him into the nearby building. It had been a shop before the war, but it was abandoned now. *Juif* was painted in yellow scrawl on the boards nailed into place over the broken storefront windows. I had found the building upon returning to Lyon, and the upper floor was comprised of five apartments, empty save for the barest of furnishings.

"Sévèrin." Owain's voice was a raw, ragged whisper.

I responded to him in English, remembering how elementary his French was. "She is safe."

He was difficult to carry, all arms and legs pared down to bone and sinew from the starvation he had undoubtedly suffered in the hands of the Gestapo. I remembered the strong boy he had been when I first met him, quick to smile but quiet and reserved. I had mistaken him for a *schwächling* until I realized it was not weakness I sensed in him but kindness. His hands had given away his background even before I learned that he hailed from a sheep farm in Wales. He would not be using those hands, reduced only to palms and thumbs, any time soon.

I managed to get him up the stairs and into the barren apartment I had set up camp in while I waited and watched to see if Klaus remained in Lyon even with the Allies firmly entrenched in the city. I had stolen medical supplies from the very hospital where I had taken Owain's wife, and I was well stocked. I knew that if he were still alive after being in Klaus's company, he would need medical attention. I had been correct on that account.

I removed the bullets from his arm and leg while he remained unconscious, cleaning the wounds and sprinkling sulfa powder over them. I bandaged his hands and his face, coating the gaping hole of his empty left eye socket with the powdered drug as well before I wrapped the bandages around his head. I felt a surge of disgust for Klaus's methods. Rococo, frivolous, and utterly lacking in subtle nuance.

Once More Unto the Breach

I coaxed Owain into swallowing several sulfa pills and then dragged one of the two chairs in the room close to his cot to wait. I would allow him time to rest and begin to recover before I performed my own interrogation.

25 December 1943

Dear Nhad,
Nadolig has been a difficult time since leaving home.
But today, I became a husband.
I look forward to the day I can bring Sévèrin home.
-Owain

XXii

"She needed multiple transfusions, and we are still concerned about septic shock. We are giving her penicillin for the infection."

I followed the dour-faced nurse into the recovery ward. Otto trotted at my heels.

"You expect her to recover, then?"

She hesitated. "The surgeon who worked on her was a student of Dr. Churchill in America. I believe we can hope."

The recovery ward was quiet and empty save for the bed in the far corner.

"She has not awakened yet, but that is not unexpected."

I nodded, unable to speak, and she place a hand on my arm before retreating.

Otto approached the bed cautiously, sniffing Charlotte's fingers. She lay on her back, a sheet tucked around her, arms alongside her body. Had she had any awareness, she would have hated the position. I had never seen her sleep on her back.

Otto licked her fingers and then climbed gingerly onto the bed to curl around her feet. I pulled a chair to the bedside, wrecked by how small and fragile and wounded she appeared. Her hair was spread across the pillow, and the honeyed gleam was dulled. The freckles on her nose and cheeks stood out in stark relief in her colorless face, and dark shadows formed bruised half-moons under her eyes.

I folded her hand between mine, flinching at how cold her fingers were. I breathed a warm gust of air over her skin and rubbed her hand until it was pink and no longer chilled. I reached over her and gathered her other hand to repeat the process.

She never stirred for the rest of the day and throughout the night. Otto and I left her side only when necessary, and nurses stopped at Charlotte's bedside regularly.

The abbess came and sat on the other side of Charlotte's bed early the next morning. "My nephew has been asked to accompany a military transport to Chambéry. There was a prison held by the Germans in the city, and the conditions are deplorable. They need more doctors there."

I hung my head and rubbed the back of my neck.

"I spoke with him, and you could catch the transport with him and the other doctors."

"When do they leave?"

"This afternoon. It would place you a hundred kilometers from Lyon."

I felt her gaze on me but could not draw my eyes from Charlotte's still face.

"I will watch over her for you." Her voice was gentle.

"Thank you for arranging this."

She stood and rested her hand on Otto's head. "It is the least I could do."

Once she left and we were alone once more in the ward, I leaned forward and pressed my face into Charlotte's hip, wrapping my arm around her legs. The crisp white sheet beneath my cheek grew damp.

It took several long moments for me to register the cool hand resting on the back of my neck. I lifted my head and met Charlotte's gaze. Seeing those blue-gray eyes open only tightened my throat, choking off the words I would have said.

"Where are we?" Her voice was weak and hoarse. She glanced from me to Otto and then peered around the room.

I caught her hand and pressed it to my face, my mouth against the pulse of life in the fine blue veins at her wrist. "At the hospital in Cluses." I recounted the events to her and told her of the abbess's

274

news.

"Owain?" she whispered.

All I could manage was a shake of my head. I cleared my throat. "Only Sévèrin. And I do not know what state she is in, only that she is in a hospital in Lyon."

"You have to leave."

My eyes closed. "Aye. This afternoon. The abbess has arranged transport to a town called Chambéry, and then I will continue from there."

"I am sorry I cannot go with you."

I clasped her hand between both of mine and rested my forehead on our interlaced knuckles. "And I am sorry I must leave you behind," I whispered.

"I know." Her free hand came up and followed the line of my brow before dropping to trace along my jaw. "You look tired. Will you lie with me for a while before you leave?"

I untied my boots. "Aye."

The bed was too small for the three of us, but I lay alongside Charlotte and let my feet hang off the end beside Otto. I was careful not to nudge against her, but she caught my arm and drew it over her body. "Come closer."

"I do not wish to hurt you," I said as I obeyed.

"You could not." She sighed as I fit my body against hers as well as I could lying on my side while she lay on her back. My chin rested against the crown of her head, one of my knees tucked under hers, Otto warming our feet.

"I will miss you sorely."

I brushed her hair away from her forehead and then folded my arm under my head. "And I you. I regret that we did not find the answers you sought."

She turned her face into my chest and clasped her hands around the arm I draped carefully over her. "I found something else along the way."

275

She was delicate and soft, warm and bright, gentle and possessing endless courage. I could have held her forever, lain beside her until the twilight of the last day. I closed my eyes and pressed my lips against the crown of her head. She was still an enigma to me, and even though we had spent the last fortnight together, I realized I knew very little about her. But what I did know was that she was fierce and fearless and constant, and I could not bear the thought of parting from her.

The hours passed too quickly. Neither of us slept, we simply lay quietly alongside one another, holding each other. When midday arrived, I could hear the military convoy assembling outside.

"I would wait for you."

"I know," she whispered. "But you have to go now."

I untangled myself from her, smoothing the blankets around her. I placed her Colt under her pillow, and then I sat on the edge of the bed and donned my boots once more. Otto repositioned himself over her feet to drape his chin over my thigh as I tied my laces, and when I sat up, I stroked his head, parsing the black curls, fingering his ears. "You are a good lad," I said softly to him. His brows twitched. "I am thankful you found us by the river and took this journey with me. I know you care for Charlotte as much as I do, so I will not be selfish and ask you to come with me further. Stay here with her and look after her." Those dark brown eyes studied my face with an almost human keenness and understanding. His tail thumped against the bed, and he nudged my hand with his nose. I bent my head and pressed my lips to the ridged bone of his skull, rubbing my hand along his flank. When I drew back, he licked my cheek.

I stood and turned to Charlotte. I braced my hands on either side of her and leaned over to rest my forehead against hers. She made a sound at the back of her throat and reached up to cup the back of my neck. Silent tears made silvery tracks down her face.

"You are the most lion-hearted of women," I whispered.

Her breath caught on a sob. "I will come find you after the

276

war."

"I will count on that and watch for you. *Hwyl fair am nawr.*
It means goodbye, but only for now." Cupping her face in my hands, I
pressed my lips to hers. They were warm against mine, damp with the
trace of her tears. Then I forced myself to let her go.

I paused at the doorway of the ward and looked back. Otto
sat upright on the bed, head cocked, ears pricked as he stared after me.
Charlotte's head was turned on the pillow to watch me, a hand pressed to
her lips, her face damp with tears. My vision blurred as I lifted a hand to
them, and then I turned and walked away, the salt of her tears lingering
on my mouth.

The truck was crowded, and I sat shoulder to shoulder with
the abbess's nephew and a French soldier. I rocked back and forth
as the truck labored over the rough, hilly terrain. A glance out of the
back showed that we were third from the last in the convoy of a dozen
vehicles.

I closed my eyes and allowed the sway of the truck and the
quiet murmur of French to lull me. Exhaustion settled about me, and
I could feel my head growing weighted, my chin dipping toward my
chest.

*I could feel the lice creeping over my scalp. When I clawed at
my head, my fingers came away with the nails limned with blood. And
still there was no relief from the itching.*

*A rat investigated my boot, and instead of kicking it away,
I merely watched it, mind blank. Something like pity or envy for the
creature moved through me, for he was trapped in the filth as well but
immune to the fear and sorrow and boredom. He stopped his progress
around my foot to bite at his haunches with the same vigor with which
I raked my fingers over my head. The pity and envy morphed into
empathy.*

*The sound of flesh being furrowed by nails drew my attention,
and I glanced at Arthur. He dozed restlessly, sprawled on the fire-*

step beside me. I looked to the lad across from me in the trench. He whimpered as he clawed frantically at his scalp, and he clambered suddenly to his feet.

"Je ne peux pas le supporter." His eyes were wild and red-rimmed. He met my gaze and then turned and scrambled up the side of the trench.

"No!" I lunged for him, but the German bullet had already found its mark between his eyes. His head snapped back with the force of it, and the back of his skull exploded, sending shards of bone and clumps of brain raining down on me. I could taste his blood and feel the heat of it on my face.

I caught him as he fell backward in a boneless sprawl, and his weight took us both to the mud.

"You bloody fool," I whispered, kneeling in the mire, holding him in my arms.

But when I looked at him, he was no longer the French soldier. He bore the face of my son.

I moaned. "No, no, you cannot be here, Owain." I cradled the back of his shattered head in my hand and could only feel wet, warm gore. "No, no, no."

His eyes snapped open, as green as my own. "Dadi." His voice was that of Owain's when he was but a child. "Help me."

I lurched into wakefulness violently, almost falling off the bench.

"*Monsieur?*"

I blinked, and the wary gazes of the French soldiers sitting across from me came into focus. The abbess's nephew clasped my shoulder, his grip firm.

"*Etes-vous bien?*"

I met his concerned gaze. "Thank you, I'm well, I am."

He searched my face and then nodded, relinquishing his grip. I sighed and rubbed my hands over my face, struggling to remove the disturbing image from my mind.

I did not allow myself to fall prey to sleep again for the remainder of the journey. It was a four- or five-hour trek from Cluses, and we arrived in Chambéry in the early evening.

When I leapt down from the back of the truck, it felt as if I were stepping off a boat. It took me a moment to steady my legs beneath me. The temporary military camp was a hive of activity.

I approached one of the drivers of the convoy. "I am in need of transportation. Do you know who can assist me?"

He eyed me. "You are not a doctor?" His accent was so thick I had difficulty discerning his words.

It struck me suddenly that without Charlotte and her ambulance, my movement through the country would not go unquestioned, and I could not afford to be detained.

"I am. Thank you." I did not look back as I walked away. I could feel his stare following me and did not want to rouse his suspicion further.

Once out of sight, I cut through the camp, commandeered a bicycle leaning against the side of a building, and slipped into the tangle of Chambéry's streets.

It had been years since I had ridden a bicycle, and my start was a fitful one. The front tire wobbled back and forth as I sought to maintain my balance on the contraption. By the time I reached the outskirts of the city, though, I had found a rhythm and steadiness.

There were still a couple of hours of sunlight left. The way was hilly, but the kilometers passed far more swiftly under my stolen tires than they would have under my feet.

The sun was bright in my eyes as it set over the trees, and a spire stood over the village ahead. Dusk was deepening into night when I reached the small cathedral, and I wheeled the bicycle into the vestry.

I lay on a bench in the chapel, watching as the stained glass darkened from its multi-hued beauty to a jumble of blacks and grays. I expected to lie sleepless throughout the distance between the sun's set and rise. But when I opened my eyes, feeling as if only a moment had passed, a prism of color from the stained glass played over me.

I wasted no time getting back on the road. As I pedaled west, the steep inclines and declines softened into rolling slopes punctuated with long, flat straightaway stretches. The forests became interspersed with fallow fields.

Storm clouds developed in the east, skirting the sun's rise and soon veiling her ascent into the sky as they overtook me. The clouds were leaden and heavy, burgeoning with rain and shifting in shape and color as they developed overhead. They surpassed me with a deep rumble of thunder, and within an hour, the western horizon was a blue-black bruise of color, threaded with white rents of lightning.

I reached Lyon at midday after several hours of hard pedaling. The storm had moved further west, leaving the streets of the city cool and rain-washed. It was as chaotic as when we had left it only days earlier: milling with gaunt citizens, teeming with soldiers, ringing with gunfire. Uncertain of my destination, I walked, pushing the bicycle alongside me.

The soft sound of muffled crying drew my attention down the alley I passed, and the sight of the huddled figure in the depths of the narrow through-way gave me pause. I leaned the bicycle against the mouth of the alley and approached the small figure.

"Are you well?"

It was a child, a young boy who looked up at me as I drew near. His face was tear-streaked and cradled in his hands was a wounded bird. The sight brought me to an abrupt halt, and for an instant, as memories flooded me, the boy bore a different child's face.

A water-logged sniff brought me back to the present, and I knelt beside the boy. "What has happened here?"

His chin trembled, and he stroked the serin's quivering yellow breast. "*Je ne voulais pas.*" A sob shook him.

"There now," I said, voice soft as I took in the damage. One of the little finch's wings hung low and lifeless. "His wing is broken, it is. With some care, he will be able to fly again in a matter of weeks." I drew the knife from my boot, and the boy hid the bird against his chest. I smiled my reassurance, cut a strip of fabric from the tail of my shirt, and tucked the knife away. I held out my hands to the boy. "May I?"

He wiped his damp face against his shoulder and hesitantly offered me the serin. I cupped the fragile creature in my hands, stilling its flutterings by rubbing my thumb over the delicate tufted cap of its skull. The boy shuffled closer as I gently folded the broken wing against the side of the bird's body and secured it in place with the swath of cloth. I ensured the makeshift bandage was tight enough to hold the wing in place but loose enough for the bird to breathe easily. The boy watched me work with a rapt expression as his tears subsided.

"If you will take care of him, give him seed and grubs and water, once his wing heals, he will be able to continue on his journey."

I had no idea if the boy understood anything I said, but he suddenly leapt to his feet and raced down the alley. "*Attendez!*" he called over his shoulder as he disappeared around the corner.

I waited, kneeling in the alley, drowning in memories. He was back in minutes, clutching a basket to his thin chest. When he thrust it out toward me, I saw that he had filled the basket with a blanket. I placed the bird in the center of his child-made nest and watched the boy smooth the blanket around him. Owain had shown the same care and concern for the creatures he had found wounded or ill.

He smiled up at me. "*Merci, monsieur.*"

I returned his smile, and he followed me onto the street, where I retrieved the stolen bicycle. I turned back to him and carefully pronounced the name of the hospital the abbess had told me of. "Do you know it?" I repeated the name.

His brow wrinkled and then cleared, and he nodded vigorously. He started to race down the street but then remembered his cargo. He motioned for me to wait and darted through an open doorway. He returned without the basket and beckoned for me to follow.

He dashed through the streets, and even with my longer strides, I had to hurry to keep up with him. He led me through the tangle of streets toward the city center until he stopped abruptly and waited at a busy corner for me to catch up with him. He pointed, and I eyed the grand building across the street. My chest felt tight, and I rubbed the space over my thrumming heart.

I turned back to the boy and tilted the bicycle toward him. "Thank you."

He touched the handlebars and glanced up at me uncertainly. When I nodded and stepped back, his gap-toothed smile grew. A torrent of French was directed at me along with a wave as he ran alongside the bicycle before leaping onto the seat as if swinging himself into the saddle on a horse.

I stared after him for a moment before I crossed the street and entered the hospital.

It took several minutes to find a nurse who spoke English and when I told her of the reason for my visit, she checked her records and eventually led me to a quiet ward on the second floor. "The third bed," she said, voice low.

The occupant appeared small and childlike, curled on her side in the narrow bed. Her hair was a dark tangle, and one foot peaked from beneath the sheet drawn over her. It was small and pink-soled, and a crescent of grime ringed her heel. I pulled the sheet over her foot and rounded the bed.

I staggered when I reached the far side of her bed and faced her. Her knees were drawn up, and one splinted arm curved around the swell of her belly. My legs barely carried me to the chair before they collapsed under me. I leaned forward and braced my elbows on my knees. My eyes burned, and I pressed my palms against them to keep the emotion at bay.

"You are so far from me at times."

Aelwyd's soft whisper brought my head around. I responded with raw honesty. "I do not mean to be."

"I know." She crossed to me, moving from the cool gild of moonlight in the lawn to the dark swaddling of shadow as she reached

where I sat atop the stone wall beneath the tree.

I lifted her into place beside me and then retrieved my cigarette. I took a slow, deep drag, letting the smoke fill and heat my lungs before releasing it into the night. From the corner of my eye, I caught the way Aelwyd turned her head aside. "It bothers you?"

She cleared her throat. "It did not prior, but of late the smell has turned my stomach."

I extinguished the burning paper and tobacco on the rock. "Are you unwell?"

"No." She reached out and grasped my hand where it rested between us on the wall and drew it to her stomach. Her nightgown was soft, the fabric warm from her skin. "I'm with child, I am."

My gaze flew to her face, but I could not make out her expression in the darkness. I tried to withdraw my hand, but she pressed it harder into the soft flesh of her belly. "Please." Her voice caught. "Please, Rhys. Let this bring you the rest of the way home. To me. To us."

I was silent, but when she relinquished her grip on my hand, I left it on her stomach and closed the distance between us where we sat on the stone wall.

A sound from the bed brought my head up. Sévèrin still slept, but she whimpered and her brow creased. Rage welled within me as I studied her. A bracelet of raw welts and abrasions ringed her wrists. Her arms bore scrapes and scratches. Her face had been met with a fist so many times over I could tell nothing of her features. One eye was swollen shut, the livid purple bruise extending down over her cheek. There was a lump on her jaw, and her lip was split. Her nose was broken, blackening the eye that was not swollen shut. My own fists clenched, and when she whimpered again, curling in on herself and wrapping her broken arm tighter around her stomach, I said her name softly.

She jolted awake, the one eye she was able to open going wide. Her gaze locked on me, and she struggled to push herself upright. "*Owain?*" She paused and studied me more closely. The tears welling in her good eye and the tremor in her busted lips gave me the answer I had traveled across France to find.

"His father," I said, voice rough, and she nodded, breath hitching. She was propped on the elbow of the arm that was not broken. "May I assist you?"

"*S'il vous plaît*. Please."

I stood and eased her upright. In another time, I imagined she was tall and svelte, but she felt skeletal now under my hands, and I propped the thin pillows behind her so the battered girl could recline more comfortably. I dragged the chair closer to the bedside and watched Owain's wife study me.

"My son is dead."

Her face worked. "He is."

I turned my head and took a deep breath. *I do not want to see your face again until you have learned to be a man who accepts his duties.* The weight in my chest grew heavier. "Will you tell me how?"

I turned my gaze back to her when she remained silent to find her eyes closed. "Owain is…was a strong man. As his father, you know this." The knot in my throat grew larger, harder. "He would not tell them. He said nothing, no matter what they did to him. And they hurt him." She opened her one good eye, but she did not meet my gaze and instead stared blankly at the opposite wall. "The man in charge…" A shudder wracked her frame. "He said the easiest way to break a man is to hurt a woman." Her hand crept to her face, and she fingered her bruised and swollen cheekbone. "He…he just kept hitting me and h-hitting me. I was so afraid. For me and the baby. For Owain." Her hand dropped and fisted in the sheet. "And then one of the guards… He…" A tear slid down her battered cheek.

I leaned forward but made no move to reach for her. "You do not need to continue."

She shook her head. "*Non*. I do. You should know." She took a deep, shuddering breath and cupped her hand over her rounded stomach. "He told Owain he would…he would c-cut the baby from my womb. I could hear Owain screaming the entire time. I have never…

284

It was like the sound of a tortured animal." She looked up at me, gaze beseeching. "I do not know how he freed himself. He was always so gentle. He could never bear to see even the slightest creature hurt."

I remembered the countless injured animals he had brought to me when he was a child: his triumph when we could save them, his devastation when we could not.

"He broke his bonds," she whispered. "And beat the man to death with the chair. It was like something wild was unleashed in him. The guards could not pull him away." She extended a trembling hand, and I clasped it in my own. "They shot him. The guards. They k-killed my Owain. Our Owain." A sob escaped her, raw and broken. "*Je suis désolée.* I am so sorry."

She clung to my hand, and I left the chair to sit on the edge of the bed. She did not flinch away from me, and when I settled beside her, she leaned into me. I wrapped my arm carefully around her slight shoulders, and she sagged, slumping against me.

The sounds tearing from her throat were painful to hear. I ran my hand over her hair and cupped the back of her head in my palm as I had done countless times in the past to comfort Owain. "Shh now. Shh."

I rocked back and forth. My shirt grew damp under her cheek, and I held her as she wept herself into an exhausted sleep. My own eyes burned but remained dry.

24 April 1944

Dear Nhad,
The bombings in the 18th arrondissement
have killed over 600 people.
Yesterday, Pétain returned to the city for the funeral.
Even after all of this, he is still revered by the people.
-Owain

xxiii

Grief and I had long been acquaintances, but now it met me in an unfamiliar guise. When I lost Aelwyd and the twins, and later my father, I had been gorged to excess on pain and anger. Grief had been a wolf pacing within the confines of my chest, gnashing at my heart, howling and feral and bitter.

This new grief flayed me down to bone and marrow. It whittled me to husk. My cleaved, bloodless heart pulsed only out of habit, not out of want. Where before my grief had been a rage and torment, now it felt like a biting wind sweeping across a barren expanse. I was hollowed out to emptiness.

If I allowed myself, I would drown in the vast desolation. I could not allow myself to consider that temptation. Not when someone depended on me.

Sévèrin woke screaming in the night, her cries flaying me as I thought of what she had suffered. What Owain had endured.

She clung to my hand in the aftermath, breath uneven, swollen face damp. I pulled my chair close to her bedside told her stories of Owain's youth, of the bright, caring, inquisitive young boy he had been. When she finally drifted into a peaceful sleep, I started to withdraw my hand, but her fingers tightened around mine and her eyes fluttered open.

"Will you take me home?" she whispered, voice raw.

Underneath the violent bruising, behind the swell of child at her midsection, she was little more than a girl, barely twenty years of age.

"Aye. Paris is a mere two-day journey from here. Once you are well—"

"*Non.* Not to Paris." She swallowed. "Owain and I…we planned to return home after the war. His, your home. He spoke of it often." I turned my face away to hide my emotion, and she hesitantly touched my arm. "Will you mind? Is it not agreeable to you? I do not—"

I clasped her fingers gently. They felt as fragile as a child's. She carried a remnant of my son within her and was my one connection to the man he had grown to be since I had cast him out. "I would be pleased to take you home."

Her smile was tremulous, a shadow of what it once was, I was certain. But the tension in her shoulders eased.

The next day, I set about securing our passage home. I had transport arranged to take us north with a medical convoy headed to the Siegfried Line. We would leave the convoy as they branched to the east, and Paris would be a day's journey to the northwest. I could find transport to the coast from there, and if need be, I would steal a dinghy and row us across the Channel. I did not think it would come to that. But then, I had not expected to cross France in an ambulance and climb the Alps on the cusp of winter either.

And I had not expected to return home without my son. It ate at me, and I roamed the streets of Lyon for two days. Searching for what, I did not know. Finding his body would be an impossible task. Séverin knew nothing of where they had been held, only that it was dark and cold.

It was during my second day of searching the city that I came across a familiar face. "Colonel."

The American officer studied me for a moment. "The man with the ambulance from Paris. You aided us at the hospital."

"Rhys Gravenor." I took in the dozen men behind him, all soldiers who appeared ready for action. "Are there German holdouts still in the city?"

"We've searched every hideout in this city, but there have been some rumors of activity."

"May I join you?" The colonel's gray eyebrows arched. "I am searching for my son. He was held by the Gestapo in Lyon."

The American's gaze was shrewd and assessing. After a moment, he said, "Walk with us, Gravenor." I fell into step beside him. "We have heard word that the Butcher and others are in retreat to Bruyères."

"The Butcher?"

"Man by the name of Barbie. He was the head of the Gestapo here in Lyon. From reports, the title of Butcher was well earned." We soon entered an area of the city that was reduced to rubble from the air raids. The destination appeared to have once been a school. "Our information says he's in retreat, but there have been reports of renewed activity around these remains of their headquarters." He waved his squad of men forward. "Wait here."

They fanned out and swept the area with such careful, choreographed precision that I knew they had performed this task a number of times. I waited as they disappeared into the bowels of the rubble and kept an eye on the street and surviving rooftops.

Long minutes passed before I heard a sharp whistle. The colonel gestured for me.

His face was grim as I approached. "We've found something."

He led me down a crumbling staircase. In the basement, a false wall had been removed to expose a heavy iron door. The door stood open, and a young soldier was bent double to the side of the threshold, vomiting.

The colonel squeezed his shoulder.

"Fucking Krauts," the young man gasped, wiping his mouth with the back of his hand.

"Take some air, son." The colonel met my gaze. "I hope your boy is not here."

I had to duck my head to clear the doorway, and the tightness of the hidden passageway assaulted my senses at the same time the smell hit me like a physical blow.

The smell threatened to choke me, and I staggered over the putrid dead who lay rotting where they had been felled. The stench clung to the man draped over my shoulders, though he was not dead. Not yet.

My breath was loud in my ears, and I could taste the overwhelming odor cloaking the landscape at the back of my throat. Arthur whimpered, and then I heard it as well: voices speaking in German.

I gripped Arthur's knees and arm as I ran through the slight cover of the woods. Most of the trees had been mown down as ruthlessly as the men, and I could only hope the shadows of the gloaming cloaked us.

They also cloaked the deep wound in the earth, and when the ground disappeared beneath my feet, I had to clench my teeth to hold in my shout.

We fell, tumbling with a shower of loose earth and severed limbs. I lost my grip on Arthur, and though my fall was cushioned by the bodies in the bowels of the trench, the landing drove the breath from my lungs. The smell that plumed from the bodies when I landed made my stomach revolt and try to crawl into my mouth.

Arthur groaned somewhere nearby, and I forced myself upright, scrambling over the dead to reach him. There was still enough light to make out the terror etched into his face. The breath rattled in his lungs, and I lifted him to lean against my chest. His legs lay in a tangle, rendered useless along with his arms by the bullet that had struck his spine.

"This is...not..." He struggled for a breath. "The adventure... you promised."

I gripped fistfuls of his tattered uniform and pressed our foreheads together. "I am sorry. I never should have talked you into coming with me."

He wheezed a soundless laugh. "If it was...an adventure... couldn'...let you go...alone."

I forced the sob welling in my chest into submission. "Quiet now. I can hear them in the woods."

"Rhys." I drew back and met his gaze. "Don'...let them...take me. End it...now."

"No, Arthur, no. Do not ask that of me."

Blood snaked from the corner of his mouth. "Please."

I stared at him, at the face whose softness had been shorn away to hard lines. It was a face I knew as well as my own, a face so similar to his sister's. We had done everything together, born days apart, bonded as friends from birth. I had always led, and he had always followed. Always. Even to this hell.

My hand trembled as I drew the knife from my boot. His face blurred before mine.

"Marry...my sister...when you...get...home," he breathed.

"I intend to," I promised him.

"Already...brothers."

"We are. We always were." My voice was choked by a sob. "Close your eyes now."

"Thank—"

The blade I slipped between his ribs and into his heart interrupted him. The last breath left him on a sigh, and his head lolled against my shoulder.

I slung the knife away and gathered him in my arms, rocking back and forth, clutching him to me.

It began with a fine tremor that shook through every muscle and fiber within me. My chest worked like a bellows. The stench around me clogged my throat and sank deep into my skin.

It filled me to overflowing, and I threw my head back, screaming and raging at the blackening sky.

"That way is a dead end." I blinked, returning to the present, and the colonel gestured to the right with a jut of his chin. "The rooms appear to have been used as storage and bunking. The rest...Come this way."

It stank of misery, fear, and pain in the tunnels. The deeper we ventured into the cave-like structures, the stronger the stench grew.

I breathed through my mouth, shallow and slow, and could taste the desperation. I focused on placing one foot in front of the other, gaze centered on the colonel's back ahead of me to keep the illusion of the walls closing in around me at bay. Owain could be here, and I would not leave him to rot in this harrowing place.

The first room I entered appeared to be an office, a mundane room furnished with a small desk and four chairs. One of the chairs was overturned in the center of the room with a girl tied face-down over it. She was naked, her back, buttocks, and thighs flayed and pulverized to meat and bone.

"*Esgob annwyl*," I breathed, and started toward her.

The colonel stayed me with a hand on my shoulder. "She's dead, Gravenor. They all are."

And they were. All three dozen prisoners kept in half as many small rooms off the dark, narrow corridor. All tortured until they were twisted, misshapen lumps of broken humanity. Each killed with a single bullet to the head. Men and women, young and old. The youngest was a girl no more than fifteen and much had been done to her before death was meted to her. The sound of retching echoed in the tunnel.

"Sir?" The call came from the last room off the corridor. "There is something here you should see."

The room was slightly larger than the others. A table, the surface polished with the brown stain of old blood, stood in the center of the room. A man was sprawled on the floor, the place where his face should be a black mass of shattered gore. A broken chair lay splintered around his caved skull. His uniform marked him as a member of the Wehrmacht.

"He broke his bonds," she whispered. "And beat the man to death with the chair. It was like something wild was unleashed in him. The guards could not pull him away."

I rubbed my forehead and pinched the bridge of my nose. The blood stains on the floor haunted me.

"They shot him. The guards. They k-killed my Owain. Our Owain."

"I think my son was here, but he is not among the dead."

The colonel did not ask how I knew but instead led us in our retreat up to the street. Each man's face was tight and drawn.

"Take some air, gentlemen," the colonel said. "And then we are going back for those poor souls."

"Thank you, Colonel."

He turned to me. "I am both sorry we did not find your son and glad he was not in that hellhole. Good luck to you, Gravenor."

"And to you, sir."

He took a deep breath and faced his men. "Let's go get them, boys. Not a one is to be left in that place."

I walked the streets in a daze, unable to rid myself of the sight of that small, rank room with the bloody table and floor. Of the sightless eyes and mangled bodies. Of the smell of the horrors that had been committed there. I staggered and turned into an alley, bracing myself against the stone wall. I gagged and coughed, but my stomach stayed in a knot and did not empty itself onto the cobbles at my feet.

I leaned my head against the rough exterior I braced myself against, the stone cool against my forehead. Fury coursed through me, hot and swift, and the temptation to drive my fist against the stone almost overwhelmed me. A broken hand would only be a hindrance, though, and one I could not afford right now. I closed my eyes and breathed, and the rage abated, leaving behind only numbness. I found myself fervently wishing for Charlotte's presence by my side, her cool hand on my arm.

I straightened, pushing myself upright, and followed the tangle of streets back to the hospital. I passed a nurse in the corridor as I reached the ward where Séverin recovered.

"You only just missed the other gentleman, *monsieur*."

It took a moment for her words to register, but when they did, I stopped and turned back, attention sharpened. "What other gentleman?"

My tone made her pause, and her forehead wrinkled. "The man who brought the young woman in a few days ago."

Sévèrin had no memory of how she arrived at the hospital, and when I asked the orderlies, none knew the details. I glanced down the empty corridor. "He was here?"

"*Oui.* He wanted to know the condition of the young woman."

"I would have liked to thank him." And ask him where he had found Sévèrin. It could aid my search.

"I told him that, but he would not stay."

"How long ago was this?"

"Only moments."

"What did he look like?"

She spread her hands. "Like the usual man. Not short, not tall. Not thick, not thin. I am sorry, I do not recall any details."

I waved away her apology and rubbed the back of my neck.

"Although, he did wear a homburg hat. I noticed, because it was black." She said it with enough skepticism for me to know the color was significant, but the significance eluded me.

I retreated back down the corridor and stairs in ground-eating strides. I rushed out into the street, glancing first to the north. Seeing no one wearing a black hat, I looked to the south, just in time to see a man capped in black turn east.

I hurried after him, breaking into a run. When I turned the corner and caught sight of him again, I started to call out. The way the man moved, though, caught my attention and stilled my voice.

He was, as the nurse had said, neither tall nor short, thick nor thin. He was indistinct aside from the hat, moving with the flow of people. He did not meander along, but neither did he rush. He pace was measured, but it was purposeful enough that I could tell he had a destination in mind. He lifted the hat from his head and held it in his hand by his side. After a few steps, he causally dropped it on a doorstep without ever altering his pace.

I followed him. I kept well back, knowing my height set me

apart from the crowd on the walk, and did not allow my gaze to rest on him for more than an occasional, sporadic second. He continued east, away from the river, into the same area from which I had just returned.

The crowd thinned to nothing, and I hung back, ducking into the recess of an entryway when he stopped and spoke to a woman. Their exchange lasted only moments, but when he continued, she fell into step beside him. She was gaunt to the point that her dress hung from her shoulders like a quilt draped over a sagging line to dry. I could tell no more about her from this distance.

I kept a street corner between us as I followed the pair, and within a kilometer, I watched from a narrow alley between buildings as he led the woman into a shop.

It appeared abandoned, vandalized and on its way to becoming derelict. I studied the building, noting that there were more windows on the second floor. Perhaps an office or apartments. It reminded me of the shop with the red awning on Rue Pavée in Paris. How long ago that seemed, I wondered.

There was no movement on the street around the shop, no shadows moving before the windows on the upper floor. I slid my hand within my shirt, eased the Luger from the holster at my side, and checked the box magazine. It was full. I kept a careful eye on the building as I crossed the street. The façade was abutted on either side by two taller buildings. I did not know if there were a back entrance, but I did not care to delay and find out.

I checked the door and eased it open when I found it unlocked. It swung soundlessly on its hinges. The smell of staleness and dust greeted me in the dark, and I nudged the door closed behind me.

I dropped into a crouch in the entryway. It took a moment for my eyes to adjust. All was quiet, and the shadows within gradually took shape and revealed themselves to be overturned shelves. I straightened and crept along the wall, glass crunching underfoot, gaze darting along the darkness.

I froze when I heard movement, the creak of footfall, but as I strained to hear, I realized it came from upstairs. I eyed the ceiling, listening closely to the footsteps, hearing a murmur of voices I could not distinguish.

And then the screaming began.

19 May 1944

Dear Nhad,
I'm to be a father, I am.
-Owain

XXIV

Henri

He was awake when I returned from inquiring about the woman. It had been a risk, going back to the hospital, but her condition concerned me. I thought of Mila and pressed my hand to where the cigar box rested over my heart in my shirt pocket.

I was relieved to hear Owain's wife was recovering. That she had been found by her husband's father did not surprise me. He had struck me as a tenacious man.

There was a careful, subtle flex in Owain's forearms, and I knew he was testing the bonds where I had tied him to the chair. He studied me, his one eye squinting and then going wide as recognition swept over his battered face.

"I thought you were dead." His voice was raw and sounded as if it were being dragged over glass and barbed wire on its way out of his throat.

"I did as well for a time." I rubbed my chest and could feel the knotted scar under my palm. I had always liked this boy. I knew he had been suspicious of me. He was intelligent, though, fearless and honorable but biddable and naïve. Or so I thought until he had put a bullet close to my heart in a shadowed attic two years ago. I felt no ill will toward him. Men killed one another all the time, especially in war. Our opinions simply did not align over what was worth killing for. "Lucky for me, your aim is not perfect."

His chuckle was a wheeze of air. "I always knew you were not what you claimed."

"You did, and I can respect that." I drew my chair closer until our knees touched. "But I need you to tell me what you know now."

His one eye was bloodshot, but it met mine evenly. "You will get no more from me than they."

I studied him. "I believe that. You are tougher than they gave you credit for, I imagine. And I am not so much the animal Klaus is, so I will not make you watch what is done to her."

His eye went wide, and he yanked at the rope bindings. "No. *No*. You said she was safe." His chin trembled. "Please."

I stood and walked to the door. "And she will be, once you tell me what I need to know." I opened the door and leaned my head out. "Proceed."

The screaming was painful to hear, but even more so was Owain's. He howled like a ferocious animal, fighting his bonds so fiercely his chair tipped over. His head bounced against the floor and still he struggled. I could not blame him. I would have been just as wild had it been Mila.

"*Stop!*" It was a roar that tore from him so violently I started. "*Stop*. I will tell you. I will tell you anything you want to know. Just please…" His voice broke. "Please do not hurt her anymore."

"Very well." I retrieved the sack I had left by the door and exited the room. The young woman standing down the hall cut off mid-scream when she saw me. "Perfect performance, *mademoiselle*."

"Is that all? Do I still get paid?" Desperation was plain in her gaunt, sallow face.

"*Oui, bien sûr*." I handed her the sack of food I had taken from the farmhouse, pity piercing me when she clutched it to her chest and scurried away as if I would snatch it back from her.

When I returned to the room, Owain's head sagged against the floor, his breathing ragged. I heaved his chair upright and helped him take a drink of water from a canteen. He drank too quickly and choked, and I returned to the chair across from him, waiting until he calmed and regained his breath.

"That was to gain your attention and ensure your cooperation."

He lifted his head, and I almost recoiled at the look in his eye. Gone was the boy I had known at the beginning of the war, when he was naïve but seeking purpose. Instead, a man stared back at me, gaze hard with resolve and tempered with an underlying steel the last years had forged. "You are one of them, then."

"German, yes. But I am not part of the Gestapo. I leave that to lesser men. Their concerns are not mine."

His face was blank. "If their concerns are not yours, then I do not understand what you wish to know."

"About the paintings!" I leaned forward. "The paintings from the attic where you shot me. Where are they?"

"The paintings?"

The confusion in his voice frustrated me, and I shoved my chair back to stand and pace. "There were three, all by Caspar David Friedrich. One was his final black painting. I need to know where they are."

He stared at me and realization slowly dawned across his face. A smile pulled at the gash on his swollen lip. Blood dripped down his chin. "They are still in the attic."

It was my turn to stare. "You did not take them."

"No. I left them. I had to get the children to safety."

I studied him. "You worked tirelessly to keep those collections out of Nazi control. And now you would just give me these pieces?"

"My wife, the baby she carries." His throat worked as he glanced toward the door. "They are all I care about now. Art means nothing to me."

"Art is the only thing that survives," I said absently as I crossed to the window. I peered out at the roofline of Lyon. I had searched every hidden storehouse in Paris, but I had never thought to return to that attic. I threw my head back and laughed. *"Was für ein Trottel!"*

7 June 1944

Dear Nhad,
Word of what has transpired at Normandy has reached Paris.
An uprising is being organized even now.
-Owain

XXV

There was an undercurrent in the screams, a second, lower voice that sounded tortured past the limits of humanity. It raised the hair at the back of my neck.

"*Stop!*"

The shout was loud enough, forceful enough to thunder through the entire building. It reverberated through me.

The screaming went suddenly silent, but the echo of it pulsed in my ears. Footsteps fell hollowly above me, and a murmur of voices drifted down from the floor above.

I edged toward the stairs but fell back into the shadows when I heard a clatter of descent.

The young woman rushed into view. She looked no worse for wear than she had when the man approached her on the street. She clutched a bundle to her chest, fumbling within as she tripped through the shop and out onto the street.

I waited for several moments, watching the stairs. No one appeared, and I could still hear a murmur of voices. The timber of one made my heart knock painfully and forcefully in my chest, but I took the stairs with care. I ascended slowly, cautious of any creaks in the wood, gaze watchful on the space above me.

The second floor was better lit than the one below. Five doors led off of the hall, and low light spilled through the thresholds. Dust and the flotsam of interrupted lives littered the seams of the hallway and the corners of the apartments. I stayed close to the wall, glancing into each small, deserted home as I passed, gaze continually darting to the

307

doorway at the end of the hall.

It stood ajar, and though the voices were low, I could distinguish two. Both male. One so familiar I almost forgot to breathe.

I placed my feet cautiously with each step. My heartbeat was cacophonous in my ears, and each breath seemed to have the force of a gale.

The apartments were all empty, save for the last one. I stayed in a slant of shadow, angled to peer between the gap in the door. I could just make out the edge of a bandaged profile. A young man sat canted to one side, held into the chair by the rope binding his arms to the back and his legs to the feet.

"Art is the only thing that survives."

The English words spoken by the other man gave me pause. I could only see a shadow of his movement as he paced away from the young man held captive. The voice held no discernible accent, and the tone was strangely courteous.

The sudden burst of laughter startled me, and I took the risk of easing the door open a few breaths more. Only two men occupied the room. The man I had followed from the hospital stood across the apartment at the window, his head thrown back with the force of his guffaws.

His next words were undeniably German.

I stepped from the shadows into the doorway and leveled the Luger at him. When he turned, still chuckling, I fired a carefully aimed bullet into his chest.

19 July 1944

Dear Nhad,
If the war draws to a close, I will be able to finish my work here.
Home calls to me.
-Owain

XXVi

Henri

I turned back to Owain, still chuckling, and the bullet caught me in the chest. Almost in the same spot Owain had shot me, I thought as I fell. The bullet pierced the cigar box, and I imagined I felt the splinters being driven deep into my heart. I reeled back into the wall and slid down, the world tilting on its axis. My vision wavered, blurred, but I blinked and for a moment was able to focus.

The man I had seen in Paris and followed across France rushed into the room and knelt at Owain's side. Light from the window spilled over the pair as the father cupped the back of his son's head in his hand and pressed their foreheads together.

I slipped my hand into my pocket and wrapped my fingers around Gerhardt's collar. I smiled, and my breath was a gurgle in my chest. It was like a painting, the scene before me, and I hoped I remembered it.

2 August 1944

Dear Nhad,
You spoke the truth.
It does not matter what a man believes himself to be.
In times of war, we are all soldiers. Sometimes violence is necessary.
It is simply a matter of finding what you believe is worth defending.
-Owain

Meghan Holloway

XXVÏÏ

I did not pause to watch the German fall. I rushed into the room and knelt by the side of the young man tied to the chair. "Owain." The word felt as if it cracked my chest wide open. "*Machgen i.*"

He stared at me. Half of his face was swaddled in bandage that had a spreading yellow and russet stain centered around where his eye was hidden. His uncovered eye held an expression of disbelief. "Nhad." His whisper, weak voice filled with hope and uncertainty, felt like a benediction.

His eye slid closed, and a tear escaped from the corner to slide over the pulp of his raw, battered face. I cupped the back of his head in my hand and pressed my forehead to his.

I eased him upright in the chair and drew the knife from my boot to slice away the rope binding my son. The breath left me when I caught sight of his ruined hands. My gaze jerked to the bandage on his face and the depression beneath the dressing. His clothing was tattered, ripped and bloodied, but there were clean dressings around his arm and leg. "What have they done to you, *machgen i?*" The words were a breath of sound, raw and shaken. Only the foolishness of wasting bullets kept me from unloading the Luger into the body of the dead man across the room.

I tucked the pistol back in its holster. There was an unfurling in my chest, a loosening of a years-long vice, even as the pain and rage over what had been done to him was as sharp as a splinter driven into my heart.

He tensed. "Sévèrin—"

The import of the screaming hit me, and I glanced at the fallen German. A slight smile still lingered on the dead man's face. "Is well.

315

Both she and the babe. They are in a hospital nearby and have been for days now."

He sagged against me, his forehead dropping to my shoulder. The breath that escaped him shuddered with a sob as I wrapped him tightly in my arms. A tremor coursed through the both of us, and I was not certain if it originated in him or in me. I had found him. Broken and not left whole, but alive. And now, in my arms, he was safe. I passed a shaking hand over my face. My fingers came away damp.

I draped him with care over my shoulder and gained my feet. I stood still for a moment, adjusting his heavy, welcome weight. My grip on him was secure and tight, and if need be, I would carry him like this all the way through this battered country across the sea to the hills blanketed in heather and skirted with sheep. "It is time to come home now."

27 August 1944

Dear Nhad,
I do not know if any of these letters will find their way home to you.
I fear I will not find my way home either.
I love you, Nhad. And I know even in your anger,
you have always loved me.
-Owain

Meghan Holloway

Epilogue

Owain

October 1945

It was a challenge, coming home.

Germany had surrendered to the Allies in May. Four of the ten children who had come to the farm with the evacuations from England had not received word from home yet. For now, for however long was needed, they were enfolded in the fabric of our family. My daughter made for the fifth Gravenor child. Aelwyd Charlotte. For the mother who remained in my mind as only a faint memory of warm hands and a soft smile. And for the woman who aided my father's journey.

Sometimes I was not certain if the pain Sévèrin and I had been forced to watch one another bear tethered us irrevocably together or drove an irreparable wedge between us. Perhaps it was both. Perhaps there was no return from witnessing unspeakable horrors done to the one you loved. Perhaps there was no solace from the knowledge that neither of us had been able to save the other. Perhaps one day, if we lived long enough, we would be able to look at one another without seeing our suffering.

Some nights, her touch was still tender and welcoming. We sought solace and forgetfulness in one another's arms on those nights, and our second child would be born with the lambing in the spring.

319

The war may have been declared over, but it still lived on for me. It was on the nights that the pain was too great between Séverin and I to allow us to touch one another that the war visited me with the most vehemence. I staved off sleep by roaming the starlit hills. And every time, my father fell into step beside me.

He became my sanity's lodestone, his presence quiet and stalwart and constant. There were times when my mind felt broken, times in which I wept and screamed. Times when it seemed as if I stepped outside of myself. Times in which the pain was as real and present as it had been back in the cell in Lyon. It was always his low voice and hand on my shoulder that brought me back.

"Does it ever end, ever leave you?" My words had been pleading, voice raw.

He cupped the back of my head in his hand, crouched beside me. "No, *machgen i*. But you learn to live with it and stay home in your mind more often than not."

I wept, hot with shame and shaken with remembered fear. He held me as if I were still a small boy.

And when I would have allowed myself to waste away to bitterness and self-pity, he refused to allow it.

"You are still strong, and you will not lie idle when there's work to be done," he said once at midday when he came in and found me still abed. "You may not be able to hold shears any longer, but you can manage everything else."

And so I did. I learned to work around my ruined hands and canted vision. Gradually, my strength returned. I found the more I breathed in the smell of river and moor, hills and heather, sheep and loyal dog, the less I smelled the memory of my own blood and sweat and fear. The more I worked in the hills at my father's side, the quieter my mind became. He gave me the dignity and purpose to begin stitching myself back together again.

Since coming home, though, there were times I caught my father gazing down the lane with a look on his face I could not decipher. It seemed to be a mixture of grief and tenderness. It made me wonder what had transpired in France on his journey to find me.

We were in the hills mending the stone fence in the north pasture on a crisp autumn day when I caught the faint hint of peppermint on the wind. I straightened and turned, searching the slopes.

A woman and dog stood downhill watching us. They stood together like both knew they belonged to the other, her hand on his head as he leaned against her legs.

My father and the boys were further along the fence, so I approached the pair. As I drew close, I paused, moved by the expression on her face and the dog's as they stared at my father. This was the same expression I had seen on his face when he stared down the lane, and now I recognized it for naked longing.

When I reached her, I could see the effort it took her to draw her gaze from him. Her eyes caught me, the colors as changeful as a winter sky with a gathering storm, and her gaze was straightforward and assessing as she studied me.

A softness came over her face when she met my eye, and the smile that curved her lips was arresting. The smile made her seem lit from within, and what was a pleasant face became striking in its brightness.

I remembered the face from the furtive exchanges of art that had been arranged along her routes to and from the camps outside of the city. I realized I had never seen the smile.

"Owain." Her voice was warm, and the American accent was low and soft. The poodle was a handsome dog, his black hair trimmed neatly around his face and feet. His tail thumped, and I ran my palm over his head when he stepped forward and nosed my fingerless hand. "I am glad to see he brought you home."

The words shifted something inside me. "He has watched for you."

Her gaze moved past me and locked on my father once more. "He told me he would."

321

I followed the direction of her gaze. My father had noted my absence and straightened from his crouch. He turned, searching the hills, and I saw the moment of recognition. A stillness swept over him.

The dog whimpered.

"Go on, Otto," the woman whispered to him, and he launched like an arrow from a bow. He bolted across the field, scattering sheep in his wake.

My father knelt with open arms, and the dog bounded into them with such force and exuberance, he rocked backward. The woman touched my arm and smiled once more before following the poodle, her pace more measured but no less eager.

I called for the boys, and though they stared at the woman with unabashed curiosity, they followed me down the hills. I glanced back once, in time to see my father straighten from embracing the dog, who leaned against his legs and stared up at him with blatant adoration. My father gazed down at the woman as she reached him, and when she walked straight into his chest, he bent his dark head over hers, the color of honey, and enfolded her in his arms.

I climbed over the stone wall and followed the boys home. Mamgu, Sévèrin, and the girls were completing the harvest of their vegetable garden. Sévèrin raised a hand in greeting when she caught sight of me. Today her face was clear and untroubled, free from memories. I would hold her in my arms tonight and for a few hours, all would be well with us. Tomorrow would be another day, and I had learned to take them as they came.

My daughter was festooned with dirt, and she squealed in delight, racing toward me as quickly as her short legs would allow as I crossed the yard. Bess's young litter of six scrambled after her, barking in glee at the chase. I swept her up into my arms, kissing her plump cheek, and knelt in the midst of the frolicking pups. Bess left her perch beside my grandmother and loped over to keep her offspring in check. I draped an arm over the collie, and she leaned against my side.

I took a deep breath and passed my palm over my daughter's

dark curls. She giggled, tucking her head against my shoulder and filling my ears with the music of her indecipherable speech. Peace, like a waft of smoke from the chimney, slipped between my ribs and settled in my chest, edging aside some of the shadows as it did so.

I knew now why my father loved these hills so, why home was his own lodestone. It had become my haven as it was his as I learned his truth: the open hills kept the memory of tight, dark spaces at bay; the scent of heather and sheep drowned the rank odor of pain and fear; the crisp wind swept away the dark heaviness within chest and mind.

And it was as the woman said: my father had brought me home.

Author's Note

No engrossing historical fiction tale is accomplished without thorough research and a wealth of resources.

I would like to thank the Military Vehicle Preservation Association for directing me to Ian Young. Mr. Young recommended the movie *Ice Cold in Alex* and sent me a number of his personal photos to use for my study of the Austin K2/Y, affectionately known as Katy—or in Charlotte's case, Kathryn.

Ms. Fabienne Gelin was an invaluable resource in Vichy in regards to the history of the libraries in the city. She graciously shared her academic paper, entitled *Histoire des bibliothèques de Vichy 1866-2016, 150 ans de péripéties*, with me.

The Welsh were instrumental in WWI, and I have my protagonist as part of the 38th Infantry Division. The 38th fought at the Somme in 1916, at the third battle of Ypres in 1917, and was instrumental in ending the war on the Belgian front in the Hundred Days Offensive in 1918. Even though the 38th was originally thought to be poorly trained and ill led (and they were), they eventually were considered one of the army's elite units. At the beginning of WWII, Wales received thousands of evacuees from London, Liverpool, and Birmingham, and Aberystwyth was a main center for children to be evacuated to from the northern industrial cities. The Heritage and History of Wales group on Facebook, and Mr. Adrian Price in particular, was helpful when it came to the Welsh language I have incorporated into the story.

My aim with ONCE MORE UNTO THE BREACH was to create a story that is as authentic to the time as it is a gripping story. I spent two years researching before I set pen to paper, and I hope that I have created a tale that feels transportive and immersive. That said, I have taken some liberties throughout the story.

General Patton and his Third Army formed the extreme west front of the Allied invasion of France. The Third Army attacked from Brittany and began a spearhead race across France toward Germany. I played a bit with the dates, but it is still possible that Charlotte and Rhys could have crossed paths with the Old Man and his Third.

There is no mention of whether Camille Claudel's work was hidden from the Nazis in WWII. It is likely Charlotte would have never seen the artist's work and therefore would never have recognized it. In March of 1913, Claudel was institutionalized at the initiative of her brother. Though doctors frequently made a plea to her family to release her, they refused, and she died in isolation in 1943. She destroyed much of her work, though about ninety statues, sketches, and drawings survived. In 1951, her brother organized the exhibition of her work at the *Musée Rodin* in Paris. In 2017, France opened a national museum dedicated to her work.

The *Maison du Missionnaire* in Vichy is indeed known for its library, but I appropriated it for my story and the young librarian who betrayed Rhys's son is entirely a figment of my imagination. I know of no association with the missionary house and any resistance efforts or Nazi collaboration.

The poem quoted in the story is one by Victor Hugo, *Demain dès l'aube* or *Tomorrow at dawn*:

Demain, dès l'aube, à l'heure où blanchit la campagne,
Je partirai. Vois-tu, je sais que tu m'attends.
J'irai par la forêt, j'irai par la montagne.
Je ne puis demeurer loin de toi plus longtemps.

Je marcherai les yeux fixés sur mes pensées,
Sans rien voir au dehors, sans entendre aucun bruit,
Seul, inconnu, le dos courbé, les mains croisées,
Triste, et le jour pour moi sera comme la nuit.

Once More Unto the Breach

Je ne regarderai ni l'or du soir qui tombe,
Ni les voiles au loin descendant vers Harfleur,
Et quand j'arriverai, je mettrai sur ta tombe
Un bouquet de houx vert et de bruyère en fleur.

Translation:
Tomorrow, at dawn, in the hour when the countryside becomes white,
I will leave. You see, I know that you are waiting for me.
I will go by the forest, I will go by the mountain.
I cannot stay far from you any longer.

I will walk the eyes fixed on my thoughts,
Without seeing anything outside, nor hearing any noise,
Alone, unknown, the back curved, the hands crossed,
Sad, and the day for me will be like the night.

I will not look at the gold of the evening which falls,
Nor the faraway sails descending towards Harfleur.
And when I arrive, I will put on your tomb
A green bouquet of holly and flowering heather.

Poodles were used as war dogs by the US Army until 1944. The Germans used shepherds, Dobermans, Airedales, and boxers as war dogs, but as the poodle is a breed that originates in Germany, I took the liberty of creating the character of Otto. My own love of the breed made it necessary to include a standard poodle in the story.

The village of La Balme-les-Grottes exists as do the caves on the eastern side of the town. The magnificent subterranean labyrinths were used by the Resistance during the war, but my incorporation of them—and the massacre of the village—is fictional.

The piano piece Charlotte plays in the farmhouse is Rachmaninoff's *Vocalise.* I do not mention whose transcription she

plays, as my favorite is Alan Richardson's, though it was not written until 1951.

The "Monsieur Jaujard" Charlotte mentions is Jacques Jaujard, Director of the French Musées Nationaux. With the help of curators and art historians, particularly Rose Valland, Jaujard was instrumental in the evacuation and protection of the Louvre art collection. He was awarded the *Légion d'honneur* and the *Médaille de la Résistance* for his actions, and the main entrance of the *École du Louvre* bears his name.

"Mongoloid" is a dated term for Down syndrome. I used it in this story because the term "Down syndrome" was not used until the 1970s, and during WWII, "mongoloid" would have been the common term used to refer to the syndrome.

Antibiotics first became available during WWII, and I made specific mention to both penicillin and sulfa drugs in the story. The Dr. Churchill mentioned is a reference to Dr. Edward Delos Churchill, an American surgeon who was renowned for his surgical practice and education.

Klaus Barbie was the head of the Gestapo in Lyon. His title of "the Butcher of Lyon" was well-earned. After the war, he was employed by the US intelligence services in South America. When Henri finds him at the demolished headquarters, it is likely given the timeline of events that he was already in retreat from Lyon to Bruyères. This slight tweak in the timeline was to suit my purposes for the story.

Caspar David Friedrich was a nineteenth century German Romantic landscape painter. Though the man himself died a century before WWII, the use of his work in Nazi propaganda almost destroyed his reputation. I found no evidence that his art was in France in WWII, hidden or otherwise, and my inclusion of his work in the plot is purely fictional.

What Charlotte said to Rhys is true: the Jews had some of the most priceless art collections, but when the Nazi laws rendered the

Jews stateless, they lost property rights. Everything they had previously owned was considered ownerless. The Reichsleiter Rosenberg Taskforce (or the ERR) engaged in an extensive and elaborate art looting operation in France. According to documents from 1944, the art seizures in France totaled 21,903 objects. A substantial amount of looted art still remains lost today, but there were numerous efforts throughout the war and at its close to save the art from Nazi possession. I encourage anyone interested in the ongoing efforts to find art looted in WWII to look up the Monuments Men Foundation.

Though the Gravenor Network did not exist, the Marcel Network—and a number of others—did. The Marcel Network is what inspired me to use the plot line of a young man and his wife risking their lives to save children. Syrian immigrant Moussa Abadi was only 33, and his future wife, Odette Rosenstock, 28, when they found themselves trapped in Nazi-occupied France. Risking their own lives and relying on false papers, the Abadis hid Jewish children in Catholic schools and convents and with Protestant families. In 1943, their clandestine organization—the Marcel Network—became one of the most successful operations of Jewish resistance in Europe. By the end of the war, 527 children owed their survival to the Abadis.

About the Author

Meghan Holloway found her first Nancy Drew mystery in a sun-dappled attic at the age of eight and subsequently fell in love with the grip and tautness of a well-told mystery. She flew an airplane before she learned how to drive a car, did her undergrad work in Creative Writing in the sweltering south, and finished a Masters of Library and Information Science in the blustery north.

She spent a summer and fall in Maine picking peaches and apples, traveled the world for a few years, and did a stint fighting crime in the records section of a police department. She now lives in the foothills of the Appalachians with her standard poodle and spends her days as a scientist with the requisite glasses but minus the lab coat.

Follow her at @AMeghanHolloway.